KT-512-287

4721800025613 4

FALSE FIRE

Recent Titles by Veronica Heley from Severn House

The Bea Abbot Agency Mysteries

FALSE CHARITY
FALSE PICTURE
FALSE STEP
FALSE PRETENCES
FALSE MONEY
FALSE REPORT
FALSE ALARM
FALSE DIAMOND
FALSE IMPRESSION
FALSE WALL
FALSE FIRE

The Ellie Quicke Mysteries

MURDER BY COMMITTEE
MURDER BY BICYCLE
MURDER OF IDENTITY
MURDER IN HOUSE
MURDER BY MISTAKE
MURDER MY NEIGHBOUR
MURDER IN MIND
MURDER WITH MERCY
MURDER IN TIME
MURDER BY SUSPICION

FALSE FIRE

A Bea Abbot Agency Mystery

Veronica Heley

This first world edition published 2016
in Great Britain and 2017 in the USA by
SEVERN HOUSE PUBLISHERS LTD of
19 Cedar Road, Sutton, Surrey, England, SM2 5DA.
Trade paperback edition first published
in Great Britain and the USA 2017 by
SEVERN HOUSE PUBLISHERS LTD

British Library Cataloguing in Publication Data
A CIP catalogue record for this title is available from the British Library.

ISBN-13: 978-0-7278-8678-1 (cased)
ISBN-13: 978-1-84751-781-4 (trade paper)
ISBN-13: 978-1-78010-850-6 (e-book)

All Severn House titles are printed on acid-free paper.

Severn House Publishers support the Forest Stewardship Council™ [FSC™],
the leading international forest certification organisation.
All our titles that are printed on FSC certified paper carry the FSC logo.

Typeset by Palimpsest Book Production Ltd.,
Falkirk, Stirlingshire, Scotland.
Printed and bound in Great Britain by
TJ International, Padstow, Cornwall.

ONE

Bea Abbot counted the number of guests at the dinner table. Thirteen! Most of whom she didn't know. She told herself that she was not superstitious. However, when the two birthday girls were taken up to bed by their nanny, Bea heaved a sigh of relief . . . and then laughed at herself for doing so.

More wine was served. Neither of her dinner companions was particularly good company, but she didn't expect the evening to last much longer. She relaxed.

Crack! A firework? Outside the house. In a neighbour's garden?

The pretty blonde opposite put her hand to her throat. 'Fireworks starting early, aren't they?'

Josh – their host – was in a genial mood. 'My granddaughter and her little friend wanted to let off some fireworks in the garden here but I forbade it. Too risky. They've been given some indoor fireworks. That should satisfy them till they get back to boarding school. They'll be going to some sort of display there, I suppose.'

Woosh . . . crackle! There was definitely a fireworks party nearby. Bea liked fireworks, at a distance. Would it be impolite to ask if they might draw back the curtains over the window to watch?

Woosh . . . crackle.

Crack! Wasn't that very loud? And close . . .?

Swoosh!

Bea turned her head to see . . .

. . . a fiery rose blossom at the top of the curtain behind her.

Someone screamed. One of the waitresses?

Mouths gaped, wine spilled.

Chairs were thrust back.

Bea started to her feet. The curtain was on fire? How? Surely not a firework indoors?

Josh clutched at his chest.

At the other end of the table Daphne, his daughter, threw herself backwards, her arm sweeping glassware and cutlery off the table. A glass shattered.

Bea's good friend Leon was sitting next to Daphne. Blood spurted from her arm. He recoiled. She'd cut herself?

One of the guests grabbed a jug of water from the table and sprayed the flames. Too little, too late.

Crack! Crackle . . . swoosh! The fireworks continued outside and in.

A thin scream from someone.

Bea projected her voice through the chaos. 'Fire extinguisher! Anyone?'

One of the men nodded and darted out of the room.

The heat from the burning curtain was intense. Bea stepped away from the table.

Daphne was having hysterics, throwing herself around.

Leon tried to calm her. 'Someone, help me!'

Bea would have gone to his aid, but the pretty blonde opposite got there first. Scarlet blotches sprang out on Leon's face and hands.

Daphne had severed an artery?

'Dad?' A cry of alarm from one of Josh's sons. 'Where's your pills?'

Josh. Heart-attack city, right?

Woosh! Splat! The firework party nearby had got going in earnest.

Bea froze.

The two waitresses had also frozen where they stood, plates and bottles slipping from their hands.

Crack! Not so loud.

Was that outside?

No. An echo? A firecracker. In the hall?

One of the waitresses turned her head to look. Had she, too, heard . . . whatever?

Bea gasped. The children, Alicia and Bernice! They'd been sent up to bed some ten minutes ago, maybe a little longer.

If a second firework had been set off inside the house, they might be frightened by it.

She took a hesitant step towards the door. Risked a glance back at the curtain, which was being devoured by the flames. If someone had gone for a fire extinguisher . . .? Josh was being attended to by one of his sons, so . . .

Should she ask Leon to check on the children? One of them – Bernice, his great-niece – was his responsibility, after all.

No, he was struggling to wrap a napkin round Daphne's arm, helped by the blonde girl.

Daphne's free arm caught the blonde a right old thwack!

Echoed outside. Swoosh and splat!

One of the young men – a son of the house? – returned with a fire extinguisher. He directed the nozzle at the burning curtain and pressed the plunger. The flames flickered and died.

Pop, pop, pop! Crackle and woosh! The fireworks continued outside.

A babel of voices round the table. 'How awful!'

'Josh, are you all right?'

Daphne had stopped screaming and was lying limply back in her chair, eyelids fluttering.

Bea tried to distinguish between the various cries of alarm inside and the snap, crackle and pop of the fireworks party outside. Had she or had she not heard a second firework go off inside the house a moment ago?

The waitress had heard something, too. Hadn't she? Somewhere in the hall or . . . upstairs? Bea skirted the table to look out into the hall.

No, nothing seemed amiss. Could she have been mistaken? She put her hand to her heart, telling it to calm down. False alarm. The children would be perfectly all right. Their nanny had seemed a sensible soul.

Perhaps she ought to see what she could do to help Leon with Daphne? Except . . . she hesitated. Her instinct was to check on the girls.

Another guest, an older man, joined her in the doorway. He was not panicking. Like her, he was frowning. Listening.

Swoosh, pop, pop, pop! That was outside, yes?

The man looked a question at her. What was his name?

Leon had been held up in a meeting that afternoon, meaning that he and Bea had arrived late and introductions had been hurried. This man was something double-barrelled?

She said, 'I'm worried about the children.'

He nodded. He stepped into the hall, the better to hear what was going on.

The dining room was on the ground floor. Across the hall was the fine, pillared reception room in which they'd met to celebrate the girls' joint birthdays with champagne and the unwrapping of a small mountain of presents.

Bea hadn't been to this house before. It reeked of wealth and privilege. High ceilings, tall windows in huge rooms, brocaded curtains, polished furniture, parquet flooring. Money no object.

Bea said, 'I thought I heard . . . I must have imagined it. What do you think? The nanny should be looking after the children.'

'Not a nanny. Part-time housekeeper, looking after them for the half-term holiday. What did you think you heard?'

'A firework similar to the one that went off in the dining room, but out in the hall here or . . . somewhere inside the house?'

He grunted and led the way to the stairs. Bea didn't know her way round this splendid mansion but the man seemed to do so.

She hitched up her long skirt to climb the stairs behind him.

Here's a how-de-do! Two guests taking off to search their host's house in the middle of the night . . . surely there's no cause for alarm . . .!

Pop, pop, pop! No, that was outside.

Broad, shallow stairs led up to a spacious landing. A full-length window faced them, with another brocaded curtain drawn across it. Corridors led off right and left.

This would be the main bedroom floor. Master bedrooms, family bedrooms, guest bedrooms. Every room en suite. Gold-plated taps and walk-in dressing rooms, no doubt.

Outside, Bea could hear another set of fireworks being let off. Further away. In the next road?

The man took two right-angled turns and led the way up the

next flight of stairs. A narrower staircase. Ah, of course. The top floor would contain staff quarters and nurseries for children. This mansion had been built when children were meant to be seen and not heard.

Was that a cry for help? Bea's silk skirt slipped from her hands and she trod on the material, tearing it loose from the waistband. She stopped for a moment to tie a knot in the material. It didn't matter how she looked. It was more important to find out if there really had been a cry for help.

It was hard to hear anything but the hubbub below . . . screams and shouts . . . a mad jumble of voices . . . and the snap and swoosh of fireworks outside. Surely only outside!

Bea sniffed. Something acrid?

Another couple of turns in the stairs. They were coming up to another landing. In front of them was another floor-to-ceiling window, covered by another brocaded curtain. Déjà vu. Flames were running up and down this one, too.

Had a second fire been started here by another firework? Was it this they'd heard from the dining room?

Gunpowder, treason and plot? But why?

No time to reason why, ours but to do or die.

A middle-aged woman lay sprawled on the landing, mewing, trying to crawl away from the flaming curtain. The nanny-cum-housekeeper. She heard them and lifted her head.

'The curtain! I tripped and fell. Broke my leg! Get the girls?' She pointed down the right-hand corridor.

Bea heard someone screaming. The girls? The birthday girls!

The man bent over the housekeeper, hauling her to her feet. 'Can you manage to hop down the stairs if I lift you . . .?' He set her on the top of the flight leading downwards. She clutched the banister, saying, 'I can manage! Get the girls!' She started to hop down the stairs, trailing one leg, leaning heavily on the banister.

Bea hesitated. The curtain was furiously aflame, reaching out across the landing for something else to devour. Blocking the way to the corridor and the girls' room.

Bea had always been afraid of fire.

Screams! From below or from the corridor? The girls?

The man took a running jump to pull down the curtain pole and with it the blazing curtain. He tore the fabric off its hooks, and stamped on it. The flames sizzled and died, flickered and turned black.

Bea felt acid hit the back of her throat, and coughed.

'Hurry!' The man heaved a cough, too. 'No time to . . .!'

They couldn't spare precious minutes in order to extinguish the flames completely. The carpet might catch and burst into fire again, but in the meantime . . .

Thin screams. Children for the use of.

Bea began to pray, *Dear Lord keep them safe, Leon's great-niece, Bernice, and . . . what was the other child's name? Alicia, that's it.*

The man plunged down the corridor, disappearing into tendrils of smoke which curled about his figure and obscured him from Bea's view. She stumbled after him, straining her eyes to see through the mist, which thickened and darkened as they advanced.

Faintly came the sound of a child coughing.

The man doubled over. Coughing. Choking. Stopped to lean against the wall. Bea tried to see through the smoke. There were a number of doors along the corridor. Which was the children's room? Perhaps more important, which was the bathroom?

The man would know.

She gasped, 'Bathroom? Water! Which . . .?'

Smoke. Thicker. Choking.

No more screams. The girls . . .?

He gestured to the second door along, stumbled to it, leaned against it, opened it and shot through. Bathroom. Thank God. Clearer air here.

The lights went out.

Her phone would give them a light!

She felt for her purse. Not there.

She must have dropped it when she left the dining room. So, no phone, no light.

Coughing, the man produced his own mobile, pressed buttons. A weird blue light.

She located a washbasin, ran water.

Seized a couple of hand towels, dropped them into the basin. He dipped towels in water, too.

How many towels would they need? One each for them, one each for the children.

If they were not too late.

They should have phoned for the fire brigade before they left the dining room.

They ought to have gone straight for the girls before they fiddled around with towels and water. She turned off the taps. No need to add flood to fire.

'Ready?' His voice was a croak. Almost her nerve failed her. She'd always dreaded fire. She imagined a fireball shooting out at them as they opened the door of the children's room. She imagined herself running back down those stairs now, safely, to safety.

She nodded.

They wrapped wet towels around their mouths and noses, took a second one each. She wanted to scream that they shouldn't go any further, leave it to the professionals.

Back to the corridor, now thick with smoke. No lights.

He held up his phone and it hardly made any difference to the gloom.

She dropped the towel from her mouth for a moment and the smoke hit the back of her throat. It reminded her of the killer smogs of her childhood. She pulled the towel back up again.

Smoke inhalation kills quicker than flames.

Don't think like that! They're not dead! Dear Lord, keep them safe!

Smoke. Dense. Menacing. Surely the family must have called the fire brigade by now?

The girls were only ten years old, for heaven's sake!

Happy Birthday to you, squashed tomatoes and stew . . . a mound of presents from people who could afford expensive toys . . . including a box of indoor fireworks.

The man rattled a doorknob along the corridor. Was that the girls' room? The door didn't budge. The door was locked?

He stood back and charged. He rammed the door with his shoulder. He was well built, but . . . Ouch! That must have hurt.

And again!

The door shifted but didn't open more than an inch.

He gave a hoarse cry. Bent down, pushing . . .

One of the girls was lying in a huddle behind the door?

He shoved hard, got the door halfway open, dragged a doll-like figure up and thrust it into Bea's arms. The towel fell from his face. He flapped his arms to tell her to get going.

She didn't want to leave him.

Correction. She did.

She wanted to run, as fast as she could, but she couldn't leave him and the other child to burn. The room behind him was filled with a dense, black smog. He hitched the towel up around his face again. The smoke reached out to smother everything in its path.

Bea had one of the girls. Which one? She couldn't tell in the dark.

Was the child breathing? Yes, her chest was heaving. She was whimpering.

Bea screamed at herself. Why hadn't she learned first aid? What do you do for smoke inhalation?

She wrapped the wet towel around the girl's head loosely, and was thrilled when the child tried to fight her off. 'Go . . .!'

The man held something out to her. A glimmer of light.

A child's mobile phone. Pink and sparkling.

Ah, that would help.

Holding up the pink phone, half carrying and half dragging the child, with the towel slipping from her face, Bea set off to the landing . . . how many doors along? They'd flown along here in a couple of seconds, but it seemed like an hour before they reached a wide, open space. The window, which had been covered by the burning curtain, now let in moonlight of sorts. London is never totally dark. The curtain was a blackened shroud at their feet.

Was that a hint of flame reviving?

No, probably not. Hopefully not.

In which direction did the stairs lie? She was disorientated in the dark. She held the child's phone up high, and still couldn't see which way to go.

The child in her arms coughed and cried out in a choked voice.

'It's all right,' said Bea, trying to keep the towel over her mouth and nose, hold up the phone *and* keep an arm around the child. Which way lay the stairs?

She risked a look back. A humped-back figure was following her, swaying. He must have the other child over his shoulder. Presumably he'd lost his own phone? No light.

Bea had the only light. But she was so tired!

If she stopped to rest . . .

The smoke would get her if she did.

The man pushed past her, led the way to what turned out to be the top of the stairs. How come he knew the layout of the house? He wasn't one of the family, was he? Or was he? She couldn't remember.

She hitched her bunched-up skirt higher, took a firmer hold of the child who was slipping out of her arms . . . don't do that, dear, or you'll end up in the morgue . . . keep going, keep on, keeping on, one foot after the other . . . the air will be clearer as we go down . . . won't it?

It was so dark! The light she held was hardly helping at all. Low on battery?

She bumped into the banister. Good. She put her elbow on it, and it helped her to feel for the next step . . . and the next . . .

A pause to take a breath and hoist the child up again. Yes, it was slightly easier to breathe here. She let the towel drop around her neck.

The child – it was Alicia – moaned and coughed and wept.

'Not much farther,' gasped Bea, not believing it, but thinking it the right thing to say. How we lie to children! For their own good, of course. And to bolster up our courage.

The man had stopped moving. He reached back to take the silly little pink phone off her. 'I'll lead the way. We turn here.'

Still no lights, except for the glow-worm in his hand.

Down, down. Feel for the next step. The child coughed and cried, a dead weight in her arms.

'Turn again . . . careful!'

Who was he to tell her to be careful? Teach your grandmother . . .

Her tied-up skirt was coming undone. She could feel it flop around her feet. She tried to hitch it up again, nearly lost her balance and fell awkwardly against the wall. Ouch. That hurt. No time to rub it, even.

Bea didn't think she could get Alicia up and over her shoulder. Even if she did, she'd probably collapse under the weight. She felt like collapsing, anyway. However many steps? They came to another flat space and turned . . . however many turns? She'd completely lost her sense of direction. Surely they'd gone down past the main bedrooms by now.

They hadn't met the nanny on the way. Presumably she'd got safely downstairs and the others would have . . .

That was weird. There was no sound of people below.

She listened hard. Faintly came pop-pop, swoosh and pop. Outside. Some distance away.

Bea didn't understand the silence. If not the guests, then surely there should be firemen and policemen and paramedics . . .

Instead, there was a dense, dead quiet.

Faintly came another set of pops and crackles. Some distance away.

There had been thirteen people at supper, plus a couple of waitresses. Where were the waitresses? Had they gone when the lights went out? Or before? Bea thought of sci-fi mysteries in which the inhabitants of a mansion disappeared without trace . . . and then told herself not to be absurd. There'd be a perfectly rational explanation for what had happened.

Only, she couldn't think what it was.

TWO

Was that a flicker of a light to their left? They were in a larger space, weren't they? Her night sight was poor.

A whimper. From the other girl, not the one Bea was carrying. Poor little Bernice, such a brave little soul. Hadn't she had enough to put up with in her short life already?

Bea cleared her raw throat. 'Are you all right, Alicia? Bernice?'

The man coughed. 'We've got to get out.' The glow of the phone passed Bea as he moved away from her.

Where were they? Could they be in the hall? No, they couldn't, or she'd hear all the other guests. No one moved, no one coughed or spoke.

She could hear the man trying to open a door. Were they in the kitchens, which presumably would be in the basement of the house? The battery was fading in the child's phone he was carrying.

She could hear him breathing hard.

Alicia was struggling feebly, coughing now and then. Bea hefted Alicia higher in her arms and spoke, or rather, croaked, 'We'll be out in a minute.'

Surely someone must have called the fire brigade? Surely one of the guests must have missed them? They wouldn't have abandoned the house without calling in the fire brigade, would they?

Bea mopped her face with the wet towel and let it drop to the floor. She began to distinguish black from grey. There was a faint change in the air, a doorway outlined in grey instead of filthy smoke. A dim light beyond. Yes, they were in the hall.

The man, hampered by carrying Bernice and the phone, was trying and failing to open the front door. The fire must even now be crawling down the stairs behind them. Unless they could get out pretty soon . . .

She didn't want to think about that. Tamping down fear,

she took an incautious step and trod on something that slipped under her foot. It gave a loud crack and broke. China? Plates from the dinner party?

She tried to orient herself.

She and Leon had been ushered straight through the hall and into the drinks party in the salon, which lay to the left of the front door. The party was to celebrate the two girls' birthdays. The girls were close friends and had their birthdays within a week of one another. Champagne for adults and Coca-Cola for the children. The men were in black tie, the women in evening dress. The birthday girls – the stars of the show – were showered with presents.

Then they had all crossed the hall to go into the dining room. She closed her eyes to shut out the faint light of the phone and opened them again. Her night sight was returning.

Was that a faint glow she could see across the hall? The fire, reignited? Her heartbeat went into overdrive.

The man held up the child's pink phone, checking the lock on the front door. Such a weak light. He was a figure from a nightmare, hunched over, powerful. Taurus, the bull?

Bea's arms couldn't hold Alicia any longer. She let the child slip to the floor where she crouched, pressing against Bea's thigh, quivering and coughing. But alive. Praise be.

The battery in the phone was definitely fading. The man's voice ditto. He gasped, 'I'll try the fire brigade. Ought to have tried earlier. Can you take the child . . . if I can get this door open?'

He dumped Bernice in Bea's arms. As if she could manage to look after one child, let alone two. Her eyes went to the glow in the dining room, which seemed to be moving . . . was that another fire?

Permission to panic?

Panic not allowed.

Bernice stirred in Bea's arms, coughing weakly.

Alicia stirred, weeping, coughing.

The children had lost the towels they'd soaked in water in the bathroom . . . abandoned on the flight down the stairs?

Bea let Bernice down on to the floor to join Alicia. She knelt, cuddling them both. Her mouth was dry. That flare of light in the dining room . . . Why hadn't the man seen it? Possibly because he was holding another light in his hand, which meant his night vision was even worse than hers?

The children were wearing velvet dresses, one black, one midnight blue. Their long hair, one nut-brown and one nearly black, had been in shining falls down their backs. Now their dresses felt gritty. Dirty. Their hair was tousled, their cheeks tear-stained.

Bea tried not panic, but . . . they had left the fire on the top floor to roar unchecked through the top storey. How soon would it crawl down the stairs?

She wanted to scream that they must smash a window and get out of the house. Why was the man still trying to get out of the front door instead of looking for another way out? What about trying to get out through the kitchen quarters?

She told herself to be patient. He was doing his best. She trusted him, didn't she? Yes, but in a minute she'd have to point out the obvious . . .

She listened to the children's breathing. Not perfect. The odd gulp now and then. It was amazing how quickly children recovered from trauma.

A clock in the salon opposite chimed the quarter-hour. A sweet sound reminding her of a previous age when dinner parties didn't end in death.

The snap, crackle and pop of fireworks being let off had receded into the distance. The fire brigade would be busy tonight.

The man stood back from the door. He was breathing hard. 'I think the front door's been double-locked or bolted. Can you keep the children here while I try to find the door to the kitchens and get us out that way?'

'Don't leave us!' Bea thought it, but it was one of the children who said it. Bea angled her wrist to look at her watch. She couldn't see it in the semi-dark. The glow from the dining room was growing brighter . . . or was it that their eyes were becoming used to the dark?

She glanced back at where she knew the stairs to be. Was that a wisp of smoke curling down from above? No, she was imagining it.

A phone rang in the dining room. They all jumped.
Someone swore.

'Faye!' said Bernice, and without warning stood up, facing the dining room.

Alicia also scrambled to her feet. 'Don't leave me!'

'Come on then!' Bernice, extending her hand to her friend.

Was that Bea's own phone ringing? It sounded like it. Bea said, 'Stop!' She staggered to her feet and gathered the remains of her skirt around her.

'Boo!' cried Bernice, jumping into the dining room.

The phone stopped ringing. Bea leaned against the doorway, her hand pressed to her heart.

The man came up behind her, surveyed the scene and said, 'Humph!'

With which sentiment, Bea agreed.

The pretty blonde who'd been helping Leon to control Daphne was on all fours under the table. The children's appearance startled her so that she jumped up, hitting her shoulder on the dining table. 'Ouch! You didn't half give me a fright!'

Faye something. Wasn't she supposed to be a model? Girlfriend of Gideon, one of the sons of the house and therefore not family exactly?

The man asked, 'Can you show us how to get out? Is a fire engine on the way?'

'What? No! Why should it be?'

'There was a fire, two fires—'

'The fire was put out ages ago.' Faye sounded so sure of herself that, in spite of everything she'd seen, Bea relaxed.

The man said, 'What! Have they been and gone? So quickly? But . . . well, where is everyone?'

'Hospital, of course.'

'Hospital? What, everyone?'

'Sure. The old man was having another heart attack, so off he goes with his entourage. Ditto Daphne. There was blood everywhere. She'd done her best to sever an artery, always the drama queen. Look!' She indicated some spots of blood on her arm and shoulder. 'My dress is ruined.' Her little black dress was minimalist, and very tight. If it was spotted with blood, Bea couldn't see it in that light.

'Mum's in hospital?' Alicia's voice quavered.

The man patted her shoulder. 'Best place, if she's hurt herself. Faye, we need to be sure. Did everyone get out safely?'

'Of course they did. Help me look for my pearls, why don't you?'

'Pearls?'

'Daphne broke my string of pearls, so when they abandoned me, I bolted the front door and stayed behind to look for them.'

Bea was confused. There'd been a real fire on the landing, hadn't there? Yes, the man had stamped it out. And all that dense smoke had been coming from the children's room, hadn't it?

The man frowned. 'Was Steve able to find a second fire extinguisher?'

Who was he? Ah, Josh's other son. He had two sons, didn't he: Gideon and Steve?

Faye was back to searching the floor. 'What on earth for?'

Bea tried to work it out. The fire which had attacked the curtain in this room had long since died out. The remains of the expensive fabric hung in shreds at the window. The fire extinguisher which had been used on the curtain lay on the floor nearby. Faye seemed to be saying that Steve had dealt with everything. The curtain on the upper landing as well?

Wait a minute! How could he have been in two places at once? Bea's brain zigzagged, trying to make sense of the situation. Faye was so calm, surely there couldn't be anything to worry about now. Could there?

The girl held up a wineglass with what looked like white beads rolling around in it. 'Don't just stand there! Come and help me! I need to find all my pearls so they can be restrung.'

Bea cast her eyes around the room. Even in that poor light, she could see there was a trail of loose pearls behind one of the overturned chairs, and a couple more under the table. There was also a broken glass, smashed plates, and food on the floor. There was what looked like splashes of blood on the table, the carpet and the chair where Daphne had been sitting.

A phone rang again, plaintively. Bea looked around. Hers? Where was it? She'd left her pashmina and evening bag hanging on the back of her chair, hadn't she? She'd been sitting on the far side of the table, with her back to the window. Ah, there was her bag on the floor.

'I've found one!' Bernice darted forward to pick up a pearl. A fragment of glass shattered under her shoe and Alicia squealed, 'Watch out, Berny!'

Berny? The girls were indeed good friends if they'd got as far as shortening their names.

'Careful, kids,' said the man. 'Broken glass. Faye, we need to be sure—'

'I'm flying out to the States tomorrow,' said Faye. 'I have to find all my pearls, now!'

Bea rescued her evening bag and retrieved her phone, which had stopped ringing. She switched it on and held it up high, doubling the amount of light in the room. Good. She hesitated. Who should she ring first? Leon. She tried his number.

Faye was aggrieved. 'I asked Gideon to stay behind and help me find my pearls, but his father twitched his little finger and that was that.'

Gideon? Bea thought, let's get this straight. She'd been seated between two beautiful young men at the table. The one on her right had been absorbed in entering a note of everything he ate into his iPhone. Bea had understood he was Daphne's toy boy. His name was . . . no, she couldn't for the moment remember.

The one on her left had spent the meal texting someone on his phone, and receiving texts in return. Bea had eventually worked out that he was texting Faye, the blonde sitting opposite him on the other side of the table. Sly glances, and lots of eye-rolling between them. Honestly! At a family dinner party!

So the man on Bea's left was one of the sons of the house, and called Gideon.

Leon's phone was engaged. Bother. A sudden nasty thought. Bea said, 'Faye, what happened to Leon? He's not gone to the hospital too, has he?'

'Yes, of course. He took Josh and Gideon.'

Bea relaxed again. At least Leon was safely out of the house.

Sir Leon Holland had been part of Bea's life for some years. Now and then he said he would very much like to be more than just a friend, and at one time she'd been tempted to encourage him. Nowadays she was content with things as they were.

Leon had been invited that evening because Bernice was his great-niece and there were no other members of her family available to attend this splendid grown-up 'do' for Bernice and her best friend, Alicia.

Bernice had been staying with Alicia for the half-term holidays because her much younger half-brother had the chicken pox, and her mother was unable to cope. Leon had suggested taking Bea to the party because he liked her company and because she knew the Holland family's past history, which had made boarding school the only option for Bernice. Also because he could get Bea to do the boring bit by buying presents for them to take.

Bea's phone rang under her hand. 'Hello? Leon?'

'Where are you? Why didn't you answer your phone?' Then speaking to someone at his end, 'No, I'll . . . in a minute.' Then back to Bea, 'I thought you'd follow me.'

'What?'

'The doctor's just . . . but Steve needs . . . I'll ring you back shortly.' He switched off.

The man said, 'Girls, come away from there. There's broken glass everywhere and you don't want to land up in hospital, too. Faye, I must have dropped my phone upstairs. Can I use yours for a moment?'

'Can't you see I need it?'

He said, 'You said Steve put out the fire down here, and I put out the one on the landing, but . . .' he stopped and stared at Bea, who stared back.

'You think we ought to check the top floor?' she said. 'What made all that smoke in the girls' room?'

Bernice said, 'It frighted us.' She had a surprisingly deep voice for a young child.

Alicia said, 'It crawled all over us.'

'A lot of smoke doesn't make a fire,' he said, but began to move to the doorway.

Faye was sharp. 'For heaven's sake, I told you! Steve put the fire out! And, as you're here, you can help me find my pearls.'

Bea said, 'Steve put the fire out down here, but there was another, perhaps two more, upstairs.'

'Don't be daft,' said Faye. 'We all saw it. A firework. These two stupid girls tried to upset us by playing a practical joke, and look at the trouble it's caused! They're going to be in deep doo-doos for that, aren't they? So—'

'Not us, honest!' The girls shook their heads, wide-eyed.

Faye wasn't listening. 'Ninette was useless as usual, weeping and wailing because her husband wanted to see that Daphne was properly looked after and Gideon said . . . Honestly! He thinks far more of his father than he does of me!'

Who was Ninette? Oh, the anorexic blonde opposite, married to . . . someone else at the table. Married to Daphne's first husband? Is that right?

'And no sooner had they all cleared off and I started to look for my pearls, than the lights went out and—'

'Everyone went with them?' The man wanted to be sure he'd understood.

'—I said, how was I supposed to get back home, and Gideon said I could get a taxi, couldn't I?'

Bea surveyed the room. 'What happened to the waitresses?'

'They refused to deal with broken glass and blood and left.'

The man said, 'Faye, which hospital?'

Faye pounced. 'There's another of my pearls. And two more. Hospitals. Plural. The old man wanted private treatment and Daphne's going to need cosmetic surgery by the look of it. Ah,' she swooped, 'there's another one.'

Bea's phone rang. Leon, again. 'Bea, where have you got to? Why didn't you answer your phone?'

'Leon, I'm still at the house, looking after the girls—'

He broke in, 'Steve needs help looking after Daphne. She's in a terrible state. She won't let them sedate her or stitch her up till they've produced a plastic surgeon. At this time of night! She's lost so much blood that . . . She needs someone to calm her down. Steve's hopeless. I said you'd do it. She's got two ex-husbands in tow . . . no, one of them's current, isn't he? Worse than useless, both of them.'

'Leon, listen! We rescued the children, but—'

'I really can't deal with hysterical women. You know how to treat—'

'Leon, I've got to ring off. I'm worried about the fire here. It may be out, but I'd like to be sure. I'll ring you back.'

The man was holding on to his temper, just. 'Faye, leave your treasure hunt for the moment. Who went with whom? They did take the housekeeper to hospital with the others, didn't they?'

Bernice started for the hall, calling out, 'Mrs Frost?'

Alicia followed her. They stood in the doorway, hand in hand and wide eyed, looking up into the darkness.

Faye shrugged. 'What a waste of space that woman is, letting the children set off fireworks inside the house. She'll be lucky to have a job in the morning. I'm sure she's perfectly all right. Her kind always are. I've got to get all my pearls. If it hadn't been for the lights going off . . .'

The man pushed the children gently aside, and started across the hall. Bea caught up with them. She held up her phone to light the space.

He peered into the darkness, head cocked to listen. The light in Bea's phone hardly made any difference.

He said, almost to himself, 'There was a fire, we saw it. Not just on the landing – which I hope to God I managed to stamp out – but in the children's room. I didn't see any flames. But something set off those clouds of smoke. Maybe it was just smoke? But . . .'

Bea confirmed, 'We have to check.'

Was that a faint cry from upstairs?

Bea clutched her phone tightly. She didn't want to let go of it. If she gave it to him, she'd be left in the dark with the two children. But, he needed it more than she did. Be brave, Bea. She handed it over to him.

'Take it.' She wanted to add, 'Be careful!' but shut her lips firmly on the words. He was no fool. He'd take care. He wouldn't play the hero without assessing the risks. Probably.

He took her phone, holding it high as he started up the stairs. Bea stayed where she was. The children clung to her, watching him turn the corner and start up the next flight. Bea wondered if she ought to have summoned an ambulance before he went upstairs. She wondered if they were making too much of the housekeeper's non-appearance. She thought that this was a nightmare and she'd wake up soon. Shadows lengthened and hovered as he turned another corner and the light retreated with him.

Faye stood in the doorway. Indignant. Sharp-voiced. 'What are you doing! I'm still short of some pearls. I don't know why the housekeeper's not here to look after them. It's not my business to look after naughty children who set fireworks off for a joke. And I am not going to be held responsible if the old man dies, or Daphne—'

A wail from Alicia. Josh was her grandfather and Daphne her mother.

Bernice made no sound, but tightened her grip on Bea. Bea knelt, holding the children to her. The stairs were uncarpeted. They could hear the man's footfall continuing up through the house. He was possibly not moving as fast as earlier in the evening.

Don't try to be a hero! If there really is a fire, you should wait for the firemen!

Faye said, 'Oh, for heaven's sake! What is it with this family? And isn't it more than time those two naughty children were in bed?'

Bernice appealed to Bea. 'We did phone for the fire brigade, we did! Mrs Frost said we could watch the telly while she went down for a hot drink for us. She said she'd help us light our indoor fireworks when she got back and not to touch the box till then—'

Fay pounced on that. 'So of course you disobeyed her, you little horrors!'

'We didn't open the box, honest we didn't!'

'It went bang—'

'It frighted us!'

Faye snorted. 'As if I believe that! It went on fire all by itself, did it? Pull the other one!'

'Something whizzed and then there was black smoke and we screamed—'

'And Bernice rang for the fire brigade, and they said we were playing silly games—'

'And I tried to ring Mummy to tell her, and we thought Mrs Frost would come to get us out but the smoke choked me and I couldn't breathe, so I laid down and did a little pray.'

Two dirty little faces. Two tired, white faces.

Faye snapped, 'Serve you right if you'd fried to death!'

'They nearly did,' said Bea as, to her enormous relief, the man came down the stairs, treading one at a time, tiredly, with Mrs Frost over his shoulder. He knelt and let his burden slide down on to the hall floor. He wheezed. 'She's still alive, I think. I found her against the wall on the next flight up. Looks as if she took a tumble and knocked herself out. When we were coming down, we kept close to the banisters. We must have passed her in the dark. The smoke is gradually sinking down through the house. It's thick up where she was.' He coughed, but had the presence of mind to hand Bea back her phone. 'Will you . . .?'

Alicia whimpered, 'Is Mrs Frost going to be all right?'

The woman didn't stir; eyes shut, hair flopping over her face, sensible clothing disarranged, one shoe off and one shoe on. Out for the count. Not dead, hopefully.

Bea pressed the emergency number on her phone. Tried to think what address they were at. Gave it. 'Yes, that's right. Fire brigade and ambulance, please. As quick as you can. Yes, someone has been hurt.'

The man drew a difficult breath. 'Is there another fire extinguisher in the house? Not that I think one will do much good.'

Faye said, 'What's wrong with the woman? I suppose she's been at the drink!'

Bea freed herself from the clinging children to kneel beside the unconscious woman and touch her throat. 'There is a pulse. She's warm. We ought to get her out into the fresh air, but it's such a cold night . . . Perhaps we could find something to cover her? A coat, perhaps?'

Bernice knelt, too. And touched. Bernice was a bright child, and brave. She looked up at Bea with a question in her eyes.

'Yes,' said Bea, 'the sooner we get her to hospital, the better.'

Alicia whimpered. She was not as brave as Bernice, was she? Both children were in shock, but thankfully not coughing as much as they had been.

The man said, 'We can't fight the fire. You're right. We'd best get out. Now, if we open the front door, it may accelerate the flames, but it's the quickest way.'

Faye screamed, 'You can't leave me! I haven't got all my pearls yet!'

Bea was sharp with her. 'Lose your life, or lose a pearl or two. Claim it on insurance.' She gathered the two girls to her. 'Come on, my darlings. Have you got a coat or some sort of wraps down here? No? Well, I've left my pashmina somewhere and we'll—'

The man said, 'I can't see how . . . can you unbolt the door for us, Faye?'

Faye screamed, 'You can't leave me!'

Alicia's face screwed into a frightened mask. Bernice put her arm around her friend's shoulders. Bernice was frightened, too, but just about holding on to her sanity. In a moment the two of them would lose control and be more difficult to handle.

Bea ran back into the dining room, lit by Faye's torch. It was in disarray, but still recognizable as a room in which moneyed people had eaten well. She grabbed her pashmina and swept the two little girls to the front door. The man had got the top bolt undone, but was struggling with the bottom one.

Alicia's eyes were fixed on the stairs. She yelped and pointed. Black smoke was rolling around on the landing . . . or was that a trick of the light?

The man stood back, panting. He'd finally managed to wrestle the bottom bolt open. He opened the door. Fresh, cold air flew in.

'Out!' Bea thrust the girls outside.

The man picked up the housekeeper and followed them.

Faye, in the doorway to the dining room, screamed, 'You can't leave me!'

Bea hesitated.

'Swoosh!' Fed by an intake of air from the outside world, flames ignited under the pall of smoke on the landing.

Bea grabbed Faye by the wrist and towed her out into the night, scattering pearls as they left.

THREE

'**Q**uick!' Bea slammed the door shut behind them.
Oh, baby, it's cold outside!
Street lights! What a relief!

Two warm bodies pressed against her. The children, shivering.

'My pearls!' Sobbing, Faye sank to her knees, beating at the closed door.

Bernice gave a little hiccup. 'She really isn't very sensible, is she?' Her voice wobbled.

'You are wonderful children,' said Bea, shepherding them on to the gravelled driveway. 'Brave beyond belief! I am so proud of you!'

Traffic moved on the road outside. It was a tree-lined street of expensive houses lit by the very latest in heritage lamps. Here were mansions individually designed for wealthy nineteenth-century merchants; solid houses, three or four storeys high – sometimes higher – plus a basement. Some had been left in red brick, others were finished in cream-painted stucco, some had coach houses and walled gardens, some had been adapted into flats. All were smugly conscious of their proximity to the world-famous Kew Gardens.

Give or take ten million or so, such houses would be worth the attention of an oil millionaire. Hopefully they were insured.

Bea told herself she was rambling. Disorientated.

A bus rumbled past. A silver moon, high in the sky, could be glimpsed through the bare branches on lime trees that had been planted when the world was a lot younger.

Ordinary, everyday traffic noises. Wonderful!

Faye was still beating at the closed door. Idiot!

The man's breathing sounded harsh. He laid the house-keeper down on the gravelled surface of the drive, took off his jacket and laid it over her. She was as limp as a rag doll. He stood over her, feet well apart, hands on thighs, bent over, taking deep breaths. Recovering.

A spit of rain.

Bea shivered. She had her pashmina over her shoulders, and round the children, too. It wasn't enough to protect them.

As for Faye, her black silk shift started halfway down her fake boobs – pardon the term, but! – and finished just below her apology for a bottom. She was too bony to have a proper, rounded bottom. That shift wasn't going to keep her warm, was it?

The man said, 'How . . . long . . . ambulance?'

Bea tried them again. 'Fireworks parties mean more accidents.' Ring-ring, ring-ring. They were supposed to answer within so many seconds, weren't they? Or was it minutes?

It was beginning to rain. A nasty, cold, penetrating rain. They'd all catch their deaths if they stayed here.

Another bus passed.

If they caught a bus . . . but where would they go?

Faye walked down the steps, slowly, as if on the catwalk. 'You, Mrs Abbot, or whatever your name is! I'm going to sue the pants off you. You've not only caused me to lose my pearls, but you've assaulted me and exposed the children to the elements without a thought for anyone but yourself.'

Bea blinked. Was that how it looked to Faye? She looked down at the children, who looked up at her with identical, enquiring, tearful faces. 'Let's find a neighbour to give us shelter, shall we? Alicia, do you know who lives next door?'

A shrug. In a neighbourhood of detached houses, you might well not know your neighbour.

Prompt on cue, an elderly man appeared from the house next door. He was holding up an umbrella with a spoke missing. He wore an overcoat which flapped around pyjama-clad legs and carpet slippers. He was holding up a mobile phone.

An elderly retired academic? 'Are you all right? Have you all got out safely? We saw the smoke when we went to let the cat out and the wife said she'd heard all the cars go out earlier, so we thought there might be no one left at home to ring the fire brigade, so she did, just in case. Oh, come in, do, or you'll catch your death!'

'About time!' said Faye, stalking up the steps to the open front door of the tall, brick-built house next door.

The neighbour spotted the housekeeper lying on the ground and tried to hold his umbrella over her. 'Dear me. She doesn't look too good, does she? I don't know if my wife phoned for an ambulance as well.'

'I did,' said Bea. 'Children, why don't you go inside? I'll wait here till the ambulance comes.'

The man adjusted his jacket around Mrs Frost. 'I'll stay with her, and you see to the kids. Be good, Lissy!'

This was only common sense. Bea didn't like leaving him, but it was true that the children needed to be under cover. Both were shivering with the cold and from shock.

She handed her phone to the man. 'Take it. Just in case.' Sweeping the children before her, Bea followed in Faye's footsteps.

Oh, warmth! A tiled hallway, an all-purpose living room with old-fashioned, sagging chairs and china ornaments on the mantelpiece. Somewhere to sit down!

A bright-eyed little woman in a maroon velvet housecoat over a flannelette nightie welcomed them. Her husband darted back outside to the pavement, looking this way and that for the ambulance and fire brigade. He was high on adrenaline, having the time of his life.

Within a few minutes Bea and the children were provided with hot drinks and swathed in coats and cardigans . . . which, Bea noted with concern, would all have to be cleaned before they could be used again, for of all the dirty, soot-encrusted ragamuffins, you'd find none worse on the streets of London that night! Bea had been wearing a brand-new dress in gold silk, with a softly folded bodice and a long skirt which she'd tied into a knot at the waistline after it had got torn. It was past repair. Tough. Worse things happen at sea.

Only Faye looked almost as bandbox perfect as she had at the dinner table. True, she complained that the bodice of her dress had been saturated with blood, and there were some red blotches on her arms, but she got on to her phone straight away. 'Giddy, where are you? You've got to come and get me, you've no idea! And my pearls . . .!' A choking cry, a realistic sniff. 'I've never been so frightened in my life . . .'

Bea tuned the girl's voice out, until she heard Faye cut off that conversation and start another, saying, 'Can you come and get me . . .? Yes, I told you where I had to be tonight. I couldn't very well refuse. It was those naughty children's birthday party, a three-line whip, Giddy needed me there, but it's all gone wrong!' Gulp, gulp! 'The children set the house on fire! Yes, they did! I only just got out with my life, manhandled by some harridan, one of the guests, who . . . Yes, it's true! And my fabulous pearls lost! So can you come and . . . No? A fine friend you are!'

The girls turned their faces up to Bea and whispered that they hadn't done it, honest! Bea believed them and said so, but there was no stopping Faye from giving her version of the story to her friends. No sooner had she finished one phone call than she made another, trying to get someone to collect her. Each time her lost pearls seemed to increase in value, as did the terror of the assault by 'that harridan, the Abbot woman!'

Faye only came off the phone to request something stronger to drink than the sugared tea which their kind hostess had provided for them. She was served with a tumbler of whisky, somewhat to Bea's disgust, as she wouldn't have minded something stronger herself . . . but not with two little girls at her knee, one of whom – Bernice – was still trembling, and the other – Alicia – weeping gently.

The householder irrupted into the room to announce that the fire brigade had arrived at last, but there was no sign of an ambulance, which he was in the process of hurrying up, he didn't know what the world was coming to, did he! And then, even in their sanctuary they heard the wail of a fire engine. Still talking on her phone, Faye drew back the curtains so that they could all see the lights flash, flash, flash . . .

Not one, but two fire engines. Their host bobbed back in. 'The paramedic's come, and is working on your friend.'

A third fire engine arrived. Alicia yawned and fell asleep on the floor at Bea's feet. Bernice leaned across Bea's lap; not properly asleep, but drifting in and out of consciousness.

Back came their helpful neighbour. 'It's raining worse than ever. That poor woman hasn't come round yet, so they're taking her straight off to hospital!' The neighbour was enjoying this in a way. Not so his elderly wife, who remarked that it was long past the children's bedtime, wasn't it? Meaning it was also past hers? Yes, probably. Bea tried to think what to do with the children. Didn't she need to talk to someone official about the fire, and the children?

The neighbour bobbed back in again. 'They think the fire's taken a good hold. It might all go up. Good thing we've detached houses, eh? They want to know if everyone got out of the building in time. Your friend said everyone was out. That's right, is it?'

Bea nodded. Yes.

'The ambulance wants to know if anyone's going in the ambulance with the woman?'

Bea shook her head. Where was her phone? Had she lost it again? No, she'd given it to the man, hadn't she, so that he could chase up the fire brigade and the ambulance? She needed it now to . . . to do what? She had to let the girls' families know what had happened. And Leon. And Alicia's mother, Daphne . . . provided the woman had been released from hospital. What a mess!

She said to their hostess, 'Is there a phone here that I can use? I'd better find out what to do with the children tonight.'

'Poor Mrs Frost,' said Bernice, opening her eyes, and then closing them again. 'She went to fetch us some hot chocolate, and she didn't come back. Where are we going to sleep tonight?'

That indeed was the question. It was half-term week and the children were home from boarding school. Bernice's mother lived in a cocoon of happiness with her new family, which excluded her clever, difficult daughter. And then there was the chickenpox.

Bernice seemed happy enough at her boarding school, and in the holidays lived either with her great-uncle Leon or her great-aunt Sybil, who was currently in America. Leon wasn't exactly nanny material. Which was why Bernice had been staying with her good friend Alicia.

And what about Alicia? Her grandfather, Josh, and her mother, Daphne, were both in hospital, and her family home had gone up in flames.

The ambulance departed, siren wailing.

The man came in, weary to the bone. Sodden clothes. Dark hair slicked to his head. A well-shaped head. A jaw that said he was not to be trifled with. He thanked their kind hosts, and said, 'You heard the ambulance leave? They confirmed Mrs Frost has a broken leg. Also, probably, concussion. They're taking her to St George's Hospital. I'll ring them later, to see how she's getting on. I've asked the paramedic to check on the children before we take them away.'

'Yes, yes,' said the householder, still high on excitement. 'The children will be all right after a good night's sleep, won't they?'

The paramedic bustled in. 'I have another call . . .'

'Please,' said the man. 'The children were exposed to dense smoke earlier. Can you check them out?'

Bea said, 'I think they're all right. Their breathing seems easy enough now, but they are exhausted.'

The paramedic gave each child a cursory examination. 'No problem. You must have got them out in time. Keep an eye, won't you? And if . . . give us a ring. Now, if you don't mind . . .'

Faye, tears pooling on her splendid cheekbones, said, 'I'm the one who needs attention. Look at my bruises, here and here!' Indicating the shoulder which she'd bumped when she'd been searching for pearls under the table, and her wrist which Bea had grabbed in getting the girl out of the burning house. 'How can I work with these injuries? Mrs Abbot assaulted me. I need photographs to prove it, so that I can take her to court and sue for damages.'

'What nonsense!' said Bea, but was herself too exhausted to complain further.

The paramedic looked harassed, but examined Faye and even consented to take some photographs of her bruises on her phone. Then he disappeared to answer his next call.

Faye preened herself. 'Now that's settled, I've got a lift arranged and I'll be off. But not before I have a word with the firemen. Someone's got to tell them that the children caused the fire!' She swept out without a word of thanks to their kind hosts, leaving Bea worried about what Faye might have to say.

No, surely, no one would take Faye seriously, would they? And she herself had something more urgent to worry about. What were they to do with the girls?

The only answer that occurred to Bea was to kidnap them and take them home with her, which she didn't think would be allowed. And, in fact, she wasn't sure she had enough strength to cope. Perhaps the man – it was ridiculous, but she still didn't know his name – might have something to suggest?

When he got off the phone again. And it was *her* phone, after all!

Their kind hosts were looking at their dishevelled guests and then at the clock, clearly feeling their age and wanting their bed. At their age, a little excitement went a long way. The householder went to look out of the window. 'There's no fewer than three fire engines working at the house now. Will you go to a hotel or something?'

The man clicked the phone off. 'I've spoken to Steve and told him what's happened. He's on his way back home as we speak. Daphne's being kept in, and so is Josh. Steve asked if I could take care of Alicia tonight, and I agreed. I've told the chief fire officer what I know, and given him my card. I asked if he needed to see you, Mrs Abbot, and the children tonight and he said "no", but to leave him an address where he could contact you tomorrow. Is that all right?'

Bea nodded. 'I'd like to take Bernice home with me, if no one objects.'

Her phone rang again. The man still had it in his hand, so answered it. Shortly. What a tower of a man he was. Solid. Reliable. Sensible. He handed the phone over to her. 'Leon, for you.'

Leon was impatient. 'Where the hell are you, Bea? And who's that using your phone? I've been waiting for you to ring back and—'

'Sorry, Leon.' Though why she should apologize, she didn't know.

'Josh is being kept in, and I was about to go home because Gideon's staying with him, when Steve rang to ask where you were because he can't do anything with Daphne and I'd told him you'd be glad to help with her. Every time he tries to leave, she gets into a terrible state. She's being kept in overnight, and seeing the cosmetic surgeon tomorrow but, even though they've sedated her, she needs someone to—'

'Leon, stop! Perhaps you hadn't heard, but after you left, another fire broke out at the house. We got the children out and the fire brigade on to it, but there's no way anyone is going to be able to sleep at the house tonight. I know Bernice can't go back to her mother's, what with the chickenpox and all, so what would you say to my taking her home with me? Unless you'd like to look after her yourself?'

'What! What? I can't . . . my sister is back in the States, you know that! You're right, the child's mother is hardly . . . well, yes. You don't mind looking after her tonight, will you?'

'If you give me permission to do so, yes.'

'Well, I suppose, if you're looking after Bernice, you can't help with Daphne.'

'She has a husband or two in tow, hasn't she? I believe I sat next to one at dinner.'

'Humph. The toy boy? He was here, yes. Left some time ago, saying he has an allergy to the sight of blood. Would you believe! Steve said Daphne's current husband – called Alaric – promised to accompany her to the hospital but never bothered to show up.' He grumbled himself to a standstill and Bea switched off the phone.

Bea's brain felt numb. Daphne, the sexy brunette who was Alicia's mother, had been married three times, or was it four? Husbands number two and three had both been present at the dinner, hadn't they? Or was Daphne still married to number two but intending to marry number three? Bea sighed. Perhaps she'd misheard. Introductions had been rushed when Bea and Leon arrived, so . . . Bea decided to think about that tomorrow.

First things first: get Bernice to bed. But what about Alicia?

Prompt on cue, Alicia started awake and cried out. The man stooped to lift the child into his arms. 'There, there! Safe now.'

Alicia snuggled into him, whimpering. 'I thought . . .'

Bea struggled to make sense of everything. 'So where do you fit into the family?'

'I'm Alicia's paternal grandfather. My son is her father.

Lissy, poppet; I'm right out of ideas. Where are you going to sleep tonight? Can you go to stay with Bernice's people?'

Bernice was out of it. Fast asleep.

Bea said, 'Sorry, no. Not appropriate. Bernice is Leon's great-niece and he's agreed she can stay with me tonight. I've got a bed to spare. Will you let Alicia come home with me, too? I live just off Kensington Church Street. I've just thought; it's lucky I retrieved my evening bag or I wouldn't have had a key to get back in with.'

He held out his hand. 'Give me your phone and I'll order a cab.' She handed over her phone again, wondering for the first time where he lived. Out of town? If he went to a hotel looking as he did now, would they give him a room? His jacket was in poor shape, his black tie – a properly tied black tie and not a made-up one – was hanging undone round his neck. A well-cut suit. Silk mixture. His shirt was filthy. She hoped he had some cards on him to pay for the taxi.

Yes, he was thinking the same thing. He handed her back her phone and, hampered by Alicia clinging round his neck, checked his pockets. Produced a wallet. Yes, he had cards and enough cash on him to pay for a cab.

He thanked their hosts for their kindness, saying he'd be back tomorrow – giving them his card – and said they must make sure to send the bill for any cleaning that needed to be done to him. He asked Bea if she had a card on her, and when she produced one from her bag, he said he'd give it to the firemen so that they could contact her on the morrow, and for her not to take the children outside into the cold until the cab arrived. Thoughtful of him. He handed Alicia back to Bea and disappeared into the night again.

Their host stood in the window to see what was happening outside and to give them a running commentary. 'It's amazing how a crowd collects, even at this time of night. Dog-walkers, teenagers with nothing better to do.' He flattened himself against the window, the better to see what was happening. 'I must say, they do seem to know what they're doing. All those hoses, you'd think they'd get them mixed up. Do they have a height requirement, do you know? I always wanted to be a fireman when I was younger.'

'Come away, do,' said his wife. 'You'll catch your death.'

He took no notice. 'Can't see any flames now, but there's lots of black smoke. What a mess! I wonder if they're going to be able to save the upper floors. I expect they'll have to keep one of the engines here all night, to make sure the fire doesn't start up again.' And, to his wife, 'Ought we to offer the firemen some refreshments?'

'No,' said his wife. 'It's long past our bedtime.'

Their cab came. Bea feared that in their soot-laden clothes, they'd probably spoil the upholstery. The driver thought so, too. The man pacified him with a couple of large denomination notes. Bernice slept as Bea bore her out to the cab; the man carried Alicia, who was fighting sleep.

Home, James; and don't spare the horses.

How strange it seemed to walk back into her own lovely house and switch on lights that worked. The children woke when they were lifted out of the cab. Both made it up the steps and into the hall on their own two feet. Disorientated, half awake. Filthy.

'Upstairs,' Bea said to the children. 'First floor. Big bedroom on the left. Bathroom en suite. Shed your clothes on the landing, get into the bath. Use masses of bath oil. Wash your hair. I'll find you some T-shirts to wear.'

Wearily, the girls pulled themselves up the stairs, holding on to the banisters. Bea knew how they felt.

The man hesitated. 'May I stay for a while?'

'Please do.'

'Is there somewhere I can wash?'

'Can you make it to the top floor? There's a flat up there which my adopted son uses. Spare bedroom and bathroom. You might even find a bathrobe which will fit you.'

He followed the girls upstairs.

Bea felt something press against her leg. Winston, her big, black, fluffy cat, letting her know he needed to be fed. She picked him up and cuddled him. He allowed her to caress him for the ritual five seconds, then wriggled out of her arms and made for the kitchen. He knew where his food was to be found, even if she seemed to have forgotten her role as carer. She obeyed him. A sachet of his current favourite. Fresh water.

She followed the others upstairs. She would give the children her own big bed tonight because they would sleep better if they were together. She always kept the spare-room bed made up, so she'd doss down there. She shucked off her jewellery, added her torn and dirty clothing to the pile of children's things on the landing and went to shower in the guest room next door.

She could hear bathwater running in her own bathroom . . . and then the water gurgled down the outside pipe from the top floor, too. She removed the remains of her makeup, found herself a long cotton nightie, shrugged on her grey velvet winter housecoat, brushed her hair, and put her head round the door of her bathroom to find the girls still were in the bath, one at either end. They'd used her best bath oil. Good. She hoped it would take the stink of fire out of their nostrils. They looked as sleek as seals, with long wet hair clinging to their scalps.

'We used two lots of bath water,' said Bernice, in her deep, grown-up voice. 'We hope that's all right.'

'Sensible girls. The hairdryer is already plugged in next door, and I'll find you a couple of T-shirts to wear. When you're ready, pop yourselves into my big bed and I'll bring you up some hot chocolate to drink.'

'We can sleep together?'

'Definitely.'

Bea laid a couple of T-shirts out on the bed and went downstairs to make four mugs of hot chocolate. She set aside two to cool while she took the others upstairs. She considered putting some whisky into the chocolate, but decided against it. The girls were near enough sleepwalking as it was. Two clean little girls, eyes wide with strain.

Ah, she knew what would help. She rummaged in a cupboard to find . . . she knew she hadn't thrown it away . . . her old teddy bear. She'd been given it as a child. It had had its growl replaced and was large enough for a child to hug. She handed it to Alicia, who was the first to climb into bed.

'Mm.' Alicia put her nose to the bear and breathed deeply. 'He smells funny. What's his name?'

'Teddy. What sort of "funny" does he smell? Funny good?'

'Dunno. All right.'

'Let me.' Bernice climbed in beside her and they both had a go. 'Mm. Yes. Funny. Like wet wool, a bit. But nice.'

'Hot chocolate, both of you.' Bea handed them their mugs. 'I'm going to leave the landing light on, just in case you need to go to the loo in the night. You might find my cat wants to sleep with you. I hope you don't mind?'

Alicia addressed the toy bear. 'Teddy, do you mind if we have a cat to sleep with us?'

Bernice put on an extra-low voice, pretending to be the bear. 'I don't mind, if you don't.'

Alicia said, 'Why don't we call him Nosey-poo!'

'That's a silly name. She said his name is Teddy.'

'That's her name for him. He has to have a name of his own.'

'No, he doesn't. He's already Teddy.'

The children giggled. They'd perked up nicely, but would probably have nightmares.

They settled down, one on either side of the bear, talking to him in low voices. 'Now don't be afraid, Teddy. Nothing's going to happen to you—'

'We're quite safe here . . .'

'Mrs Abbot won't let anything awful happen to us . . .'

The children's eyes were closing. Bernice gave an enormous yawn. Alicia put her thumb in her mouth and sucked. She probably hadn't sucked her thumb since she was two years old, but this was not the moment to remonstrate.

Bea decided to sleep next door so that she could hear them if they called out in the night. She collected all the dirty clothing which had been abandoned on the landing, and went downstairs to see whether or not her male guest was still around.

She found him in the kitchen, contemplating the microwave and two cooling mugs of hot chocolate. He was wearing – just about – her adopted son's white bathrobe, over his own trousers. Bare feet. His dirty shirt and socks were on the floor. She picked them up to put in the washing machine, together with the children's things. She buried her ruined evening dress in the rubbish bin. She'd never wear that again.

He said, 'A cat keeps nudging my ankles. Yours?'

'Winston. I fed him a while ago, but he reckons guests can always be bamboozled into giving him extra. I'll give him another sachet to shut him up. Can you work the microwave, and do you want me to put something in your chocolate?'

'I'll have it straight. Thanks.' He microwaved and handed her a mug of chocolate so hot it almost burned her hands. She didn't mind. She cupped her hands around it, and savoured the aroma. She closed her eyes for a moment.

There was something she had failed to do. What was it? She said, 'I know it's ridiculous, but I can't remember your name. I'm sure we were introduced but . . . and then someone was sitting between us at table.'

'Morton. William.'

'Abbot. Beatrice. Call me Bea.'

Was that a cry from one of the girls? The both lifted their heads to listen. No, all was quiet except for Winston noisily ingesting his food, and the swish of the washing machine.

She said, 'It's getting late. I don't know where you live. Do you want to stay here tonight, in the flat upstairs?'

'I'd like that. I was supposed to stay at Josh's tonight.'

She had a ridiculous impulse to laugh. Why? Totally inappropriate. She suppressed the urge with difficulty. 'You haven't even a toothbrush to your name, then?'

'I could go to an hotel.'

A phone rang. Her mobile? She looked wildly around. She must silence it, immediately, or it might wake the children. Where had she left it? Ah, her evening bag was sitting on the table in front of her and her phone was in it. She extracted it. 'Bea Abbot speaking.'

Someone screamed. 'He's dead!'

FOUR

Bea said, 'What!'

The phone went dead.

William asked, 'What is it? Bad news?'

She handed her phone over to him. 'I think that call was meant for you. A man shouted that someone was dead.'

He checked. 'That call was from Steve's phone. I'd better speak to him. If I may?' She could hear the phone ring at the other end until it was answered. At the same moment she heard a child cry out. Bea hurried up the stairs.

Alicia was fast asleep but Bernice was out of bed, holding the bear by one hand, swaying with fatigue.

Bea gathered the child up in her arms, and rocked her to and fro. 'There, there.'

'I thought I heard . . . was that Mummy ringing to see if I was all right? Or Aunt Sybil? Can I speak to her?'

Oh dear, neither of them had been informed. Bernice's mother, Dilys, was a sweet-natured, not particularly intelligent woman, whose default position was to dither.

Sybil Holland was Bernice's great-aunt, a billionairess; a painted, cigarette-smoking, red-lipsticked dragon who'd discarded three husbands so far. Her mind was as sharp as a razor, and her mantra was, 'Never look back.'

Even before her mother had remarried, Sybil Holland had taken Bernice under her wing and acted as her guardian although, as far as Bea knew, the position had never been made legal. Sybil was made of tungsten and understood Bernice, but Sybil spent most of her life in America and was living there now.

Bea wondered what to say. 'I don't want to disturb them at this time of night, poppet. We'll speak to them in the morning, both of us, and tell them not to worry because you're managing beautifully.'

Bernice was a brave child, who would, hopefully, respond to the challenge.

Bea said, 'Let's get you back into bed with Teddy, so he doesn't catch his death of cold. Do you say your prayers when you go to bed?'

Bernice obediently got back into bed. Nice child that she was. 'Is Mrs Frost all right? She taught us a prayer, but I can't remember how it goes. Can you say it for me?'

Panic. Bea had forgotten all about poor Mrs Frost, and it was years since she'd used a child's prayer when she went to bed. Nowadays she talked to God whenever she felt like it, at any time of the night or day. Also when she was in trouble. This poor little mite was in trouble, all right . . . especially if that telephone call meant what Bea thought it might mean.

She tucked Bernice under the duvet, and smoothed her hair back. 'I don't know which prayer Mrs Frost taught you. The one I used to say is:

> '"Now I lay me down to sleep,
> Guardian angels round me keep.
> Watch about me through the night,
> Wake me safe with morning bright."'

Bernice's eyes were bright. Too bright. Tears were about to spill over.

Bea tried to think of something to distract the child. 'How do you imagine your guardian angel? Is he just hanging around behind your left shoulder? What does he look like? Mine has wings that aren't pure white, but have flashes of pink and orange in them. When I'm on the verge of sleep, I think of him standing behind my bed and stretching out his wings to shelter me.'

'There's bits of blue in the white,' said Bernice. 'Different blues: some sky-blue and some a bit violety. I didn't know grown-ups could see angels as well. Alicia's angel has got some green in hers.' The child snuggled down, clutching Teddy. 'When Mummy rings, will you tell her I'm all right, really? And not to worry. She does tend to panic, you know.'

Bea kissed the child's forehead, wondering if Dilys would ever be able to find room in her new life for her daughter. Possibly not. But this was not the time to say so. 'Of course

I'll tell her. Now close your eyes, and ask your guardian angel to look after you through the night. Tell her to be careful not to bump into Alicia's angel. We don't want a heavenly fight over the bed, do we?'

Bernice giggled. 'Silly . . .!' She closed her eyes. Her breathing slowed. Bea didn't move until the child's regular breathing told her she was deeply asleep.

Downstairs Bea went. William was on her phone, still. Walking around, monosyllabic. Listening to a voice which sounded scratchy, hysterical.

Bea took the clothes out of the washing machine and put them in the drier.

William finished the call, and put her phone on the table. He looked stunned. 'I can't believe it. Josh, my old friend . . . we were at school together, our children went to the same schools, and we . . .' He passed his hand across his eyes. 'He's dead. I can't take it in. I mean, we all knew his heart was damaged. He'd had a by-pass last year, but . . . I could see his colour was bad at table, when the firework went off behind us, but Gideon was attending to him, and . . . did I do the wrong thing in leaving Josh so we could look for the girls? No, that was the right thing to do. We would have been too late to get them out if I'd stopped to help Josh. Gideon was there and got him to hospital.'

Bea set the drier to work. The children probably wouldn't want to wear those dresses again, but they'd need their other things. She said, 'You are a family friend?'

He nodded, bringing his thoughts back from some faraway place. 'It had never crossed my mind that . . . he's been a creaking gate for years. I wonder, ought we to have done things differently? Taken him to a different hospital? No, what am I saying? It could have happened at any time, and he was in the best possible place . . . Where was I? Oh. Yes. They'd planned to keep him in hospital overnight. Just as well, as he couldn't have returned to a home in flames. He never knew about the fire. I'm glad he didn't.'

'You told someone who was with Josh at the hospital about the fire, didn't you?'

'We were all on our phones, calling one another. I told

Steve, who told your friend Leon. Then Gideon rang Steve and got the details. They decided not to tell Josh about it for the time being. Leon did well, didn't he? Keeping everyone calm. They decided Steve should see his sister Daphne settled down so that he could get back to the house . . . she was in quite a state, apparently. She is a bit of a drama queen.'

Bea said, 'Leon rang me, wanted me to go and look after Daphne, but by that time we had the children on our hands.'

He wasn't listening. 'There was no immediate danger, they thought. But then, Josh had another heart attack. Out of the blue. They did their best, they worked on him for quite a while, but it was no good. Josh has gone. He was a good man, you know? Always tried to do his best.'

Steve and Gideon were Josh's two sons. Bea had a feeling that Steve was the elder of the two. 'Was that Steve on the phone, or Gideon?'

'Steve. Gideon had rung him to break the news, so he rang me. Steve's usually so calm and capable, but losing your father so unexpectedly . . . No, it's not surprising. I'm shocked, too. He was one of my oldest friends and . . . Daphne!' He shook his head. 'She'll take it hard!'

'They won't wake her to tell her, will they? Time enough for her to hear about it tomorrow. I suppose it will be best for Steve to break the news? Perhaps he'll tell her husband and he can tell her?'

He took a deep breath. 'Yes, sufficient to the day. Steve is still at the house. He says the fire is out but they're keeping a crew on overnight to make sure it doesn't break out again. He rang me because . . . I suppose I'm the only one of the older generation around to rely on, now that his father is . . . Steve says Gideon is taking it badly. An understatement, I should think. Gideon was always his father's favourite.'

Bea didn't reply. There was at once too much to say, and nothing helpful. She put Winston's dirty plate in the dishwasher, together with the mugs they'd used.

The man tramped around the room. She could read the signs. He was distressed and was going to pick a quarrel with someone if he could. He started by saying, 'You don't panic easily, Mrs Abbot?'

'Have you checked on Mrs Frost?'

That rocked him back on his heels. He reddened. He'd forgotten poor Mrs Frost. 'May I borrow your phone again?'

She nodded. At least he'd had the courtesy to ask.

He reached the Reception desk at the hospital. Got short shrift. Shut off the phone. He was annoyed with himself and everyone. 'They wouldn't give me any information because I'm not family, or even a friend. What can I do? I don't know who her next of kin would be. Josh would have known. Daphne? No, she's out of it for the moment.'

'Try Steve. He might be able to throw some light.'

He threw her a dark look, but followed her suggestion and used her phone again. 'Steve, sorry to bother you, but do we know who Mrs Frost's next of kin might be?'

He listened. At length. Shook his head. Clicking off the phone he said, 'Steve hasn't a clue. The top floor of the house where Mrs Frost and the children slept has been burned out, and the stairs leading to it. Whatever's left up there is going to stay up there. Josh had a study on the ground floor at the back, overlooking the garden. With any luck that's still intact. There'll be some paperwork there which will give us her next of kin. They ought to be told so that they can visit. Steve will see if he can gain access tomorrow. Any other helpful suggestions?'

In a meek tone, she said, 'It seems a long time since supper. Could you eat something?'

He was going to say that that was a ridiculous sugges-tion, but changed his mind. He even managed to produce a smile. 'Apologies. What do you suggest? Shall I send out for something?'

'What about some home-made soup and a roll? I always keep some in the freezer for emergencies.'

He lifted his head. Was that a cry?

She listened, too. The cry was repeated. 'Grandpa!'

Bea said, 'Alicia. Your turn. I'll have the soup ready by the time you come down again.'

He went off up the stairs and she set about defrosting and heating up some soup and rolls. By the time he'd soothed

Alicia back to sleep and returned to the kitchen, she'd sorted out what to say to him.

'Sit down and eat. Take your time. I'm sleeping next door to the girls, so if they wake in the night, I'll see to them. If you'd like to stay here, too, then you may sleep in the spare room at the top of the house.'

'Thanks. I appreciate it.' He spooned soup up and attacked the rolls as if there were no tomorrow.

She said, 'Tomorrow I'll tell Bernice's people what's happened and find out what arrangements they want to make for her. You'll do the same for Alicia? When are the girls due back at school?'

'Tuesday, I think. I doubt if Daphne will be able to look after them meanwhile. Perhaps they'll let me take Alicia back to my place.' A sigh. 'Then there'll be funeral arrangements to be made for Josh. If Steve doesn't pull himself together, I may have to help out there.' He sat back, temporarily sated. 'You're a good cook, Mrs Abbot.'

'Don't sound so surprised.' She stowed the dirty plates away, and rescued the dried clothes from the drier. 'We'll talk in the morning. Best get some sleep, now.'

Faye is going to tell everyone that the girls set the fires. But we won't talk about that now.

He said, 'If you don't object, I'll bring down a duvet from the top floor and sleep on a chair in the girls' bedroom, just in case Alicia wakes in the night.'

She checked her watch. 'All right, but if Bernice wakes, rouse me to deal with her. I'll be next door.'

William started up the stairs ahead of her, while she collected Winston and the girls' clean clothes and shut off the lights downstairs. By the time she reached the first floor, he was humping a duvet on to a chair beside the bed in which the children were sleeping. She paused on the landing to watch as he leant over Alicia, to push the hair back from her forehead.

She caught her breath. For a second there, William reminded her of her own much-loved dead husband. He'd been a big, well-built man, too. Yes, they were the same physical type . . . which, she told herself, did not mean anything.

She still occasionally wore the diamond engagement ring which her husband had given her, and had never removed his wedding ring from her finger.

Leon? Well, he'd crept into her life through a business contact and become her good friend. He'd asked her to marry him several times. She'd grown fond of him as a companion and escort, but over time she had come to understand that she was keener on Leon when he had other things on his mind, and that she withdrew when he wanted to commit to her.

She turned into the spare bedroom. The cat Winston leaped on to the bed, turned round three times, hesitated and looked through the open door, across the landing, and into the master bedroom opposite. He was trying to decide where he would sleep – with her or with the girls. She wouldn't wait for him to make up his mind. She got into bed, turned out the light and tried to relax. She was very tired. She hoped she'd sleep but feared she wouldn't. She prayed in snatches, aware of problems hovering on the edge of her consciousness.

For a start, she didn't think the fires had been started by accident. Someone had timed them to go off during the dinner party and after the children had gone to bed. The girls had been allowed to stay up later than usual. If they'd gone up at their usual time, they'd have been in bed when the fire started upstairs. And died. It had been intended they should die.

No, no! She must be wrong. Who could be so callous as to think up such a scheme?

She was wide awake, aware of the minutes ticking away, trying to pray . . . finally recalling what she'd told Bernice about a guardian angel.

Before that night, Bea hadn't thought about guardian angels for ages. Years. She'd told Bernice that her own guardian angel had white wings with pink and yellow feathers. Bea smiled. Was that true? She supposed it must have been or why would it have come to her? But why not blue or green? Why not completely white?

She liked the thought of someone watching over the children as they slept. Too, too Babes in the Wood. Hansel and Gretel. Well, why not?

A bird trilled a pre-dawn song in the garden below. She slept.

Saturday morning

She started awake. It was full daylight. Why was she not in her own bed?

Ah, she remembered.

She peeped in on the girls, who were still fast asleep. Good.

The chair William had slept in was empty. The cat Winston heard her, and jumped down from the girls' bed to butt at Bea's legs. She was late getting up, and he was informing her that he needed to be fed, now! She dressed quickly, brushed her hair, put on the minimum of make-up, and stole down the stairs to find a note on the kitchen table from William, saying he'd borrowed her phone again, had gone out to get a replacement but would be back shortly.

She fed Winston and made coffee. She could hear voices in the agency rooms down below. The domestic agency she ran was usually busy at weekends, and recently they'd had two people on duty on Saturday morning and occasionally on Saturday afternoons as well.

Bea took her coffee and went downstairs to see who was on duty that day. By great good fortune, it was Betty, her office manageress: a practical, reliable person. The other girl was a sweetie, but not exactly Brain of Britain. However, she could take phone messages, which was mostly what was needed on Saturdays.

Betty took one look at Bea's face. 'A problem?'

'You bet,' said Bea. 'Let me explain . . .' She did so, concluding, 'Bernice's mother is not going to be able to drop everything to look after her daughter because their little boy has gone down with chickenpox and they don't want Bernice to get it, too . . . which is why the child was staying with a friend for half-term.'

'Ouch!' said Betty.

'Uhuh! I'm pretty sure Dilys will want me to look after Bernice till she goes back to boarding school, and where we get replacement uniforms I do not know! Whatever happens, the child needs something to wear today. The same applies to Alicia, whose mother was carted off to hospital last night needing stitches in her arm. Not to mention that the family house has been burned out. So, can you find someone to go shopping for the children and to look after them for a couple of hours afterwards? Marks & Spencer should have everything they need. T-shirts and jeans, sweaters, jackets, tights, undies and toiletries. And trainers. Age ten. It would be best to get everything in two sizes because Marks will take back anything we don't use, right?'

'Age ten.' Betty scribbled on a pad. 'Payment?'

'Here's my M&S card and details. This will be an emergency package only as the relatives will no doubt want to buy more clothing from Harrods or whatever later. I'll be in touch with Bernice's family, and Alicia's grandfather will deal with hers, but I don't see him shopping for girls' undies and toiletries.'

Betty turned back to her computer. 'How about our own Mel? She's local and often does the Saturday morning slot. What do you think?'

Bea looked across the room to an unoccupied desk in the corner, and imagined the girl who usually sat there. Straight fair hair in a ponytail, big-boned, conservative dress sense. Mid-twenties? She'd been away to university but returned home to help when her mother had been diagnosed with breast cancer, thankfully now in remission. Mel hadn't been with them long but appeared to be hard-working and possessed – wow! – common sense.

'Has she any experience of dealing with children?'

Betty was busy scrolling up and down. 'Siblings, older and younger. I can't think of anyone else who's local and might be free at short notice. Also, Mel's young enough to know what fashions youngsters are wearing nowadays.'

'You've sold me. See if she'll come in. Now, what have I got on this morning?'

Betty switched files. 'Nothing I can't handle till noon when we have that super-nanny coming in, the one whose CV reads like a list from *Who's Who*. You said you'd see her, and I don't think she'll be willing to see anyone else.'

Bea grimaced. She couldn't put her finger on it, but for some reason she hadn't been altogether convinced that super-nanny was as super as she'd claimed to be. 'Right. Well, I'll be upstairs if you need me for anything else.'

Bea usually made a point of being in the agency on Saturday mornings, but today she left Betty trying to contact Mel while she went back upstairs to start breakfast, ensure the girls were getting up, make lists of who she needed to contact, and check if she had enough extra food for the weekend.

William hadn't yet returned, so Bea used her landline to contact Dilys, Bernice's mother, reminding herself to Handle with Care. Dilys was a sweetie but not the sharpest knife in the drawer. Bea had a bet with herself that Dilys would flap and worry and basically be unable to cope.

And that's what Dilys did. Flap and dither. Dilys had just got to the point of saying it would be much the best for Bernice to stay with Bea when the two girls came into the kitchen, wearing two more of Bea's T-shirts over their own clean tights, but no shoes. They'd brushed one another's hair out and looked all right at first glance.

Bea motioned the children to take a seat while saying, 'But yes, I quite understand you can't cope at the moment, Dilys. Chickenpox is awful. And you didn't get a wink of sleep? Well, of course I can keep Bernice here today and kit her out with some fresh clothes. She's just come in and is dying to speak to you.'

Bea handed the phone over to Bernice, whose stoical expression told Bea that the girl didn't expect anything much in the way of loving care from her mother. The child said 'Yes' and 'No' at appropriate intervals and, finally, ended the conversation with, 'Of course I understand. And yes, I think Aunt Sybil's in Boston this weekend. I expect Uncle Leon will tell her.'

Bea laid out breakfast things for the girls: orange juice, cereal and toast. Alicia was carrying Teddy, whom she placed on a stool beside her. Bea blinked. Something about Teddy was not quite right. Then she got it; Teddy was wearing one of Bea's handkerchiefs round his neck, and Bea's diamond earrings. Oh. The girls had made free with Bea's wardrobe, hadn't they? And her toiletries, too, by the look of it. Was that a trace of lipstick on each?

Bernice put the phone down and looked Bea straight in the eye. 'You can't rely on some people, can you?' Her eyes were heavy-lidded. Her unchildlike, deep voice didn't waver. She was indeed a little soldier, was Bernice.

Bea sighed. 'You can only rely on people to be themselves. They do love you, you know. We'll get on to your uncle Leon and your great-aunt in a couple of hours when they're up and about, and find out what plans they have for you.'

Alicia said, 'What about Mrs Frost? Mummy needs such a lot of looking after. If she's hurt her arm, she won't be able to do anything about the house. Not that she does much, anyway.' Her tone was dispassionate. Another child accustomed to fending for herself.

Bea nodded. 'I'll ring the hospital and find out how she is, in a minute. You don't happen to have your uncle Steve's number, do you, by any chance? No. Well, it was just a thought. Meanwhile, eat up, and by the time you've finished there'll be someone here with some brand-new clothes for you to wear. You can help me by putting the breakfast things into the dishwasher and then go upstairs to make the bed and tidy the room. And please return my jewellery to my dressing table straight away.'

The children tried to work out how seriously they needed to take Bea's words, and concluded that, yes, they'd better behave. Alicia pretended to feed Teddy's mouth with some cereal.

Bernice said, 'Eat up, Teddy, or you'll never grow up to be a big boy.'

Alicia pushed her lower lip out. 'He can't grow any bigger, anyway. He's only a bear.'

'He can if he wants to.'

Bea left them to it. She used the extension in the living room to ring Leon. Her call went to voicemail. Presumably he wasn't out of bed yet.

The doorbell rang. It was William Morton. He'd had a shave somewhere and dressed in clothing he'd no doubt just bought that morning; a navy blue sweater over a white shirt, well-cut dark trousers, slip-on shoes. He was carrying a holdall, also new. He hoisted a huge arrangement of flowers up the steps and into the hall. 'For you,' he said. 'Already in water so you don't need to do anything with them. How are the children?

Are they up yet? I've got myself another phone, and a spare you can use till yours is charged up again.'

'The children are coping pretty well, all things considered. And trying my patience. Thank you for the flowers, though there really was no need—'

'There was every need. I bought a couple of sparkly T-shirts for the girls. I understand they like such things.'

'They're in the kitchen, having breakfast. I've got someone going out to buy them some clothes. Come into the sitting room.' She led the way, and closed the door behind them. 'I've been on to Bernice's mother, and got permission for her to stay on here for the time being. I asked Alicia if she had Steve's telephone number, so that I could ask him about Mrs Frost. She didn't have it.'

William set the flowers down on an occasional table and fished a couple of phones out of his holdall. 'This one is new, for you. The other one is your old one. Everyone's got this number of yours, so I've been getting calls all morning. First; Daphne's been stitched up but is being kept in hospital because she's running a temperature.'

In a flat tone, Bea said, 'Alicia seems resigned to not having her mother around.'

In an equally flat tone, he said, 'Daphne's looks are very important to her.'

They both understood that Daphne lacked the maternal instinct.

He said, 'As to Alicia; I've been on to Steve, who says it's all right with him you having Alicia overnight, but I have to get Alaric's permission to take the child home with me for a few days before she goes back to school.'

'Alaric . . .?'

'Sitting opposite you last night. Daphne's second husband, who adopted Alicia when he married her mother. True, he and Daphne are in the process of divorcing, but legally he and Daphne are still jointly responsible for Alicia at the moment. So far I haven't been able to get through to him, but I've left messages on his phone, so I hope he'll get back to me soonest. Steve spoke to the hospital where they took Mrs Frost; she hasn't yet regained consciousness. He stayed at the family house till dawn and is now trying to deal with firemen and investigators and insurance people and solicitors and Josh's death. Oh yes, and a fire investigator is coming round here this morning to talk to the children.'

'They're going to try to blame the fire on the children, aren't they?'

FIVE

Saturday, mid-morning

Bea lit the simulated gas log fire in the sitting room. Her central heating was adequate, but on a cold and dreary winter's day it was a good idea to have the fire on. Besides which, Bea told herself that if she didn't light it now she might never be able to face doing so again.

William hovered, hands in pockets, frowning.

She said, 'Do sit down. Have you had any breakfast?'

'Coffee and a bun. It'll do me.' He still didn't sit down, but walked around the room, looking at the books, the pictures. He was trying to get a feel of what she was like from her surroundings? He seemed to approve of the Adam-style fireplace with the gilt-framed mirror over it; the comfortable easy chairs and the settees with their deep, loose cushions; the big side lamps. He nodded in recognition of the quality of the mahogany dining table and chairs in the bay window overlooking the street, but stopped for a while at the other end of the room to look at the portrait of her husband hanging on the wall above her writing table.

Still looking at the portrait, he said, 'How are you related to Bernice?'

'No relation. Friend of the family. Bernice's mother married for the first time when she was very young. Her husband was a no-gooder who abused her. When he was killed, Dilys found it difficult to cope. She's very sweet but she dithers. She's remarried to a decent man who looks after her beautifully, and they've produced a little boy who has gone down with chickenpox. The three of them are so bound up with one another that . . . don't get me wrong, they love Bernice, but—'

'She's surplus to requirements.'

Bea winced. He was right, of course, but nobody had put the situation so bluntly before. 'Leon is her great-uncle and he adores her, but he's not exactly domesticated. His sister Sybil has sort of adopted Bernice, but Sybil lives mostly in the States and is really too old to look after the child properly. Bernice has brains. She herself opted for boarding school, and she seems to be thriving in that environment, especially since she made friends with Alicia. It's just the holidays which can be difficult. She was supposed to go to her mother's this half-term but then . . . the chickenpox . . . which is why Alicia suggested Bernice stayed with her. I've spoken to Dilys this morning, and she's happy for me to look after the child till she goes back to school.'

'Who is the child's legal guardian?'

Bea frowned. 'I suppose her mother is, though I believe it's Sybil who pays her school fees. You are making me uneasy. Do you really think that's going to become an issue?'

'I hope not.'

Bea didn't know what to make of William Morton. He'd behaved well under difficult circumstances. No, he'd behaved admirably, but she had a feeling he was not being completely open about something.

She turned her head to listen for . . . what? Ah. It occurred to her that the girls were being far too quiet. Was this a case of 'Find Tommy and tell him to stop it'? They were nice kids but they'd been through a traumatic experience and one of the ways children let off steam was by doing something they knew they ought not to do, in order to attract attention.

Bea considered that, as of this very moment, they were being just too quiet. Making the excuse that she needed coffee, she went out to the kitchen to find the breakfast things still on the table, a chill wind blowing through the house, and the kitchen door wide open. The girls had gone down the iron staircase into the garden, where they were trying to coax Winston off the roof of the garden shed. Winston, being a canny cat, knew perfectly well they couldn't reach him, and so was ignoring them.

Bea called out, 'Alicia! Bernice! What are you thinking of! You'll catch your death of cold. Come back inside, at once!'

They obeyed, dragging their feet.

'We weren't doing any harm.' Alicia, lower lip well out.

'Teddy wanted to play with the cat. Winston could have got away if he'd wanted to.' Bernice had the toy bear in tow. Bea noticed, with some annoyance, that the bear was still wearing her earrings.

Bea shut and bolted the kitchen door, seized the bear, removed her earrings and put them on herself. 'I thought I asked you to clear the breakfast things and make the bed.'

'Don't you have a cleaner?' Alicia, on the verge of rudeness.

Bernice was sharp enough to interpret Bea's annoyance correctly. 'We were just going to do it.'

The front doorbell rang. Bea went to open it and found Mel, the fair-haired girl from the agency, on the doorstep. Mel was sensibly dressed in a leather jacket over jeans and boots, was wearing a minimum of makeup and was – thank the Lord – laden with packages for the children.

'I hope I haven't got too much, Mrs Abbot. I can always take back what doesn't fit.'

Bea drew her inside. 'Mel, you are brilliant. Did Betty fill you in about what's happened? Yes? Good. Now, the children are on edge and inclined to be mischievous. Do you think you can cope?'

'Sure. I'm one of four, well spaced out. Our house is chaos and I'm happy to escape for a few hours.'

'Can you give me the rest of the day? Bless you.' She called out, 'Alicia, Bernice; this is Mel, who's been out shopping for new clothes for you. I suggest you take her upstairs and try everything on.'

The girls inspected Mel. Mel inspected the girls.

'I hear you've had a big adventure,' said Mel. 'I'd love to hear all about it. Why don't you show me where you're sleeping and we can see if the clothes I've brought will fit you?'

The girls took Mel upstairs, chattering away about the fire and how they'd been rescued, while Bea set about clearing away the breakfast things and making some coffee.

The front doorbell rang again.

A stranger stood on the doorstep. A woman: Asian, stocky, black hair in a chin-length bob, intelligent eyes. She was wearing a dark blue suit. Not a police uniform.

Bea's heartbeat went into overdrive.

The woman produced a smile, and showed a badge. A fire investigator.

'Mrs Abbot? About the fire last night. I'm told you very kindly took the two girls in overnight. And you,' she turned to William, who had followed Bea into the hall, 'are William Morton? Is that right? You helped to rescue the girls? I understand, Mrs Abbot, that you have parental consent to look after them. Splendid. I'd very much like to have a little chat with them now, if convenient.'

William said, 'Do you have a warrant?'

'Goodness me, no. No need for that.' The woman smiled. A pleasant smile, backed by a strong personality. Bea had heard that it took years of training to become a fire investigator. You needed a background in forensics, a grounding in crime detection and, last but not least, the ability to assess character.

This woman was British born and well-educated. The slightest of sibilance in her voice? No fool. No. At present she was being friendly. Long might that last.

Bea waved the woman into the sitting room. 'Come in and sit down. I was just making some coffee. Will you have some? The children are upstairs. They've had a reasonably good night. I sent one of my agency girls out for some clothes for them to wear and they've gone upstairs to try them on. I'll call them down in a minute.'

The woman preceded them into the big room and looked around. 'No sprinkler system in the ceiling?'

Bea said, 'Putting a sprinkler system in these old houses would mean first installing a false ceiling. We've got two fire extinguishers in the kitchen, and fire blankets as well.'

The woman spread out her hands to the fire. 'You don't often see an open fire in this part of London. You have central heating, I see. Do the girls like an open fire?'

'I have no idea.' Bea felt she'd been wrong-footed. 'They haven't been in this room yet. I put the fire on for myself because I was afraid that if I didn't, I'd never be able to do so again.'

'Ah yes. You were caught up in the fire last night, too? Would you like to tell me about it?'

Bea excused herself. 'William can tell you what happened. I'll get the coffee.' She shut the door behind her and went into the kitchen to make a quick phone call. Brr, Brr. Brr, Brr. 'Leon, answer the phone!' Finally, he did.

'Leon, Bea here. Are you up and awake? I've got a fire investigator here wanting to talk to the girls. I have a horrid feeling that she'll think they started the fire. Can you get here, quickly?'

'What? Well, no, I can't. I'm on my way to the hospital right now. Daphne's had a bad night and someone's got to break the news about her father to—'

'Leon, she's got two brothers who could—'

'Steve's at the house, hasn't slept, is holding everything together, but—'

'What about Gideon? And, for heaven's sake, what about her two husbands?'

He laughed. 'Oh, come on! She only ever has one husband at a time. And I understand the present boyfriend passes out at the sight of blood.'

Bea told herself to calm down. 'Leon, I'm getting a weird idea. Is the family setting you up to become her fourth husband?'

A long pause. Then, 'It's not like that. I'm not in the market for . . . Bea, you know I'm not! But Daphne needs someone to . . . in the absence of her father . . . and Steve doesn't know which way to turn. I couldn't refuse to help.'

'Sorry. Yes. That was in bad taste.' Didn't Bea know well enough that Leon could be flattered by the attentions of a pretty woman but had no intention of committing himself to marriage?

Nevertheless, 'I don't see why you should be dragged into their affairs when your great-niece needs you here.'

'You'll be looking after her though, won't you? Of course you will. Look, I'll drop by later, when Daphne's settled down.'

'Promise me one thing, that you'll phone Sybil now, and ask her to come back straight away.'

'Sure. Sure. I'll be with you about lunchtime, I suppose. Shall we take the girls out somewhere nice to eat?'

Bea shut off the phone, made a cafetiere of coffee, put mugs and some soft drinks on a tray and took it into the sitting room. William wasn't there.

But the fire investigator was. She had a notebook out and what looked like a small recorder had been placed on a nearby table. She said, 'Coffee? Lovely. And what beautiful flowers. Your friend has told me what happened last night. My colleagues say you and he were heroic, carrying women and children out of danger. He's gone upstairs to see what the girls are doing.'

Implied criticism: *Why am I being kept waiting?*

Bea served coffee. 'Knowing girls, they're probably changing their minds every two minutes about what they're going to wear. He's brought them some clothes as well.'

The woman produced a form. 'While we're waiting, perhaps you can fill this in for me? I need parental permission to talk to the girls. Alicia's grandfather has signed for her, but I'm not quite sure what relation you are to Bernice?'

'None,' said Bea. 'I'm a family friend. However, I've been in touch this morning with Bernice's mother and her great-uncle, both of whom have asked me to take care of her until they can make other arrangements for the child. I'll give you their phone numbers so that you can contact them direct, shall I?' And she reeled them off. 'You can check with them while I go and yell at the girls, right?'

She went out to the hall and called up the stairs. 'Girls!' She clapped her hands. 'Come on down. There's someone to see you.' *William will have been briefing them, won't he?*

The girls clattered down the stairs, Bernice carrying Teddy, with William following behind. Alicia and Bernice were wearing identical blue T-shirts with a sparkly design on them, over jeans – and their own shoes. They were holding pink phones. Also new. The tops and the phones would be the things William had bought for them. Those tops were definitely not from Marks & Spencer.

Their hair was newly brushed, and they had removed all traces of Bea's makeup. Good, thought Bea. The agency girl had been a good choice.

Mel descended the stairs after the girls, smiling, at ease with the children.

Bea said, 'Mel, would you join us? The fire investigator wants a word with the girls, and I'd like you to be present.'

The girls halted just inside the sitting-room door. They looked at the fire and froze.

Bea gently urged them forward to sit side by side on the settee to the right of the fireplace. Mel took a seat near the door and made herself invisible. Bea congratulated herself on using Mel. The girl actually used her head in an emergency . . . and this was an emergency, wasn't it?

The fire investigator held up a form. 'Mrs Abbot, if you will sign here, giving your permission for me to talk to the children?' A slight baring of teeth, intended to represent a smile.

The girls were sitting close to one another. Alicia's thumb circled her mouth, but she was just about able to prevent herself from sucking it. Bernice was holding Teddy on her hip. He was still wearing Bea's hankie round his neck.

William took a chair at the back.

The fire investigator said, 'Well, girls; my name is Manisa, and I work for the fire service. I've been asked to find out what happened last night.' She gestured to the fireplace. 'Does this fire bother you?'

'Sort of.'

'No. Not really.'

It was definitely a tape recorder at Manisa's side. She was making notes in a notebook as well as recording everything the girls said. Bea supposed William had given permission.

Manisa smiled. 'Which is which? Alicia? You are Alicia? And so your friend is Bernice. Don't you like an open fire?'

Alicia shrugged. 'We don't have one in our house.'

Bernice agreed. 'We don't have one, either.'

'It's pretty, don't you think? Don't you find bonfires exciting?'

Bernice said, 'You can't have bonfires in towns.'

'But you like fireworks?'

'Not any more.' That was Alicia.

'Alicia, I heard you wanted to let off fireworks in your garden last night.'

'We were, but Grandpa . . . that's my other grandpa, not my granddad that's here . . . he said no.'

Manisa looked down at her notes. 'But you were given a whole box of fireworks, just for yourselves.'

Bernice said, 'Those were indoor fireworks to go on a tray on a table. But we didn't get the chance. Mrs Frost went to fetch us a hot drink and a tray and some matches and she didn't come back before . . . before.'

Manisa smiled. 'Oh, I know how it was. You were so excited, you couldn't wait. You just had a peep inside the box . . . right?'

Both girls shook their heads. Alicia said, 'No, Mrs Frost said that while she was gone we should start making out a list of the presents we'd been given so that we could write thank-you letters to people. But we didn't want to bother. I got out my new iPhone, and Bernice tried on her new shoes that she'd just been given. So we didn't open the box.'

'Who gave you them?'

The girls looked at one another and shrugged. 'We don't know,' said Bernice. 'We looked to see if there was a label—'

'But there wasn't,' said Alicia. 'We don't even know which of us it was meant for.'

'So you opened it up to see.'

Bernice shook her head. 'It was a big box and sellotaped up and we couldn't find any scissors to open it up. So I put it on Lissy's bed. I was trying on my new shoes and Lissy said she'd look to see what was on the telly and . . .' She gulped. 'The box exploded.'

'The telly exploded, you mean?' Manisa frowned.

'No, the box of fireworks. Things whizzed round the room and we were frightened—'

'Lissy used her phone and asked for the fire brigade—'

'But they said we were just kids making a hoax call—'

'Mrs Frost didn't come back and I threw the duvet from my bed over the fire but it didn't work—'

'I tried phoning Mummy downstairs and then there was all this black smoke—'

'I fell down. I couldn't breathe.'

'And then they came to get us out, and carried us down the stairs in the dark and it was, like, really scary. Then we saw Faye under the table in the dining room, trying to find her pearls and we were going to help her only Grandpa said not to because of the broken glass—'

'Then we asked about Mrs Frost and Lissy's granddad went back up the stairs to find her, leaving us in the dark again, but it was all right because he found her and then we went outside into the cold—'

'And the neighbours gave us a hot drink, and we fell asleep and came here and had a bath and fell asleep all over again.'

Huge eyes. Tense little bodies, vibrating with the strain. Alicia whimpered. Bernice pushed Teddy into Alicia's arms, saying, 'Teddy needs a cuddle.'

And not only Teddy.

Bea got to her feet, caught Mel's eye, and gave a hand to each of the girls. 'That's enough now. Darlings, why don't you go out to the kitchen with Mel and see if you can make some hot chocolate for yourselves. You might even be able to find the biscuit tin, if you look hard enough. Whatever you do, don't feed Winston. That cat's had more than enough food for now.'

Alicia obediently slid down to the floor and allowed herself to be handed over to Mel, but Bernice hung back. 'Can Mel take us to the shops to change the trainers she bought us? We really only like Nike.'

Bea checked with Mel, who nodded. 'If you ask her nicely, yes. She can take back any of the clothes you don't want at the same time. Don't forget your jackets. It's cold outside.'

'Hold on,' said William. He stuffed some notes into the girls' hands. 'Choose trainers you really like this time.'

Nice man.

Mel nodded, and shooed the children out of the room. A moment later Bea heard them chattering away in the kitchen next door. Bea reflected that the girls might be well behaved for the time being, but would recover and start thinking up some more mischief soon.

Bea carefully closed the door so that the children shouldn't hear what the adults had to say.

Turning to the fire investigator, Bea said, 'What the girls didn't see, and don't know about, are that two fires were timed to go off in the house after they'd gone upstairs. One started behind the floor-to-ceiling curtain over the window in the dining room. Something – possibly a rocket, some kind of firework? – shot up to the top of the curtain and burst into flames. That's the one which caused Josh to have a heart attack, and Daphne to cut her arm open on a broken glass.'

Manisa said, 'I've seen the remains of that curtain. I was informed the girls set their own curtain alight.'

Bea shivered. The supermodel Faye had got her story in first, hadn't she? 'You can't get up the stairs to the top floor yet, can you?'

'The top stairs have gone,' said Manisa.

'Ah. Well, shortly after the first fire started, I thought I heard a second explosion somewhere else in the house. William thought he'd heard it, too. He and I were concerned about the children and we went upstairs to check. On the top landing we came across Mrs Frost, who'd left the children in their room and been on her way downstairs when the curtain on the landing beside her went up in flames. Shocked, she tripped, fell and broke her leg. She begged us to leave her and get the girls out. We started her on her way down the stairs and went on to get the children. That's when the lights in the house went out.'

Manisa's eyes narrowed. 'Really?'

'Yes. You can check with Faye. She was there and can confirm it.'

'But . . . why?'

'I don't know. Perhaps the fire had reached . . .? No, that can't be right. Have you looked at the fuse box? Where would it be? In the kitchen quarters? Can you find out if that's been interfered with, or someone set a fire there, too?'

'We'll check. If I've understood you correctly, you're saying someone set up timed explosions throughout the house and shut off the electricity, but that it wasn't the girls?'

Bea nodded. 'Far too elaborate.'

Manisa wasn't sure about that. 'They can get all sorts of information from the Internet nowadays, including how to make a timed firework. Their uncle and his fiancée are convinced the girls set the fires.'

'Yes, you've been talking to Faye, haven't you? All right;

let's look at what the arsonist had to do. He had to research how to make the timers. Presumably on the Internet? He had to buy the necessary bits and pieces and construct the timers. Where and when were these two girls supposed to do that? At boarding school? Presumably you can trace what use they made of the school computers? And wouldn't questions have been asked at school if they'd had packets of chemicals delivered to them there?'

Manisa looked down at her notes. 'We'll check.'

'Very well. Suppose they had made timed explosive devices at school – which seems to me to be ridiculous, but yes, you have to check – then they had to smuggle them home, where Mrs Frost would be overseeing every movement of their lives.'

'They could have made the timers at home.'

'In the five days they had for half-term? That's so unlikely it's out of the question. Then they needed to set the rockets – or whatever they were – in place behind the curtains. When were the curtains drawn that day? Not until after dark. Let us suppose it was dark about four. What were the girls doing that afternoon? Running around the house setting explosive timers? I don't think so, do you?'

Manisa grimaced. 'I will check.'

'Of course. Then another timer had to be placed in the box of indoor fireworks which, judging from the description the girls gave, did not contain harmless indoor fireworks, but rockets or other fireworks which whizzed around the room and set fire to the bed. And why would the girls have wanted to set their room on fire? The smoke nearly killed them, remember. If we hadn't got there in time, they'd have died.'

Manisa winced. 'They might have done it for a lark. They wouldn't realize how quickly the smoke might kill them.'

'Did they also arrange to knock out the electricity? And why would they do that?'

'Their relatives are convinced that they did.'

'Perhaps,' said Bea, attempting to be charitable, 'they are not thinking clearly. Remember that the shock has put Alicia's mother in hospital, and helped her grandfather, Josh, to an early grave.'

'Have you a better theory?'

Bea shook her head. 'I think the girls were speaking the truth. I don't know Alicia well enough to judge, but I do know Bernice pretty well, and I think I'd know if she were lying. What they say happened sounds right to me.'

Manisa produced a faint smile. 'I'm afraid very few adults know when children lie. They swear blind that their children are pure as driven snow, even if we show them a video of them misbehaving.'

'And adults never lie?'

'Yes, of course they do. All I'm saying is that it's hard to tell when children are lying.'

Bea lifted her hands in a gesture of resignation. 'All I'm asking is that you apply the same rules of evidence to the adults who were present. As far as I am concerned, I don't know enough about the rest of the party – except for Leon – to suggest who might wish to throw the blame on the children.'

William spoke up for the first time. 'I can't suggest who would benefit from what happened, but I think I can start to make out a timetable of events. It seems to me that the two curtains being set on fire were meant as distractions to the main event. The distractions worked far better than they had any right to do since two members of the party – Josh and Daphne – and later a third, Mrs Frost . . . were carted off to hospital. But none of those injuries could have been anticipated.'

'So what were they meant to distract from?'

'I get it,' said Bea. 'The main event was the box of indoor fireworks exploding . . .?'

'Yes. The girls had been allowed to stay up long after their usual bedtime. Normally they'd have been in bed and probably already asleep when that box of tricks went up in flames. The smoke would have suffocated the girls as they slept.'

Bea said, 'But the electricity . . .?'

'Perhaps it was planned to go off to hinder any possible rescue attempt.'

Silence.

'Hang about,' said Manisa. 'What would be the point of that?'

William's tone was bleak. 'Alicia is a very wealthy little girl.'

Bea drew in her breath. 'Actually, so is Bernice. When her great-aunt dies, she'll come into a lot of money.'

Manisa was incredulous. 'You think this was attempted murder?'

'Yes,' said William. 'I don't want to believe it. But, yes.'

The front doorbell rang. And rang. Bea attended to the summons.

At first Bea didn't recognize the woman standing in the porch. And then she did. At dinner the previous night, she'd been sitting opposite Bea on their host's left. A stick insect in designer clothes. A fake blonde with a head too big for her long, thin neck. Last night she'd been wearing diamonds and a skimpy emerald green dress which had been designed for someone with fuller curves. Today she was wearing a pseudo-fur jacket over skinny jeans and stiletto shoes.

'I'm Ninette, remember? William rang us to say you were looking after Alicia for a while. Good of you. We're here to take her off your hands. Her father's outside in the car, waiting for her.'

SIX

As if on cue, the two girls came clattering down the stairs wearing their new jackets, with Mel carrying bags of rejected clothing to be returned to the shop. All three were animated, almost pink-cheeked, though Bernice was carrying Teddy in a sling on her back. Teddy bear as safety blanket?

'Ah, there you are,' said Ninette, beckoning to Alicia. 'Your father's outside. Say "thank you" to the lady for looking after you, and we'll be off.'

The two girls lost all their vivacity.

'Aunty Ninette,' said Alicia. 'We were just going shopping for some trainers.'

'You won't need them. You're going straight back to school.'

'But it's half-term!'

'They're making an exception. Come along, do! We haven't all day and I have a hair appointment this afternoon.'

Alicia hung back. 'We'll have to pack. Grandpa and Mrs Abbot bought us some new clothes to wear. And we haven't any school uniforms.'

'The school will provide everything you need. Bernice will not be returning.'

The two girls froze.

'Why not?' said Alicia. 'She's my best friend.'

'A bad choice. If they'd known her father was a criminal, the school would never have accepted her in the first place.'

Alicia's healthy colour faded to a greenish-white.

A stir in the doorway, and there was Manisa, holding up her ID. She announced her name and said, 'Do you have the right to remove the child?'

'William can give you any information you require. My fiancé adopted Alicia and has the right to remove her from contact with a pernicious influence.'

Bea said, 'Ninette, I hardly think you should—'

'Don't tell me what I should or should not do. It's a thorough disgrace that Bernice should ever have been allowed into such a prestigious school. Under false pretences, no doubt. If we had only known what Alicia was to be exposed to!'

Alicia struggled to keep calm. 'Bernice is my best friend. I don't want to go back to school without her. You don't understand what it's like. You never listen to anything I say!'

Ninette was not to be stopped. 'Did you think we wouldn't find out? How dare these people foist a felon's child on to—'

William loomed in the doorway. 'Enough, Ninette. You've made your point. I'm sorry, chicken,' he said to Alicia. 'While your mummy is so poorly, I'm afraid Alaric has the right to decide who looks after you. Be brave.' He bent down to give her a hug.

Alicia sobbed, 'I can't, Grandpa! Don't make me!'

He looked as if he were on the verge of tears himself. 'I'll ring you later, all right? You've got your new phone, haven't you? Maybe we can get permission for me to take you out next weekend.'

Tears stood out on Alicia's pale cheeks. She kissed her grandfather, and released him only to hug Bernice.

Bernice was not crying. She was beyond tears. She held out Teddy to Alicia in a gesture that said: You need him more than I do.

Alicia took the bear from Bernice and, sobbing, wrapped her arms around him.

Ninette snatched the bear from Alicia and threw him across the hall. 'Ugh. You're not taking that horrid, dirty thing with you. Come along, now!' She seized Alicia's arm, and towed her out of the front door and down the steps.

A car was waiting below, double-parked. There was a man at the wheel whom Bea recognized. He'd been introduced to her last night as 'One of Daphne's exes'. The second husband? The one who'd adopted Alicia?

Bernice watched as Alicia was pushed into the back of the car and the door shut. The car was driven away with Alicia's white face in the window as she looked back, keeping Bernice in sight as long as she could.

Bea shut the front door on the cold weather outside.

Bernice picked up Teddy. 'I'm perfectly all right,' she said in her grown-up, touch-me-not voice. She adjusted the bear into the sling at her back and looked up at Mel, who'd been hovering, and yes, wringing her hands. 'Mel, shall we go and get those trainers now? And later on, perhaps we can pack up Alicia's things and send them on to her?'

Bea wanted to hug Bernice and tell her she was a brave child, but feared that any attempt to console her might break down the child's fragile composure, so did nothing. What she did say was, 'Mel, once you've bought the new trainers, I think Bernice might like a hot chocolate with whipped cream on top. Or whatever she fancies. Something sweet. Carbohydrates. Her great-uncle is coming round later so perhaps you'd best be back by noon.'

Message received. Mel nodded, pushing back her own distress to look after Bernice.

Straight-backed, the child opened the front door and descended the steps to the street, followed by Mel who was – yes, she was! – blowing her nose.

'Well!' said Manisa. 'Will someone kindly fill me in?'

Bea led the way back to the sitting room and sat down. William followed. Manisa checked her recorder and turned over a page in her notebook. She looked at William. 'You first. Explain!'

William was also blowing his nose. 'Josh, he's the owner of the house that went up in flames last night; he and I go back to schooldays. Our wives were friends. Our children grew up together. When my son and his daughter Daphne got together, well, it was a happy day. Yes, we did think they were a trifle young to settle down, but – ' he threw up his hands – 'they were so much in love. We bought them a house between us; I made my son a partner in the company. They had Alicia pretty quickly but . . . maybe that was when things began to go wrong. They played at being grown-up, but neither of them was. They had trial separations and went to marriage counsellors but it was no good. Within four years they'd both moved on to other partners. It was distressing, but we couldn't do anything about it.'

Manisa said, 'They divorced?'

'Amicably. They'd both signed pre-nups. Daphne was far too young, emotionally . . . not really maternal . . . we mustn't blame her for . . . My son, likewise. He wanted to be the free and easy bachelor again, so . . . the courts gave her custody of Alicia, and he agreed to pay maintenance. Daphne handed the child over to nannies and housekeepers and married again. Alaric. A title, a family estate, well connected, a non-job in the City. Mrs Abbot, you remember him? He was sitting opposite you at dinner last night, between the supermodel Faye and your little Bernice.'

The man in the car. Yes, she remembered him all right. Today he was wearing casual clothes but last night he'd been in black tie. Liquid dark eyes, smooth dark hair and a six o'clock shadow. She'd wondered if there were Italian blood there, but apparently not. He'd been a little too well padded for his years, perhaps? Not the sort to enjoy exercise. Judging by the car he was driving today when he and his new partner, Ninette, collected Alicia, he was doing well.

She said, 'So he's the second husband? Alaric, title and estate. What happened to your son?'

'He remarried, too. She's a Californian whom he met on a business trip over there. My son is . . .' He looked down at his interlocked fingers. 'He's a live wire. Always looking to the future, working on the next big thing to hit the market. He sold our company to buy a stake in an Internet mega-business. He and his new wife live in Florida. She plays tennis to competition standard. They have a couple of little boys who are football-mad. American football.'

'When does he see Alicia?'

He shuffled his feet. 'Living in the States is expensive. My son had some difficulty paying Alicia's maintenance when he remarried. His new wife wasn't keen on Alicia visiting while she was in the throes of producing her two sons. Of course I understood.'

Manisa was ahead of him. 'You helped him out?'

He flushed, sensing criticism. Perhaps feeling that his son had evaded his responsibilities? *And what was that about his son selling the business? Over his father's head?*

'He is our only child. My wife began to be not so well

about that time. Neither Josh nor I wanted a family rift so, yes, I helped him out. When Alaric married Daphne, he adopted Alicia. To tidy things up. My son was pleased. You see, he had so much else on his plate. He felt that – as he couldn't be a good father to Alicia – it was the best thing that she be adopted by someone who was on the spot. He hadn't even seen her since she was a baby. He didn't think she'd even remember him. So Alaric is officially Alicia's father.'

Bea raised her eyebrows. 'But Daphne's second marriage hasn't worked out, either.'

'True. They separated some months ago and are in the process of divorcing. Both Alaric and Daphne have new partners. Neither Josh nor I liked what was happening, but there . . . the young ones tell us we're two old codgers who haven't moved with the times. They said that children adapt, though I'm not so sure about that.'

Manisa was sharp. 'What's Daphne's new man like?'

William's mouth twisted in distaste. 'Don't ask me. I'm biased.'

Manisa looked at Bea, who said, 'He's a stud, beginning and end of. He sat next to me at dinner last night. Looks like a Greek god. Has no interest in anything but himself. He spent the evening putting a note of what he was eating on his smartphone and calculating calories. He told me – as if I ought to be interested – what his heart rate was and how many steps he'd taken that day. I tuned him out, I'm afraid.'

'He's ten years younger than Daphne,' said William. 'Both he and she think he's the bee's knees. I believe he is involved in some competitive sport or other. Athletics? Into steroids, maybe? No, I can't say that. That's slander. He was renting a room in someone's flat till he met Daphne and she's set him up in a studio apartment of his own.'

'He didn't move in with Daphne? Where does she live?'

'When she left Alaric she bought herself a new flat not far from here, but she wanted the bathroom and kitchen ripped out and replaced so she moved back in with Josh till the work was done. The toy boy would have liked to move in, too, but Josh forbade it.'

'What does this lad do for a living?'

'He's a personal trainer. That's how they met. He wants her to sponsor him in training for the next Olympics. I don't think he's ever remembered Alicia's name in the short time that he's been around and I can't see that relationship lasting.'

Manisa was taking notes. 'So Alaric adopted Alicia. Adoption is for life. Does he intend to apply for custody when the divorce comes up?'

'I believe so, yes. And with Daphne in thrall to the Greek god, she might well agree. You'll think her very unfeeling, but the truth is that she doesn't seem to have much of a maternal instinct. She says Alaric is better for Alicia than the Greek god would be, and maybe she's right.' He twisted his hands. 'I keep forgetting that Josh has gone. I can't say either of us liked the idea of Alicia being handed over to Alaric. So far as I know, he's never shown any affection for the child.'

'Then why would he want to have custody?'

'Because . . . it's a harsh thing to say, but the only thing I can think of is that it gives him the right to administer her trust fund, which at the moment is not even covering her school fees, but with Josh's death will become considerable. He needs money and she is a considerable heiress.'

'But surely,' said Bea, 'he won't be the only trustee. He can't raid her inheritance to pay his own bills, can he?'

'I hope not,' said William. 'The thing is that grandparents don't have any rights when families split up. I know, because both Josh and I have looked into the matter. My only hope is that Ninette will take a shine to the child.'

Bea doubted it. She didn't think Ninette had the slightest interest in the child. To Bea's mind, Ninette was a perfectionist, a control freak, possibly anorexic.

'Poor Alicia. Poor little mite,' said William. 'She's been handed around like a parcel all her life. Always a loner, always polite, a little withdrawn. I thought at one time that she was being bullied at school. I took it up with her housemistress and got a flea in my ear. The school has a robust policy on bullying. Or so she said. I try to take Alicia out once a month, but Daphne says that it's better for her to be with her own peer group. Bernice has been good for her, though. Alicia has become far more outgoing, even cheeky, since Bernice made friends with her.'

Manisa looked at Bea. 'What did Ninette mean about Bernice being a bad influence on Alicia?'

The doorbell rang, three short bursts of sound.

'Perfect timing,' said Bea. 'That's Leon, Bernice's great-uncle. I'll let him tell the tale, as I suspect it was he who gave away the truth about Bernice's parentage.'

She let Leon in, accepted his kiss, and took his coat to hang up. As usual he was wearing silk and cashmere and his after-shave was a delight, even if his neck was beginning to thicken and, though she'd never mentioned it, his hair was beginning to thin. She sighed. She had no right to criticize, had she? She was also beginning to show her age, wasn't she?

He stamped his feet. 'Cold out. Are the girls ready to go out to lunch? Shall we take them anywhere in particular?' Without waiting for an answer he walked into the sitting room. And realized there were visitors. 'Hello? Morton, you here? Dreadful business that, last night. I've just left the hospital; Daphne's not feeling too good today, rather sleepy. Are the girls all right?' He turned to Manisa with the easy charm of a multibillionaire who expects to be liked. 'And you are . . .?'

'This is Manisa, the fire investigator,' said Bea. 'She'd very much like to know how Alaric and Ninette came to hear about Bernice's father. I assume you told them last night?'

'No, certainly not.' He seated himself, leaning back, pleased with himself and his world. 'It never came up. I was on Daphne's right. All she could talk about was her new man. Besotted with him, isn't she? She wanted me to sponsor him for some athletics trials or other, but I'd taken one look and decided I wasn't interested. Those light blue eyes of his, burning bright, if you know what I mean. Obsessive. Enough to scare any investor off. Daphne was drinking with one hand and hanging on to my wrist with the other. Poor girl, she's showing her age, despite the Botox. She used to be the loveliest little thing.'

'You weren't impressed by him?'

'I suspect all he sees when he looks at her is pound signs.'

'So how come Alaric has found out about Bernice's father?'

'I certainly didn't mention it to him. We don't exactly swim in the same waters. I suppose, though . . .' A wrinkled brow, 'Yes, I did tell Josh. Poor old Josh. Wasn't that a terrible thing! So sudden! I thought he was good for years yet. I still can't believe it. Steve's coping remarkably well, don't you think? A steady hand on the helm. I asked the doctors about telling Daphne her father had died and they said to wait till the antibiotics had taken effect. They're keeping her in, you know. Poor kid. And her Giorgio didn't even turn up at the hospital this morning, which you'd think he would, wouldn't you! Where was I?'

'You gave Josh the dirt on Bernice's father. Why? I thought it was agreed not to talk about him.'

'Josh asked me, he'd heard some rumour, he was worried because Alicia and Bernice were spending so much time together. I thought it better to tell the truth than to let him imagine the worst.'

Manisa said, 'Whatever was the matter with the girl?'

Leon shook his head. 'Nothing. Nice child, brave. Intelligent. Got the makings of a fine businesswoman; or so my sister says, and I believe her. The thing is that Dilys – Bernice's mother – got married far too young to a man who was climbing the ladder in the family business, global wide, Holland Holdings – you know? – that I eventually took over.'

As any multibillionaire would, he expected the reference to Holland Holdings to be understood and appreciated. Perhaps Manisa wasn't as familiar with the pages of the *Financial Times* as he'd expected, for she nodded but didn't fall to the ground and kiss his feet.

Leon recovered quickly enough. 'Anyway, he, Benton, was sleeping his way to the top. He'd discarded a wife on the way up but forgot to divorce her first, which laid him open to blackmail when he set eyes on my niece, pretty, silly little Dilys, and "married" her. He treated Dilys badly and oh, there was something about a business deal that went wrong. So yes, I did tell Josh, in confidence, that her father had been a bigamist, but that wasn't the girl's fault. I suppose the man might have been prosecuted for it eventually, but his discarded wife took her revenge by doing away with him. Dilys reminds me of Daphne in some ways. Dependent on men, petted and pampered. Not much common sense. Happily Dilys later found someone more suitable to marry her and has even produced another child.'

William said, 'I like Bernice. She's all right.'

Bea thought William had heard the details some time before, had made his own assessment of Bernice and had decided he still approved of her as a friend to Alicia. Bea liked him the better for it.

Manisa, however, was not satisfied. 'Details? What exactly is this man Benton supposed to have done? Was he ever arrested, convicted . . . and for what?'

Leon was expansive. 'I suppose we could have got him for bigamy and domestic violence, if he hadn't died.'

Manisa wasn't satisfied. 'Ninette hinted—'

Leon smiled. 'Oh, rumours. Bernice, now, she's made of sterling silver. Takes after the Holland side of the family. My elder brother and his wife – Dilys's parents – are both dead. I've done all right and my sister, Sybil, is a multimillionaire in her own right. Sybil took Bernice under her wing after her father died, partly as a companion and partly to take the place of the children she's never had. Round and round the world they went, until Bernice said she needed to settle down and get a good education, as she has her sights on Oxford or Cambridge; can't remember which. Josh must have told Daphne, who told Alaric because he was officially Alicia's father, and he told Ninette.'

Bea added, 'Benton was handsome, charming, and clever to a point, but he was a bully when his brains didn't get him what he wanted quickly enough. Bernice is pure Holland. She has integrity and courage. I'd be happy if she were my grandchild.'

'Ditto,' said Leon, shining with rectitude. 'Not that I'm likely to sire children at my age.'

Bea sighed. No, she'd long accepted that Leon was too self-centred to want marriage and children. She said, 'Leon; there's been a development. Alaric and Ninette have whipped Alicia back to boarding school early, but they say Bernice is not allowed to return.'

'What!' Leon gaped.

Honestly, he could be slow on the uptake sometimes, especially if it meant that he ought to take action. 'Leon, you promised me that you'd phone Sybil and tell her that Bernice was in trouble. Did you do so?'

'Well, I . . . no. The hour's all wrong. I wasn't getting her out of bed to—'

'Perhaps it would be good to ring her, now. Someone has got to deal with the school, and it wouldn't be any use asking Dilys . . . unless you'd like to do it yourself?'

Leon didn't want to do it. 'If fee-paying schools took only those pupils whose parents wore haloes, they'd have no pupils at all. I'll guarantee there's as bad or worse in every school. This will all blow over. Besides, Sybil won't answer the phone when—'

'Dilys and her new husband couldn't possibly have afforded the fees at this boarding school. Did you enter the child, or did Sybil?'

'Sybil did. But naturally, I'd be prepared to pay the fees if—'

'Ring Sybil now, Leon. Please. You know she'll be furious if she finds out that the school has asked Bernice to leave and that you've done nothing about it.'

He got out his phone, slowly. Manisa rapped on the table to attract his attention. 'Before you speak to her . . . Mrs Abbot was so kind as to give me permission to talk to the children this morning, but I need to cover myself. I need to know: is it you, your sister Sybil, or Bernice's mother who has parental responsibility for the girl?'

'That's a very good point.' He frowned. 'I suppose it's Dilys, but . . . I mean . . . either Sybil or I . . . yes, I see where you're going. In practice, it's whoever is on the spot.'

Manisa was not amused. 'If I ring the school and ask them who they deal with . . .?'

'I'm sure Sybil only has to wave a cheque and the school will be delighted to welcome Bernice back again. Apart from anything else, she's scholarship material. A fine brain.'

'Interested in science, is she? Chemistry, for instance?'

Manisa was probing to see whether or not Bernice might be interested in making her own fireworks?

Leon was puzzled. 'Maths, yes. Not sure about science.'

'Was it you who gave her a box of indoor fireworks for her birthday?'

'I know she and Alicia wanted some fireworks, but Josh had said "no" so we got her tickets to some pop show or other . . . what was it, Bea? You got them for me. They'll have gone up in smoke, the tickets, I suppose. Bad do, that. The fire. I was on the phone to Steve and he said the ground floor's all right and some of the rooms on the first floor, though there's smoke and water damage. I'm glad Josh didn't live to see it. The family will have to move out, I suppose, for the time being. Gideon has his own place. So it's only Steve now. And Daphne, while her flat's being re-plumbed or whatever. Who's going to look after Daphne when she gets out of hospital? The housekeeper, I suppose . . .'

So Leon didn't know Mrs Frost had also been taken to hospital?

He continued, 'Steve will arrange something, no doubt. And the insurance will pay up.' He dabbed at his phone. 'I'd better see if Sybil can get over here sharpish. I think she's in Boston for the weekend.' He held the phone to his ear. Frowned. 'Engaged. I'll try again in a minute.'

Manisa said, 'I think I'd better have a chat with Bernice's mother. To be on the safe side. Can you give me her details?'

'Sure,' said Leon, pressing buttons again. 'Bea, can you keep the child here for a few days? Just till Sybil works things out with the school? I'll be on my way in a minute, since the girls aren't here. Keep in touch, though, won't you?'

Bea told herself she ought to have been expecting that, but she hadn't. She forced herself to smile and said, 'Of course', but really all she wanted to do was to lie down in a darkened room and have a soft-footed maid bring her tea and crumpets and possibly arrange for a massage with heated oils and . . .

She laughed at herself. As if she'd ever had a maid! Perhaps she should book herself into a spa hotel for the weekend? If only she didn't have to look after Bernice, poor mite. She collected some coffee mugs and took them out to the kitchen.

William followed her with one she'd overlooked.

She tried to smile. 'I must warn you; I'm not up to polite conversation.'

'I don't suppose you had much sleep last night. Neither did I. The girls were so restless, I kept starting awake. When they dropped off to sleep, I didn't.'

Bea nodded. She'd gone in to see to Bernice who'd woken and cried out, twice. He'd been fast asleep then and snoring lightly, but she wouldn't mention that. She'd soothed the child, given her a drink and stayed with her till she'd settled down again, her nose in Teddy's fur.

The front door opened. Manisa and Leon were in the hall, preparing to leave. Leon was offering Manisa a lift. She declined. Bea went out to see them off.

'Keep in touch, Mrs Abbot,' said Manisa. And then the front door closed behind them.

Peace and quiet. Bea went back to clearing up in the kitchen.

William said, 'I used to be able to keep going for thirty-six hours without a break. I can't do that any more, but I can hang on for another couple of hours if you'd like to get your head down?'

The dear man! 'I wish I could but there's the agency . . . although my manageress is first class. No, I'd better keep going till Bernice gets back.' She dropped a mug that she was trying to fit into the dishwasher. Fortunately it didn't break.

He picked it up and finished loading. 'You were magnificent last night. You were the only one who kept their head—'

'Apart from Steve. He had the sense to go for the fire extinguisher.'

'When the curtain went up in flames, I heard Josh choke. I looked at him and he looked at me. I thought he was dying, there and then. That he was saying "goodbye". Then I saw you were listening—'

'You hadn't heard the second firework?'

'I had, but it hadn't occurred to me that it was important till I saw you glance round the table. Then I saw the empty chairs, as you did, and realized. If you hadn't acted, the girls would have died. Another five or ten minutes. I am indebted to you, Mrs Abbot. For taking us in last night, as well.'

A long, long sigh. 'I was terrified. If it hadn't been for you . . .'

'Do you think they'll give us a medal for saving the girls' lives?' He said this in such a droll tone that she spurted into laughter.

'One medal each, or one between two?'

He laughed, too. 'That's better. Now, you can trust me to wake you up if anything happens. Go and rest while you can. I promise not to leave the house till you get up again.'

She nodded. Didn't bother to thank him. Plodded up the stairs, threw open the door to her bedroom . . . and recoiled. Phrases such as 'it looked like a bomb-site' came to her mind and were rejected as being an understatement.

Two ten year olds had torn open the bags of shopping which Mel had brought them, and scattered the items over every surface in sight. Plus towels from the bathroom. Plus – Bea wanted to shriek! – Bea's toiletries.

Bea sniffed. Plus there was a layer of talcum powder over everything.

It was enough to make her weep.

She was too tired for tears. She left everything as it was, drew the curtains, let herself down on her bed – which the girls hadn't bothered to make – and told herself to relax. First the toes, then the ankles. Then the knees.

A spot of prayer. *Thank you, Lord. I can't think of the right words. Too tired. That's a good man, William. He knows how to . . . how to . . . can't think. Doesn't matter. Oh, bother Leon! Why can't he just . . .?*

Saturday noon

It seemed she'd only just fallen asleep when something heavy landed on the bed and a voice cried, 'Auntie Bea! Wake up!'

'Mm?' She forced her eyelids open.

Bernice was pressed close to her, one arm round Teddy.

William put his head round the door. 'Are you decent? We have a problem. Alicia's gone missing.'

SEVEN

Bea struggled to sit upright. She was tempted to have hysterics. She wanted someone to tell her, 'There, there! There's nothing to worry about!' She wanted this not to be happening.

But it was.

Not to mention the chaos in her lovely bedroom.

Two anxious people stood in the doorway; William was one. The other was young Mel. 'I'm so sorry, Mrs Abbot. We couldn't find any trainers that Bernice liked and then she had a worrying phone call from Alicia, and she's tried to ring her back and it's true, Alicia's not answering.'

Bea put her arm round Bernice and Teddy. Bernice's self-control mechanism had finally tripped. She shook and shrieked into Bea's shoulder. It was probably good for her to let go like this, if ruination to Bea's top. Well, tops could be washed or, in the worst case, dry-cleaned.

Bea held the child tight and rocked her, 'There, there!' The bear dug into Bea's ribs, but that didn't matter. Teddy needed comfort, as well.

Bea said, 'Spit it out, love! Scream hard enough to raise the roof if you can manage it!'

William, seeing that Bea was properly clad, propped himself up in the doorway and got on his phone. 'Steve, is that you? We have a small problem here. Yes, I know that . . . but . . .' Silence while William listened to someone talking at the other end.

Bea said, 'Bernice, can you tell me what's happened?'

Bernice gulped. 'Alicia rang me. She was crying. She said she wasn't going back to school without me. Then she rang off and now she won't answer her phone!'

Not good news. Bea reached for a box of tissues. The child blew her nose and mopped up. She was regaining her control. There was a nasty damp patch on Bea's top, which she decided to ignore.

Bernice said, 'Uncle William gave us brand-new phones this morning. We charged them up straight away. Her battery can't have run down yet.'

'Does her phone go to voicemail?'

An emphatic nod. Bernice handed her phone over. 'Press the top one. That's for Alicia. We put the numbers in this morning.'

Bea tried the number. No answer. Voicemail. She thought about it. 'Would the school confiscate her phone if they thought she'd been naughty?'

An emphatic shake of the head. 'No. They take our tablets away, but not our phones.'

'Would her father or Ninette?'

'They never have. Besides, they dropped her at school ages ago.'

'How do you know that?'

'She said she was ringing from the driveway to the school.'

William shut off his phone. 'You'd think things couldn't get worse. I've been trying to get Alaric or Ninette but neither are answering their phones. I've just tried Steve. He's at panic stations because Daphne's supposed to be leaving hospital today and he doesn't know where to take her. Her own flat has no water till next week, and the family home is . . . well! I'm not sure she knows about the fire or about her father yet. What a mess!'

'Could she go into respite care somewhere?'

'Steve's trying to arrange it but he's afraid she won't agree. I doubt if Giorgio will be willing to help, and Alaric is out of the picture.'

Bernice said, in her grown-up voice, 'Alicia is worried about her mother, too.'

William took a deep breath. 'Bernice, there is absolutely no need to panic. The most likely thing is that Alicia's dropped her phone. Or lost it somewhere.'

'Alicia doesn't lose things. She said she wasn't going back.'

Bea said, 'William, could you try the school, to see if she's there?'

'I'm sure she's all right, but . . .' He pressed numbers. 'Is that . . . am I speaking to the school secretary? Yes. This is William Morton, Alicia's grandfather. I understand she returned to school early . . .'

He'd been propping himself up against the doorframe. Now he jerked upright. 'She hasn't? . . . Yes, that's right. Her father and . . . yes, they were bringing her back by car. They set out this morning . . . what time? About eleven, I should say . . .'

He checked his watch. So did Bea. It was nearly noon. Bernice was right; the school was in Richmond. Half an hour there and half an hour back. And, if they'd had a breakdown in the car, Alaric and Ninette could have used their mobile phones to call for help and let the family know what had happened.

William said to the school secretary, 'You say you were expecting her, but . . . No, of course you would know if . . . Well, as you say, I expect there's some very good reason. They've been delayed en route. A puncture or breakdown on the way. Of course that will be it. But, would you be so good as to let me know, on this number, when Alicia finally . . .? Many thanks. Yes, and a good day to you, too.'

Bea said, 'Try Alaric again.'

William tried. Voicemail. He said, 'I can't believe it. I don't want to believe it.'

Mel was very young to be dealing with this. She bit her lip, and subsided on to the nearest chair. 'Call the police?'

Bea stifled impatience. 'No, Mel. We're not going to panic. Not yet.' And to Bernice. 'Ninette said she had something else to do this afternoon?'

Bernice straightened her back and looked up. 'The hairdresser's. She'd promised to take Alicia with her to have her hair trimmed, but she sent her back to school instead.'

'You don't know which hairdresser's?'

Bernice's face crumpled. 'Alicia would know.'

'So she would. Bernice, what do you think has happened to Alicia?'

Bernice gulped. 'Alicia hates school. I don't mind it too much, because the maths teacher is really good, but Alicia's not good at maths and she didn't want to go back without me. She used to be bullied, you see. And wet the bed sometimes.'

William breathed out. 'I knew it!'

'I was lonely, too,' said Bernice. 'I was glad to go away to school because I thought I'd catch up on lessons and make friends, and when I got there Alicia was told to take me around. She showed me where everything was and warned me to keep out of the way of the bullies. She said they're always horrible to new girls and that if I had any pocket money they'd take it off me, because that's what they did to everyone who wasn't in their gang. But I knew better than to give in to bullies, so when they started on me I said I'd spit in their milk and I'd crawl into their beds at night and pinch them black and blue and I'd do the same to anyone who tried it on Alicia. So they left us alone and after that we told one another everything. I'd never had a best friend before, and neither had she. She even stopped having nightmares.' She stared at Bea with eyes that had seen more than their fair share of horrors.

William held back anxiety to moderate his voice. 'Bernice, think! What did Alicia have in mind?'

'I don't know! And then she rang off!' Bernice buried her head in Bea's shoulder again.

Bea held her tightly. 'Bernice, love. You have to be strong. Alicia is your best friend. I think she's going to ring you again, soon. You must keep calm and be ready to speak to her when she does.'

William spat out the words. 'Bernice! Answer me. Tell me exactly what Alicia said.'

Bernice controlled herself with an effort. With her head still buried in Bea's shoulder, she muttered, '. . . run away?'

'How could she run away?'

Bernice struggled upright. 'She said Alaric and Ninette were in a hurry to get back and dropped her off by the main gates. She said she waited till they'd driven off and then . . . she said someone was coming, and she rang off.'

A sharp intake of breath from William. 'Where *could* she go?'

No reply. A shake of the dark head.

A chirrupy noise. Was that someone's phone? Not Bea's.

William hadn't heard anything? Bea frowned. Had she imagined it?

Bernice said, 'I'm going to the loo.' She withdrew to Bea's bathroom, shutting the door firmly behind her.

William said, 'I'm ringing the police. If she turns up unharmed we'll look like fools, but I'd rather it turn out that way than do nothing.'

Ho, hum! Bea played for time. 'Wait. Before we ring the police, we must contact her father and warn him. Ninette may well have turned off her phone while she was at the hairdresser's, although some people never do. Maybe she's turned it back on again now. Do you have her number?'

'No. Why should I?'

Bea tried to think. 'You said that Steve is with Daphne at the hospital. Do you think he might have Ninette's number? Steve and Gideon may have turned their phones off if they're sitting with Daphne, but this is an emergency and surely we can tell the nurses that we need to speak to Steve on an urgent family matter? Either Steve or Gideon can be fetched out to take our phone call. Maybe one of them will know how to contact Ninette. Whatever happens, we must set a deadline. We warn the family and the school, everyone involved, what we're going to do. We say that if Alicia doesn't turn up in the next hour, we *are* going to ring the police. We also tell the fire investigator.'

'Why her?'

'Because the family desperately want to put the blame for the fire on the children and if one of them disappears of her own free will, they'll take that as a confession of guilt.'

His jaw sagged. He hadn't thought of that. Then he straightened up. 'I'll get on to my solicitor, as well. If Alaric left Alicia in the middle of nowhere, without seeing her safely inside, then he's responsible for her disappearance. But I'll need proof.' He pressed buttons. 'Is that the hospital? I believe you have a patient called . . .'

Bea swung her legs off the bed, and got to her feet. William was doing the right thing; the family must be informed first. And then the police.

As for Bernice? Ho, hum. The child was handling the situation well. Wasn't she?

Bea started to pick up the girls' clothes and put them in a neat pile. Mel, glad to have something to do, joined her. Together they created some sort of order. Bea sent Mel downstairs to find a duster and some wipes, while she seated herself at her dressing table, brushed out her hair and worked on a broken nail.

Bernice returned to sit on the bed, nursing Teddy. Eyes down, shutting herself off from the world.

Bernice was no longer hysterical. Why?

Bea decided to renew her nail varnish, and did so. Rhythmical movements aid thinking.

William had settled in the chair by the bedside, to make his phone calls. Bea acknowledged that he knew how to get things done.

Mel returned, asked Bernice to get off the bed so that she could make it. Bernice wandered around the room, blank-faced, until Mel had finished, and then got back on to it.

Mel folded up the spare duvet William had been using, returned towels to the bathroom and set about wiping talcum powder off every surface.

Bea tuned back in to William's voice. He hadn't been able to reach either Steve or Gideon yet, had he? Well, he would keep on trying. That was one thing you could count on; William would keep on trying.

William hadn't considered what scenario Bernice plus Alicia plus money might create. Yes, there was a slight risk in playing for time. Scare stories about white slave traffic flitted across Bea's mind and were dismissed as ridiculous. An hour's grace should be sufficient.

William had reached Steve. Good. Bea applied a little make-up. Not a lot. Mostly around her eyes. Her dear husband Hamilton had called them her 'eagle's eyes' because they were long-tailed and saw more than most people's did.

Mel had restored order to Bea's bedroom but didn't know what to do next. 'What else, Mrs Abbot?' Mel was out of her depth but doing her best to be helpful.

Bea smiled, wryly. She thought that if Mel was too young to know what to do, she herself was too old. Definitely.

Bea checked her watch. In a moment she would have to go

down to the agency to deal with super-nanny, but what should she do with Bernice? Leave her with Mel? No. The agency girl had behaved well, but was not trained for this.

William had not convinced Steve that the situation was serious. 'But Steve, you do understand that we have to inform the police if the child can't be . . . No. No, of course the child is not your priority . . . No, I didn't know Daphne was still feeling so poorly. But they're not keeping her in? . . . Yes, of course. Ring me as soon as . . . yes. Yes.'

He shut off his phone, met Bea's eyes, and shrugged. 'Gideon is there with him. The hospital want to discharge Daphne today, even though she's not responded as well as they would like to her first lot of antibiotics. They're trying a different lot, and she should be going home . . . no, not home . . . Steve's arranging for her to go somewhere she can be looked after for a few days. There's no sign of Alaric or Giorgio, and Steve has no idea where they might be. Steve doesn't have Ninette's number but he thinks Gideon might have it. He'll find out and let us know.'

Bea took one of the children's new hairbrushes and started work on Bernice's long hair, plaiting it to keep it tidy. The child was relaxed, looked as if she were going to fall asleep. No longer under stress.

Bea said, 'I have an appointment downstairs at noon. Mel, how are you fixed? Are you free this afternoon?'

Frowning, the girl looked at her watch. 'Yes and no. I have to call in on an elderly lady who lives in a flat up the road to give her her lunch. She's scared of the microwave so I have to do it for her. Her carer doesn't work at weekends, and if I don't go in she'll never think to get anything for herself. I could be back within the hour, if that's any good?'

Bea accepted with pleasure. 'Bless you, my dear. Yes. Come back as soon as you can. Meanwhile . . .'

As Mel collected her cleaning gear, there was a knock on the bedroom door and there was Betty from the agency, looking apologetic but gesturing to her watch. 'Super-nanny is here. She says she's not accustomed to being kept waiting!'

'Two minutes.' Bea checked her appearance in the mirror and realized her top was stained beyond redemption. She stripped it off, not caring whether William caught sight of her bra or not, and fished a silky, sea-green top with a cross-over bodice out of the cupboard. Her diamond earrings were . . . in her ears. Good. No time to bother with anything else. Off we go.

What to do with Bernice? Bea tapped William on his arm. He was in mid phone call, but this was an emergency. 'William, I have to see someone in the agency. Could you wrap Bernice in my duvet and carry her down there for me? She can have a nap on my sofa while I see a client.'

He put away his phone to scoop up child and duvet and follow her. 'I've been on to my housekeeper to let her know what's happening. It's too far off the beaten track for Alicia to get there easily, but . . . just in case. Gideon doesn't have Ninette's number. Steve's given me the gigolo's, only he's not answering. Steve is desperately trying to find somewhere for Daphne to go and he doesn't need this . . . Another fifteen minutes and I'm phoning the police.'

Fifteen minutes? Mm. This was cutting it fine. So William had a house out of town? With housekeeper? Down the stairs they went, Bea leading the way. Betty briefed Bea as they went.

'Super-nanny was five minutes early, declined a cuppa, said that she never used "foreign facilities" and wiped her finger – yes, she really did – across my desk to see if there were any dust on it!'

Bea was caught up by the giggles. '"Foreign facilities?" Does she carry a pack of bacterial wipes around with her? No, I shouldn't laugh. She's probably got the right idea. Some of the "foreign facilities" I have known would frighten a health inspector into fits.'

'Yes, but ours are spotless.' Betty held the door open for Bea to enter the office. 'I could look after the child for you, if you like? Where's Mel?'

'Running an errand. Leave the child with me till Mel gets back. I'll tell you why later . . .' Bea swept into her office to greet her visitor, with William at her heels, carrying the child.

Bea greeted super-nanny – a middle-aged dumpling in dowdy clothes – with a smile. 'I do apologize. A domestic crisis. Come into my office. Yes, William, you may leave the child on the settee here. She'll be safe with me for a while. Thank you. You get back to your phone calls.'

Bea took the file which Betty was holding out to her and switched on her computer. Out of the corner of her eye she noticed that Bernice was perched on the edge of the sofa, looking uncomfortable. So why hadn't she nestled down in the duvet? She was hugging Teddy, eyes on the floor between her shoes.

However, super-nanny was making herself very much at home. With a frown at everything in sight.

Bea opened the folder. Excellent references, super-nanny had been with Lady This and before with Dame That.

What was wrong with Bernice now?

A second look at super-nanny had told Bea she'd been right to wonder whether or not this woman was going to fit the criteria for their agency. If you described her as 'jolly', you'd want to add 'Roger' as in 'Jolly Roger'. Too wide a smile, lacking warmth. Too bulbous an eye, lacking joy. The hands were pudgy and strong; good for slapping children's legs. The body was heavy – not good for running after nimble infants.

Bea thought, Oh dear. She looked over at Bernice, who hadn't moved. Ah. Bea told herself she'd been slow on the uptake. 'Bernice, do you want to take Teddy to the toilet?'

Affirmative.

Bea led Bernice to the door, and pointed to the far end of the main office. 'The loo's by the door to the steps that go up to the street. Can you see? Take your time. Make sure Teddy washes his hands afterwards. And then perhaps he might like something to eat? A biscuit, perhaps? Betty will give him one if you ask nicely.'

The child set off to the loo and Bea returned to her desk. 'I do apologize. Her little brother's gone down with chickenpox and—'

Super-nanny recoiled. 'You have exposed me to chickenpox?'

'No, of course not,' said Bea. 'The child hasn't been exposed to it, either, which is why I'm looking after her for a while. Now, I see that your last position was—'

'Well! You might have warned me. And you allow her to

cuddle that dirty old teddy bear? Harbouring who knows how many germs?'

'The child has been through a lot recently. The teddy bear seems to comfort her.'

A snort. 'My children are not allowed insanitary toys. I only permit soft toys which can be put in the washing machine every other day. Life is not a bed of roses, and the sooner children accept that and conform to what society expects of them, the better.'

Bea told herself not to grind her teeth. 'You think it's a good idea to instil discipline into children from an early age?'

'Naturally. No little liars or thieves in my families.'

Bea held back a sigh. 'In my experience children do lie now and then. To get themselves out of trouble or to help a friend.'

'It is an error commonly found among parents who have not had the benefit of proper training themselves,' said super-nanny with a supercilious smile, 'to allow their children to transgress without correction. Needless to say, that is never the case with a child placed in my care.'

'You put them on the naughty step?'

'I find shutting them in a quiet, dark place is more efficacious. A short, sharp shock works wonders and we do not have to repeat the action.' Super-nanny gathered herself together. 'That child is a liar. I smelled it on her as soon as she came in.'

Bea nodded. The woman had had many years of experience of working with children, and yes, she would have recognized Bernice's trick of sliding her eyes down and away. 'I think you are right.'

'Yet you do not see fit to interrogate and punish her? A hidden lie will fester in her mind. If she thinks she's lied to you and got away with it, she will do it again. You are going to let her walk down the primrose path to perdition?'

Bea's lips twitched. 'I know why she lied. She will tell me all about it in her own good time.'

The woman stood up. 'Chickenpox. Dust on the desk. And you have no appreciation of how to bring up a child in the way they should go. I am not willing to allow my name to go on to your agency books.'

'I understand. Let me show you out.'

By the time the woman's stout legs had disappeared up the outside stairs to the street, Bernice had left the loo, and Betty was giving her a biscuit from the office tin.

Bernice lifted her head and met Bea's eyes. A look full of intelligence and knowledge. Bea sighed. Yes, Bernice had lied, by default if not directly.

Betty looked at the clock and began to bustle around, shutting everything down for the weekend. 'All right if we go now, Mrs Abbot? There's nothing that can't wait till Monday. I've switched the phones over to voicemail.'

The second Saturday girl was already packing up for the day.

'Have a good weekend.'

Back in Bea's office, Bernice snuggled down on the sofa while Bea checked her emails . . . nothing much to worry about there. Then Mel returned, bumping down the steps from the street with a bag of children's games.

'I thought we might play Ludo or Snap or something. I told the old lady that I visit about the little girl who's all alone this weekend and she said to borrow her grandchildren's toys for the afternoon. Isn't that good of her?' Mel would enjoy it, too.

'Splendid,' said Bea.

Someone was banging on the front door and ringing the doorbell. Someone in a hurry. Someone in a temper? Now who, oh who, could that be? Not the police. The hour wasn't up yet. So, someone looking for Bernice . . . or for Alicia?

Bea made sure she had her smartphone on her, and climbed the stairs to the front door.

EIGHT

Surprise! Ninette, freshly curled and scented from the salon. In a tearing temper. Close behind her came the seal-smooth head of her fiancé, or whatever he was – the current-but-soon-to-be-divorced husband of Daphne.

Ninette had a voice like a parrot. 'Where is she! What have you done with her!'

Bea blinked. 'Who? Bernice? But—'

'Not Bernice, you stupid creature! The runaway! What have you done with her?'

Ninette thrust past Bea into the living room, shoving aside a chair which had got in her way.

'What . . .?' William, frozen to the spot, still on his phone. There was no one else in the room.

Ninette screamed, shrill as a dentist's drill. 'Where have you put her?'

Bea crossed her arms. 'Well, good afternoon, Ninette. Nice to see you. And Alaric, isn't it? I don't remember inviting you but—'

Ninette shook her finger an inch from Bea's nose. 'Come off it! You don't fool me!'

'Ninette!' Alaric took her by the shoulders, and turned her away from Bea. 'Darling, not so fast!'

Ninette gave a little scream, and stamped her foot. Yes, she really did! Out of the corner of her eye, Bea saw William shut off his phone and put it away. Bea put her smartphone down on the occasional table nearby.

Ninette twisted out of Alaric's hands. 'We'll have the law on you, you . . . you thief!'

Bea raised one eyebrow. 'What is it I'm supposed to have stolen?' As if she didn't know.

Alaric pushed Ninette down on to a chair. 'My apologies, Mrs Abbot. I had inadvertently switched my phone to voicemail and have only just heard from the school that my daughter has gone missing. Naturally I am most concerned to find her before anything, well, untoward . . . you understand?'

Bea raised the other eyebrow. 'Are you referring to Alicia, whom you removed from this household this morning?'

'Yes.'

Ninette tried to struggle out of the chair. Alaric pushed her back down again. 'Quiet, Ninette. The thing is, Mrs Abbot, that the child got some silly idea in her head, you know what young girls can be. Perhaps she's been influenced by her young friend, who should never have been allowed to . . . the thing is, the child seems to have run away.'

'After you delivered her back into the hands of the staff at the boarding school? How on earth could they let that happen?'

A tinge of colour. 'We think she must have slipped out somehow—'

'But once you had handed the girl over to the staff, it is their responsibility to look after the girl. You did hand her over, didn't you?'

'Of course.' A full-frontal lie. Wide brown eyes. A look of five-star sincerity. As false as a toupee. Alaric was accustomed to lying, wasn't he?

Ninette, however, was so aerated she couldn't keep her mouth shut. 'She only had to cross the drive, for heaven's sake. She's done it a dozen times before.'

'Do I understand,' said Bea, 'that you didn't actually deliver her to the school authorities? You left her outside? In the drive?'

'She was in sight of the front door.'

'Oh dear. How remiss of you. I do hope nothing tragic has happened to her, a small child, all alone and friendless, abandoned in the middle of the—'

'Abandoned? Nonsense. We saw her enter the school.' He glanced down at Ninette, skewering her to the chair with his eyes. 'Didn't we?'

'Oh. Yes. Of course.' Ninette was rapidly calming down. She looked around her, taking note of the furniture and furnishings, using the calculator behind her eyes to tot up how much Bea might be worth. Slightly impressed.

Bea noted that William had gone to stand at the back window, overlooking the garden. He was leaving this to her to deal with, wasn't he? And so she would.

She said, 'So you left the child there, in the school drive, without actually handing her over to anyone at the school, and then you returned to London. You had an appointment to have your hair done, Ninette? Is that right?'

'We've dropped her off there a hundred times without—'

'And Alaric . . . where did you go? When we heard the child was missing, we tried to contact you before we alerted the police, but you were unavailable.'

'I called into the gym for a coffee, and they have a policy of turning off mobiles . . . if it's any business of yours, which it is not. But there's no need for the police. None. I suggest you produce the child, and we say no more about it.'

'You think I am harbouring the child? How? Did I hire a helicopter and follow you all the way to the school – I have no idea where it is, by the way – hover overhead till we saw you abandon the child, scoop her up off the ground and tear back here to drop her . . . where? In my back garden? In a local park?'

'You have her, we're sure of that.'

'I assure you we haven't seen hair nor hide of her since the moment you took her away this morning.'

'I don't believe you.' Alaric's eyes were hot. 'Hand her over, and we'll say no more.'

Bea held up her hands. 'You think I've kidnapped the girl? Why on earth would I do that? I met her for the first time last night. Out of the goodness of my heart I allowed her to sleep here when her home was burnt out. I fed her and bought her clothes to wear, only to have you remove her without so much as saying "thank you" for all the time and trouble I've taken. The more I think about it, the worse your behaviour becomes. How dare you force your way in and accuse me of kidnapping the girl, when it is clear that you have been remiss in abandoning her in the middle of the countryside, or wherever her school is.'

Alaric tried on a smile. Not a good effort. 'I . . . we apologize for disturbing you. As you say, we are worried sick about the girl, for if she isn't here, then where is she?'

'That's your problem, not mine. We said we'd inform the police if she didn't turn up within the hour. There's five minutes left. If you don't know where she is, and I certainly don't, then in five minutes' time we will be ringing them. They will no doubt put out an All Points—'

Alaric was beginning to sweat. 'No police. We have to find her. I'm worried sick, thinking what might happen to her, out there, all by herself. You must understand; we were sure she'd come here.'

'Why on earth should you think that? What can I say to convince you? Do you want to search the place?' Fingers crossed.

Ninette said, 'Yes!' She exchanged looks with Alaric, who nodded. 'That is, if you don't mind.'

'Mind?' Bea raised her eyes upwards. 'Of course I mind. But . . . well, let's get it over with. Follow me. Yes, I'm coming with you. I don't want my home disturbed more than is absolutely necessary.' She palmed her smartphone and led the way. 'We'll start downstairs, in the agency rooms. I'll put on the light; it gets dark so early these winter afternoons, doesn't it? Through this door here, and into the main office. My staff only work Saturday mornings at the moment, and they've gone for the day. Come along, come along.'

With Ninette and Alaric at her heels, Bea threw open the doors into the loo and the tiny kitchen. 'The usual facilities. Our cleaner comes first thing in the mornings, Monday to Friday, but never on Saturday, so please excuse the mess. This is the main office, as you can see. Lights . . . more lights. And now we're going into the small side office . . . no one there, as you can see. It's not much used. The girls prefer all to be in the same room. That door there . . . you'd better look, I suppose. The stationery cupboard. The shelves are too close together for a child to hide in, but our cat – yes, do be careful, he's renowned for tripping people up – likes to hide in there during thunderstorms and firework displays. Yes, you've seen enough there? Good. And this is my office, which has French windows leading on to the garden. And here you see Mel, who is looking after Bernice for—'

Bernice was sitting on the settee with Teddy beside her, playing chess with Mel. Or, since Mel was agonizing over the board, it was possible that Bernice was teaching Mel how to play chess, rather than the other way round?

Ninette leapt upon the child. 'You wicked girl! What have you done with Alicia?'

Mel, alarmed, shot to her feet, scattering chess pieces.

Bernice gasped, and struggled to free herself.

Ninette had the child by her shoulders, shaking her.

'Enough!' said Bea, full voice, holding her smartphone up to record the moment.

Ninette took no notice. Between her teeth, she said, 'Tell me, you little toad!'

Bea said to Alaric, 'If you don't get Ninette to let go, I'll call the police!'

Alaric put his arms round Ninette. 'Let her go!'

'What! But she knows . . .!'

Mel snatched the child from Ninette's arms, and carried her to the far side of the room. Bernice's face was without colour. She stared at Ninette. Then at Alaric. Then at Bea. Did her lips twitch? No.

Bea had to hand it to the child. Bernice knew exactly how to behave. She buried her head in Mel's shoulder.

Bea found her heart was thudding. 'You . . . you . . .! Alaric, I think you'd better remove your fiancée before I have the law on her. No, wait!' Though they hadn't moved. 'You asked to see over the house, and I'm determined that you shall look into every room, and every cupboard. And then I'm going to make you sign a statement to the effect that the girl is not here, and if you ever, ever try this on again . . .!'

Ninette stamped her foot so hard that Bea thought it might go through the floor. Bea could see the woman wanted to scream with rage. Alaric's hand on her arm kept her from erupting, but Bea was in no doubt that Ninette still thought Bernice knew what had happened to Alicia.

As, indeed, did Bea.

But that was another matter.

Bea gestured that they should follow her out into the garden to inspect the garden shed, which was empty of all but tools and shadows. Returning to the house, she led the way out of the office quarters, up the stairs and into the

'Well, she wasn't. I suspect that she arranged with Bernice to come back here but not to enter the house until Bernice gave her the all clear. I think we can take it that Alicia slipped down the stairs and into the basement office when Bernice sent Mel up for some food. And the child will now be . . . where? Let's go and see where she and Teddy are hiding, shall we?'

He didn't understand what she meant but followed her down the stairs and into the agency offices. There were lights on in the main office, and in Bea's. Outside the twilight was closing in. It was a dark and drizzly afternoon.

Bernice was sitting in a sort of nest in the duvet on the settee, cross-legged, contemplating a chess problem on the board in front of her. She looked up when they entered. Wary.

'Ta-da!' said Bea, with a wide gesture. 'You see? No bear.'

Teddy was indeed conspicuous by his absence. 'William, it's still light enough for you to pick your way out into the garden. I expect Teddy's in the garden shed keeping Alicia company. She'll probably be glad of a wash and a cup of tea. And of that sandwich Mel is making for Bernice.'

William blundered out through the French windows into the garden, calling out, 'Alicia, it's only me!'

Bea sat down beside Bernice and inspected the board. Her late husband had introduced her to the game but she hadn't played it for ages. Could she remember enough of the twisty moves he'd taught her to beat Bernice? If she played the girl and lost, she'd lose respect. If she played and won . . .? It would help to keep the upper hand. Now, how was the game going? What openings were there for black?

She said, 'I suspect you're a killer player, Bernice. You beat Mel, I suppose.'

Bernice flattened her eyelids at Bea. And made no comment.

Bea fingered a pawn. 'Now, where shall I go with this? Shall I take this pawn here . . . or shall I move my one remaining knight?'

'Knights jump on people,' said Bernice. 'And bishops slide across.'

'And queens . . .' Bea skidded hers across the board. 'Take the biscuit. Checkmate.'

William came stumbling back through the room, carrying
a bedraggled Alicia in his arms. 'She's all right! Thank the
Lord! Needs the toilet, and she's dehydrated.'

Bea said, 'Take her straight upstairs. Let Mel clean her up
and feed her the food she was preparing for Bernice. And, let
the school know we've got her safe and sound, or they'll be
phoning the police themselves.'

'And Alaric? Do we tell him he's off the hook?'

'What do you think?'

William grinned. 'We keep him dangling in suspense for
a while.' He started for the stairs, shouting, 'Mel? I've got
her!'

Bea leaned back in her chair. 'Time to come clean, Bernice.
I think I know how you managed to get Alicia here, but fill
me in, will you? Start from the phone call you received when
you were out shopping with Mel.'

'Lissy said she was standing outside the school. She said
they'd dropped her on the drive because there were some
workmen's vans by the front door. She said she couldn't bear
to go in. And then she shut off—'

'And wouldn't take your phone calls when you rang back.
Which panicked you. Understandably.'

Bernice twisted a strand of hair round her finger. 'You got
Uncle William to ring the school and they said she hadn't
arrived, but you said to wait and she'd ring me. And you were
right. She did.'

'That was the chirruping sound I heard when we were all
upstairs in my bedroom. I couldn't identify it until I remembered that William had given you girls a new phone each only
that morning. You went off to the loo to take your phone call
in private. What did Alicia say then?'

'That she was on her way back here. She had the money
Uncle William had given us to buy new trainers. She'd taken
a bus to the station and was on the underground train coming
back here.'

'You told her that, once she arrived, she must wait outside
in the street till you could smuggle her in? Did you think I'd
agree to hide her, or that you could keep her here without me
knowing?'

'I thought you'd look after her till her mother got out of hospital and then it would be all right. And you did hide her from the baddies.'

'No, I didn't. I made them look all over the house, and sign a document which said Alicia was not here. I also taped those two nasty pieces of work admitting that they'd left Alicia in the middle of nowhere.'

'But you *are* hiding her now.'

'Not I. In a minute I'm going to ring her uncle Steve and tell him that Alicia is safe and sound. I shall tell him that Ninette attacked you. I shall say how worried I am that she might attack Alicia too because, after all, she's no blood relation to the girl, is she? And I'll ask if it's really true that Alaric left Alicia in the school grounds but didn't see her handed over, because Ninette was so anxious to get back to town for her hair appointment.'

Bernice blinked. 'They'll take her away again, and then she'll run away again and . . . you can't let them have her!'

Bea sighed. 'My dear, it's not as simple as that, and you know it. The law says Alaric is her adopted father and he has the right, with her mother, to decide where she lives. The fact that he doesn't seem a very caring parent gives William the ammunition to challenge Alaric in the courts. But by law, I have to hand Alicia over either to her mother or her father as soon as she reappears. I expect William is running through his options as we speak.'

'Her mother doesn't care.' A bleak tone.

'Oh, I expect she does, really.' Fingers crossed. 'But she's quite poorly, you know.'

'Perhaps Uncle William will hide Alicia somewhere.'

Bea shook her head. 'No, he won't. And you know he won't. He'll fight for her, but he won't break the law.'

Bernice sighed. 'They'll send her back to the school.'

'It's not so bad, is it?'

'Without me? She'll die.'

'I hope not.' Though Bea thought Bernice might be right. 'How about you?'

A shrug. 'I'll be all right. I suppose they'll find me another school.'

'Is this one really so bad?'

'No. It's all right, really, now I've dealt with the bullies.'

'Leon can get on to the school, get them to take you back.'

'He'll wait for Auntie Sybil to do it. Uncle Leon's not so good with people. He'll huff and puff but he never actually does anything himself if he can help it.'

An acute judgement.

The child continued, 'Auntie Sybil loves me, she really does. And I love her. But she's so old and I'm something of a trial to her, because she has to keep stopping and thinking what she should do with me when she wants to go somewhere or do something on the spur of the moment. She'll be furious that the school doesn't want me back and she'll find another boarding school for me, but I don't want to go without Lissy.'

Bea nodded. She wanted to hug Bernice, but thought it best not to touch the child lest she lose her fragile self-control.

'When I'm grown up,' said Bernice, 'I'm going to buy a house in the country and have a collie dog and a black cat for intelligent company and have some peace and quiet and only invite people in when I want to talk to them.'

'A trifle bleak,' said Bea. 'You'll need to keep that keen brain of yours from getting rusty. Do you want to be an aeronaut, or a website designer, or a mathematician or an airline pilot or an archaeologist or a ballet dancer . . . or what?'

The child smiled. 'I could be any of those things if I wanted to. Mostly, I want to be like you and Auntie Sybil.'

'Your aunt? That I can understand. She's an amazing person and brilliant at making money. But why me?'

For the first time, of her own accord, Bernice laid her head against Bea's arm. 'Some people, like Uncle Leon and Mummy and my stepdad, only have a little space inside them for loving other people. I mean; they do love people, but not very many, and they can't make that space any bigger. Auntie Sybil expanded herself to take me in. She doubled up her loving space for me. You're the same.'

Bea put her arm round the child, with care, and was not rebuffed. She thought it was a terrifying prospect for a woman in her sixties, who would normally be thinking about retirement, to be lumbered with an intelligent child. It was exciting, yes. But, on the whole, more terrifying than exciting.

Bernice said, 'I'd better go and find Teddy. I gave him to Alicia to look after and she didn't bring him back in. He doesn't like being out there in the cold and the dark.'

She vanished into the darkening garden, and was back with Teddy before Bea had put away the chess pieces in their box. Together they made sure the lights were all turned out and climbed the stairs to the kitchen.

Alicia was at the table, being fed egg and soldiers by Mel. William was on the phone. He shut it off when he saw Bea and Bernice.

'I rang Steve, told him Alicia had found her way back here after being dumped by Alaric. I'm taking Alicia to the hospital to see Daphne in a minute. My solicitor has dictated me a form which I shall try to get Daphne to sign, giving me the right to look after the child for the time being. I've informed the school that the child is with me and will not be returning until after the weekend, if ever.'

'And did you tell Alaric?'

William grinned. 'What do you think? I expect Steve will get round to it, eventually . . . but he does have rather a lot on his plate at the moment.'

'What terrible people they are,' said Mel, efficiently cleaning Alicia up. 'There, now. All done? Perhaps a biscuit and some juice to follow?'

Alicia nodded. She held out a hand to Bernice, who took a seat beside her, hoisting Teddy on to her hip.

Bea investigated the contents of the fridge. 'You need something to eat as well, William. And what do you fancy, Bernice, now that Alicia has eaten your tea?'

'I can manage,' said William, looking at his phone again. 'I've booked myself a room at the hotel down the road. I'll eat when I get back from the hospital. I must ring the hotel to change the booking so that Alicia can have a room next to me.'

'Leave her here for the night,' said Bea. 'I am not having those two girls wreck my bedroom again, but they can move into the flat on the top floor. That is . . . Mel, are you free?

Could you bear to stay on to look after these two naughty children tonight?'

'Can do. I'll let my mother know. You know, I thought my family was weird, but this lot take the biscuit.'

'You can have the run of the flat on the top floor tonight. The girls can have the room with the double bed, and you can have the single next to it. There's a small kitchen and shower room next door. Ham sandwiches do everyone? Or scrambled eggs and smoked salmon?'

William gave Bea back her phone. 'I've copied the interview with Alaric and Ninette on to my phone, so you can have yours back. With thanks. I ate a couple of bananas a while back. That'll do till Lissy and I get back from the hospital. May I pay for you to get in some ready meals, if you're going to play hostess today? Save you cooking. Come on, chicken. We're off to see your mummy.' He picked Alicia up off her stool, made sure she was reasonably tidy, and towed her out of the front door.

Peace and quiet.

Mel said, 'I'll give Bernice her tea. All right, Mrs Abbot?'

'Bless you, my dear. You didn't expect to get involved in a family feud when you came to work this morning, did you? You must say if you think it's all a bit much for you.'

'Certainly not,' said Mel, straightening her shoulders. 'It's most interesting, and I wouldn't like to leave the children without anyone to look after them. Not after all they've been through. They're managing very well, aren't they, but . . .'

'My old nanny used to say, "There'll be tears before night-fall". Yes. They're running on adrenaline at the moment, but when their batteries fail, they'll need extra care. So, thank you, Mel. I appreciate your staying . . . and that's the front door. I wonder what William has forgotten.'

It wasn't William. It was a total stranger, holding an expensive-looking tote bag. Bleary-eyed. Unshaven. Wearing a good-quality black T-shirt – which had been pulled on inside out – a leather jacket which had seen better days, and jogging trousers. Bringing with him the unmistakeable odour of a fire. A taxi was just drawing away.

A hoarse voice. 'Alicia? Is she safe?'

'Yes, she's quite safe.'

'Thank God for that.' He went limp, put out a hand to steady himself against the doorframe. Then, with an effort, pulled himself upright again. 'I have some things here for Lord Morton.'

NINE

'Lord Morton?' For a moment Bea was at a loss. 'Oh, you mean William? He's a Morton, isn't he?'

'Uncle Bill.' The visitor nodded, tried to smile.

Bea wondered if the man was actually swaying, or was it an optical illusion? 'You're . . . Steve, is that right?' She wasn't surprised that she hadn't recognized this exhausted, dishevelled creature. At dinner last night he'd been a dapper youngish man in evening dress, with curly fair hair that was beginning to grey at the temples. He'd been seated between Ninette and the supermodel, Faye, and had worn an expression of . . . what, exactly? Amused resignation? That was the nearest Bea could come to it. No wife, partner or girlfriend had been apparent.

Steve was the one who'd kept his head and gone for the fire extinguisher.

He tried to hand her the tote bag, but dropped it. 'For Uncle Bill. Tell him our insurance will pay for anything he's lost.'

'He's just gone out, but he'll be back soon.'

He swayed from one foot to the other, and almost fell. When had he last slept? He'd been keeping everything going since the fire, hadn't he? In hospital with his father . . . who'd unexpectedly died. Then back to the house with the firemen . . . seeing to solicitors and funeral arrangers . . . in and out of a different hospital to look after Daphne . . . and back to the house again to see what could be salvaged.

She said, 'You'd better come in.' She reinforced the invitation with a hand on his arm and he stumbled inside. She picked up the tote bag, and dumped it on the chest in the hall.

He said, 'Uncle Bill was staying the night with us. Shaving things. Night things. They need a good clean.' He shook his head. 'Top floor . . . stairs have gone. First floor, all right if doors were shut.' He nodded. 'Inside OK, but stinks of fire. And the foam gets everywhere. And water. In those near the stairs. Father's room . . . intact. Crazy, you know?'

She moved him, still talking, into the kitchen, where Bernice was finishing her sandwich and Mel was clearing the table.

Steve recognized Bernice, with an effort. 'Bernice! Where's Lissy? She all right?'

'Ugh, you pong!' said Bernice.

Bea steered him to a stool. 'Have a seat, Steve. Your uncle Bill has taken Alicia to see her mummy in hospital. When did you last eat?'

'Eat?' The word didn't mean anything to him. He licked his lips. Was he dehydrated?

'Or sleep?' Bea filled a glass with orange juice from the fridge and handed it to him. As he didn't seem to understand the word 'sleep' either, she tried on an order for size. 'Drink that. Slowly.'

Obeying orders, he did so. Tried to put the empty glass on the table and missed. Bea caught it as it fell. 'Now,' she said, 'do you want a ham sandwich or some scrambled eggs?'

He looked at her with a blank expression.

Bernice said, 'Tsk!' She thrust Teddy at him. 'Hold Teddy, Uncle Steve.'

He took hold of Teddy and said, in a tone of surprise, 'It's a teddy bear!'

Catching Bea's eye, Bernice said, 'Uncle Steve's too old for Teddy, really, but he's not doing well, is he? Shall we make him some strong black coffee?'

Mel objected. 'If we give him coffee, he won't sleep.'

He looked pleased. He'd recognized a word he knew. 'Sleep. Yes. Soon. Book into a hotel. My bedroom . . . no good. After . . . what is it I have to do?'

Bea whipped egg and poured it into a saucepan. 'Bernice, get him a spoon, will you, dear? Don't bother him with a knife and fork. Mel, sweetened tea, don't you think?'

'After what? Ah,' he nodded to himself. 'I remember. After I see Daphne and take her to . . . Daphne's very upset. Quite poorly. Doesn't know yet about . . . what is it she doesn't know? I've found a nice place for her to stay until . . .'

Bea plonked a bowl of scrambled egg in front of him, handed him the spoon and said, 'Don't talk. Eat.'

He looked puzzled. 'What?'

Bernice climbed on to the stool next to him, picked up the spoon, collected a mouthful of egg, and said, 'Open your mouth, please!'

He blinked, but obeyed, still holding the bear.

Bernice tipped the egg into his mouth. 'And in it goes! This little piggy went to market . . . and open! This little piggy stayed at home! Open wide! This little piggy went, Wee, Wee, Wee . . . Open! All the way home!'

Mel put a mug of tea on the table, removed one of his hands from the bear, and put it round the mug. He blinked, took his eye off Bernice as she tried to put the next mouthful into his mouth and missed, getting it to his cheek instead. She called him back to attention, and he dutifully swallowed.

'There!' said Bernice. 'Now you can drink up your tea before you have a little nap.'

He looked at the mug, but didn't seem to know how to lift it to his lips. Mel put an arm round his shoulders, and lifted the tea to his mouth as if he were a small child. 'There, there . . . there's a good boy.'

Steve's blue eyes widened and he turned his head to look at Mel, whose fair skin was no fairer than his and whose hair was only a shade lighter. He looked puzzled. Couldn't work out who she was.

Bea reflected that the whole of life must be a puzzle for Steve at the moment. 'Bed,' she said. 'We'll put him in the guest room, Mel. First floor, where I slept last night. Don't bother about clean sheets. Everyone's going to have to sleep in someone else's sheets tonight.'

'Come along,' said Bernice, taking him by the hand. 'Up the stairs to beddy-byes.'

Mel kept her arm around Steve's shoulders and urged him on, too. Awkwardly, still holding the bear, he got off the stool and allowed them to lead him back through the hall and to the stairs. And there, he stuck.

Stairs, thought Bea. His mind is back in the burned-out shell of what used to be his home.

'Come along!' Bernice was getting impatient. 'A good night's sleep and you won't know yourself!'

'Yes, come along,' said Mel, with an encouraging smile. 'You'll like to shower, and then get into a nice, clean bed. Let me have your clothes and I'll wash them for you so that they'll be fresh in the morning.'

He looked at the stairs, took a deep breath, and allowed himself to be guided up them. Stopped halfway and turned round. 'I must . . . No, I have to . . . Daphne, you know? And, Gideon couldn't have . . . could he? That would be murder!'

Mel's one idea was to get him to bed. She turned him round again. 'Up the stairs to Bedfordshire.'

Bedfordshire! When had she last heard that? Bea clutched at herself. She told herself that she was *not* going to have hysterics. Certainly not.

Another two steps and Steve stopped again, fumbling in his trouser pockets, producing . . . a smartphone, which was vibrating. He couldn't work out how to answer his phone while holding on to the bear, but at the same time he didn't want to let go of Teddy.

Bea solved that by plucking the phone from his hand. 'Let me. I'll be your personal assistant while you have a nap. I'll take messages and have them ready for you to look at when you surface again.'

'It's Gideon.' He let the phone go and, guided by Mel, staggered into the guest room. He saw the bed, tripped and fell full-length on to it. Still clutching Teddy.

And began to breathe deeply.

Mel threw up her hands. 'Can we get him into the shower?'

'No,' said Bernice and Bea together.

'We need a man for that,' said Bea, thinking . . . *Lord* Morton! Didn't he introduce himself as 'Morton, William'? Not, as it happens, that I give a damn about titles.

Mel was easing off Steve's shoes and socks. 'My brothers are the same when they overdo things. I'll strip him and tumble him into bed, shall I? Leave him to sleep it off.'

Bernice eased the bear out from Steve's arm, and gave him a cuddle. 'There, now, Teddy. Did the big man squash you? You're doing a great job.'

Bea clutched at her arms again. *Who's been sleeping in my bed? said Daddy Bear. Who's been sleeping in my bed? said Mummy Bear . . .*

She told herself to grow up. She told herself to file away Steve's remark about murder until she had time to deal with it.

She went downstairs to be quiet while she answered Steve's phone, which had stopped ringing, and had now started again . . . at the same time as her own landline began to shrill . . . and the doorbell.

She answered Steve's phone as she opened the door. It was her good friend Leon on the doorstep, looking dapper, expensive and well rested. She gestured him inside while saying to the agitated voice at the other end of Steve's phone . . . his brother? . . . 'So sorry, Steve is temporarily unable to get to the phone. May I take a message?'

'What . . . who?' said Leon, looking at his watch. 'Aren't you ready yet?'

'I have to speak to him! It's an emergency!' said the voice on the phone.

'Hold on a minute,' said Bea, hurrying to pick up her landline. 'I'm taking messages for him while—'

'Put him on, straight away!'

Bernice threw herself down the stairs and into Leon's arms. 'Uncle Leon!'

Leon picked Bernice up and twirled her around, making her laugh and sending Teddy flying through the air to land up on the floor. 'How's my little pickle?'

Bea picked up the bear and got to her landline, to hear the harsh but very welcome tones of Leon's elder sister, Sybil. 'Bea, what's going on over there! I got the strangest message from my young brother while I was playing bridge, saying you'd taken Bernice in because she'd been expelled from school. There must be a mistake!'

'Indeed,' said Bea. 'They're both here. Sort it out with them.' Bea held out the phone to Leon. 'Sybil. For you.' And to Steve's phone, 'Now, who am I speaking to?'

'I'm his brother! Who the devil are you, and what are you doing with my brother's phone?' A strident voice, the voice of a pampered poodle who got all the treats and left it to others to take out the garbage.

Bea envisaged him at the dinner table the previous night; a good-looking blonde, almost as much in love with himself as had been the gigolo Giorgio. It was Josh's favourite son, Gideon.

She said, 'I'm Mrs Abbot. I was at your house with Sir Leon Holland last night. Lord Morton and I rescued your niece and Leon's from the fire and they are temporarily staying with me. Your brother arrived here a few minutes ago in a state of exhaustion. We've put him to bed and I'm in two minds about calling a doctor to have a look at him.'

'What? That's ridiculous! There's nothing wrong with Steve. He's bombproof. I need to speak to him, and you have no right to interfere. Put him on the phone, now!'

'I regret,' said Bea in her creamiest tone, 'he's out for the count. I would guess he hasn't slept for thirty-six hours. How about you?'

'What? Me? Well, I . . . Come off it! I was at the hospital till late and . . . what has that got to do with anything? I need to speak to him, and you have no right to stop me.'

'If you would like to leave a message, I will take it and give it to him later. Or, I can turn this phone off, and whatever you want to say can go to voicemail, to be retrieved when he is able to face the world again. Possibly tomorrow morning? Or even the day after?'

That was being provocative and she knew it. She was probably going far beyond what was sensible, but Gideon's manner riled her. She cuddled Teddy and said, 'Fire away.' And then thought she oughtn't to have mentioned the word 'fire'.

Heavy breathing. He really was an angry young man, wasn't he? 'Tell my brother,' spitting out the words, 'that Giorgio refuses to take Daphne down to the spa hotel—'

'Spa hotel?' echoed Bea. 'Is that what Steve arranged—?'

'Because he's got something else on. He says.'

'Uh-huh,' said Bea. 'Is that it?'

'Are you a half-wit? Don't you understand what this means?'

'I suppose it means that you expect your brother to rise from his sick-bed and take her down there himself?'

'Are you thick, or something? He's the only one who—'

'He's out of it. Unconscious. You'll have to do it yourself.'

'You have absolutely no concept, no understanding of . . . how dare you!'

Bea sighed, switched the phone off, made sure the ringtone had been turned to silent, and hid it in one of the top cupboards in the kitchen, behind the biscuit tin. She did think of putting it in the fridge or the freezer, but that might wipe the SIM card, or whatever it was that made it function. She could put it in the oven, of course. Nice and soundproof. But, no. It wasn't up to her to destroy Steve's phone, although she had a shrewd idea that he was at the beck and call of far too many people, and it would do him good to be out of contact for a while.

Was she going to feel guilty about hiding the phone? Perhaps.

She confided in Teddy as she placed him on the kitchen table. 'I'm prepared to be very sorry about it, tomorrow.'

She could hear Leon chatting away on the phone in the sitting room, interrupted by little cries from Bernice, who also wanted to speak to her Auntie Sybil to tell her what had been happening.

Mel arrived in the kitchen, carrying an armful of Steve's clothing. She put the clothes into the washing machine without waiting for instructions.

Winston the cat arrived, smelling of fish and wanting to be fed. Where had he got the fish? Oh, well; he knew where to find food in all the neighbourhood kitchens, didn't he? Winston was a survivor, which was more than Bea felt like at that moment.

Don't think about Steve saying something had been murder.

Well, try not to think about it.

Mel hovered, with her finger on the button for the washing machine. 'Anything else to go in?'

'Can't think. Oh, Steve brought a tote bag for William. Maybe there's something in there? Everything that was in their house last night will need a wash. But I suppose we ought to ask his permission first.'

'Right. I'll set this lot going, but after that, can you spare me for half an hour while I dash home and get some things for tonight? And, shall I bring something in for supper?'

'Supper? No, we'll raid the freezer.' Bea looked at her watch. She couldn't make sense of the time it was telling her. The front doorbell rang. On her way to answer it, Bea threw a few words back to Mel. 'Yes, take advantage of the lull before the storm, though why I think there's going to be a storm, I don't know. Hold on a mo; you'll need a front-door key. There's a spare in the top cupboard in the mug with a hedgehog on it.'

The front doorbell rang again. Passing the sitting-room door, she saw that Leon was still on the phone, with Bernice on his knee. The two of them were taking turns to fill Sybil in on what had been happening.

Another stranger was at the door. A man. Tallish and well built, dark – no, black – hair. Narrow eyes. An air of danger. Cornish? Bosnian? Albanian?

'Mrs Abbot? Detective Constable Thurrock. May I have a word?' He held up his ID for a second, and stepped inside. Whatever his family background, he'd been born and educated in this country.

A plain-clothes detective? Oh dear. Wanting to pin the fire on the children?

Mel came through the hall, pulling on her jacket. She looked at the man, and then at Bea. 'Do you want me to stay, Mrs Abbot?'

'No need,' said the policeman. 'I just need a quiet word with Mrs Abbot, that's all.'

'It's all right,' said Bea, feeling jaded. This would be about the fireworks, of course. Hadn't Manisa the fire investigator said something about the police always being involved in any case of an accident with fireworks? 'Do come in, officer.' Even though he was already inside the hall. She reflected that she was getting to be like Steve, not connecting.

She hesitated at the door to the sitting room. Leon was still on the phone, talking to his sister. Bernice was listening intently. Talking about another school for Bernice? They both looked up at her, and looked away. She wasn't needed.

She led the way to the kitchen, which was reasonably tidy,

and indicated that the man – what was his name again?
Thurrock? Was that a northern name? Definitely not Cornish.
'Do have a seat. Now, what can I do for you? It's about last
night, I assume.'

He sat down and produced a notebook. 'We understand you
were present at a dinner last night, and one of the other guests
was a Faye Starman.'

'Was that her surname? Yes, we were both guests.' She put
the kettle on. 'Could you do with a cuppa?'

'Not on duty, no. Miss Starman alleges that, during the
course of the evening, two children belonging to the family
set the house on fire and—'

'That's not right. For a start, only one of the children
belonged to the family and—'

He lifted his hand to stop her. 'Be that as it may, and it is
understood that further proceedings are under way with regard
to the involvement of the children in criminal proceedings—'

'The children did *not* set the place on fire!'

A heavy sigh. 'Please, Mrs Abbot. Will you kindly let me
continue? Miss Starman alleges that in the confusion following
the fire, she found herself alone in the house except for you
and the children, and that you assaulted her, causing her to
receive hospital attention, which has resulted in the loss of a
lucrative modelling assignment—'

'What!'

'And that you stole her pearl necklace.'

The kettle boiled. Bea switched it off and stared at the man.
A hard face over a hard body, not an ounce of fat. She said,
'I don't believe it! I pull Faye from a burning building, and
she says I assaulted her?'

'She has bruises to prove it.'

'She has a vivid imagination.'

'Are you accusing her of making this up?'

Bea banged a mug down on the table, put in a tea bag and
poured hot water on it, adding milk to taste. She needed a
cuppa, even if he didn't. She sipped the tea, and told herself
to keep calm. She said, 'When the curtain in the dining room
went up in flames, Daphne, our hostess for the evening, became
distressed. Faye went to her aid. Daphne threw back her arm,

which hit Faye. In doing so, she tangled with Faye's pearls and broke the string. Two of us went searching for the children and found them on the top floor, which was also in flames.

'When we managed to get back down to the hall, we found everyone had gone except for Faye, who had been left behind, searching for her pearls on the floor. We helped her pick them up. The fire became too much of a threat to ignore, so we decided to get out. Faye didn't want to leave her pearls, but . . . yes, I admit I grabbed her arm and towed her out of the house. And yes, she was furious with me, wanted to go back to search for them. If she'd gone back in, she'd have died. Some neighbours took us in, and yes . . . Faye did complain about her bruises but . . . ought I to have left her there to die?'

'She is accusing you of assault, claiming loss of wages, pain and suffering. Also the cost of replacing her pearls. She has the evidence to back up her claim in the form of photographs of her bruises.'

'Tell her to claim on the house's insurance.'

'The house didn't cause her bruises and loss of wages. You did.' He shut up his notebook. 'Mrs Abbot, the police have enough to do without dealing with matters such as these which are best settled in the small-claims courts. When you receive a summons, I advise you to settle Miss Starman's claim quickly. You don't want this aired in the tabloid newspapers, do you? Think how it would look. "Model loses pearls and career at millionaire's party".' He flattened his eyelids at her. He really was an intimidating person.

Bea stared at the man. Thinking hard. 'I can produce a witness who saw exactly what happened.'

'I daresay. It is always good to prepare your defence in advance.' The man didn't even refer back to his notebook. 'A "friend" of yours, no doubt?'

'You mean: was Sir Leon Holland the man who helped me to get everyone out of the burning house?'

'He's your live-in boyfriend, I believe.'

A false note. What rubbish had Faye been feeding the police? 'You are mistaken. It was a completely different man. Hang on a minute. Why isn't she suing the family for the loss of her pearls?'

'They didn't assault her.'

'Or maybe Gideon isn't being that helpful to his girlfriend? Doesn't want to be bothered? He's got a lot on his plate, without her wittering on about her lost pearls.'

He slitted his eyes at her. 'You think that because you have money, you can throw a poor working girl aside?'

Bea checked herself from saying some hasty words. She picked up Teddy and stroked him. His fur was soft and tickly. A very present comfort in time of trouble. *Dear Lord. I'd like to smash this man's face in . . . not that I could. I can hardly lift my hand to my head, never mind assaulting him.*

She put Teddy down, and said, 'Sorry, mate. You've come to the wrong house. I suppose Faye reported this to the police station and flapped her eyelashes at you till you were fool enough to fall for her sob story. Tell Faye to go and get a solicitor – which will cost her money – who will advise her that Mrs Abbot has no case to answer. Tell her that if she tries to sue me for bruises or whatever, I in turn will sue her for endangering my life and the lives of the two children by begging us to search for her pearls despite the danger.'

He gave her a hard, flat stare. She had to admit he did it rather well. 'I am sure Sir Leon will be delighted to help you defray Miss Starman's costs, in order to keep his name out of the papers.'

That amused Bea. Leon wouldn't pay up. Why should he? 'Pull the other one.'

'Well, I have done my bit, and you must decide what attitude you are prepared to take when the matter comes up in court. As I say, you'd best be advised to settle her claim before it gets that far. Understood?' He got up to leave. 'I'll see myself out.'

She followed him to the door and watched him stride off down the street. She wondered if Faye were waiting in a car nearby to see how he'd got on. But he went to the end of the road and turned left. Going to the nearest tube station?

What a very strange interview. He hadn't written anything down that she'd said to him. She supposed he was off duty . . . doing a favour for a pretty girl. A bit naughty. Not a real threat, surely?

She was so tired! What a nuisance this all was. She supposed she'd have to alert her own solicitor on Monday. But she was not, definitely not, going to pay blackmail money to Miss Starman, complain she never so loudly.

Beatrice lifted her face to the sky, which was darkening. Somewhere nearby a rocket pinged into the sky and splattered green and blue stars.

She shuddered. She didn't think anyone under her roof was going to enjoy fireworks for some time to come. Nor, come to think of it, would Winston, who always scuttled for the stationery cupboard when he was frightened. No real need to worry about him, provided he was indoors when the noise began. She must check. Back to the fray.

TEN

Saturday early evening

'Ah, there you are, Bea!' Leon, smiling, with Bernice at his side.

Bernice was excited, eyes shining . . . eyes too bright, too heavy-lidded. Early to bed for this little one? Bernice jigged up and down. 'We're going to Disneyland in Paris. Lissy as well! I can hardly wait!'

Leon was pleased with himself. 'You'll come too, won't you, Bea? I don't think I could cope with the excitement of meeting Mickey Mouse all by myself.'

Which meant, Bea guessed, that he wanted her to make all the arrangements. Once upon a time Leon had been a mover and shaker, making deals here, flying there, shifting millions around the world, but he'd grown lazy since he'd sold off most of the Holland empire, and now he deputed other people to do his dirty work for him.

'Disneyland?' said Bea, trying for enthusiasm, 'I'm sure the girls will love it. Did you think we were going out to supper tonight?'

'I thought we deserved a treat, after last night. You can get a baby-sitter for Bernice, can't you?'

'I'm sorry, Leon. I have a house full. I've got Steve here as well as Bernice, and William's bringing Alicia back soon. Quite frankly, I'm bushed and could do with an early night myself. I'll have to try to find something for us all to eat here. You're welcome to join us.' His face fell, and she realized she hadn't couched the invitation in the warmest of terms.

He shrugged. 'Oh well. Perhaps I'll drop in at the club.' He'd recently been put up for some prestigious club or other, Bea wasn't sure which one. She actually thought it a good idea for him to have somewhere to go in the evenings. He really wasn't a domestic animal. Perhaps he should take up golf?

She said, 'Ring me tomorrow? Oh, and is Sybil on her way back and what is happening about the school?'

Bernice danced around the room. 'Disneyland, here we come!'

Leon consulted his watch. 'Sybil should be here tomorrow. She said she'd phone me when she'd got a flight. So . . . well, let me know how you get on, will you?'

A rocket wheezed off into the sky and burst like bullets from a gun. Bernice froze in mid dance step and Leon had the grace to look uneasy. 'Just a stray firework. Nothing to worry about. I hope you're not going to have a bad night with the girls, Bea. But there! You'll cope, won't you?' He kissed Bernice and Bea, and let himself out.

Bea looked down at Bernice, who looked back up at her, a serious little girl once more. Slightly scared but trying not to show it. Bea said, 'He's right, you know. Nothing's going to get you here.'

Bernice said, 'I know that!' Hiding anxiety. Brave girl.

Bea thrust her fingers back through her hair. 'What next? Food?'

The front doorbell rang . . . and, at the same time, someone turned a key in the lock. Mel entered, ushering in William, who was carrying a sleepy Alicia in his arms.

As per usual, thought Bea. Alicia's family make a habit of getting other people to carry them through difficult times, don't they?

'Lissy!' cried Bernice, jumping up and down like a jack-in-a-box. 'We're going to Disneyland!'

Alicia opened her eyes and slid to the floor, showing signs of returning life. 'Cool!'

'And,' said Bernice, catching Alicia by the hand and leading her to the stairs. 'We're sleeping up at the top of the house by ourselves, and there's a kitchen next door, so we can have a midnight feast! Come and see!'

Bea threw up her hands. 'I'm too old for this! Midnight feasts, indeed. What have they been reading?'

'Enid Blyton?' suggested Mel, humping in a small tote bag. She laughed. 'I'll see to them if you like, Mrs Abbot. A light supper and then . . . is there a DVD player upstairs? I brought some Disney films for them to watch. They probably know them all by heart but I thought it might calm them down before going to bed.'

'I'll see to the food and, as for a telly, there are two up there.' Bea narrowed her eyes as William propped himself up against the wall. If he sat down, he'd fall asleep. Like Steve.

Another rocket went off nearby and William blenched.

Bea looked up the stairs. The children would now be out of earshot, hopefully. 'Do you think they're going to be all right? Aren't the fireworks going to bring it all back to them?'

Mel grimaced. 'Nightmares, you think? I promise to stick to them like glue.' She went off up the stairs.

William was grey with exhaustion. 'Where did you find that girl? Worth her weight.'

Bea held out her hand to him. 'William, don't fall asleep yet. Look, Steve has brought over your night things. Would you like me to put them in the washing machine for you? They'll stink of the fire.'

'Ugh?' he said. And tried to focus on the bag. 'No, that's not mine.'

Bea sighed. He was obviously too far gone to recognize his own bag. 'All right, we'll leave that for the moment. You should have something to eat before you go to your hotel. Come into the kitchen and tell me what's been happening while I see to the food.'

He followed her, walking heavily, feeling his age as she was feeling hers. She investigated the freezer. 'I have a big fish pie here. That'll take a few minutes in the microwave. Frozen veg. Anything you don't like?'

'Celery.'

'Really? OK. No celery. Fruit and cheese for afters? If you can stay awake that long.'

He passed the heels of his hands over his eyes. 'Bless you. Daphne . . . I'm worried about her, I'm not sure why. I asked the nurses, there was no doctor available. They had talked about sending her home today but changed their minds and are keeping her in till tomorrow. The nurse said Daphne was coming on nicely. Alicia was a bit shocked at her mother's appearance, I think, but I told her hospital lighting isn't kind to women. Daphne loves Alicia. Of course she does, but she's not well.'

Bea wanted to say 'Humph!' but refrained. With an effort. William said, 'Alicia told Daphne she was staying here with you and Bernice. She did say she didn't want to go back to that school. Daphne said she'd think about it but I'm not sure she was taking it in.'

Bea set the microwave going, hoping there'd be enough for Mel and the girls as well. 'So you didn't get her to sign a letter removing Alaric from guardianship?'

A long, heavy sigh. 'I brought the subject up. She didn't seem to understand what I was on about.'

Bea took a large pack of mixed veg out of the freezer. She could only hope there wasn't any celery in it. But if there was . . . well, tough! He would have to fish the pieces out and leave them at the side of his plate. She said, 'You didn't press her to sign.'

No, of course he wouldn't. Not William. He wouldn't think it ethical to do so while Daphne was unwell. He would probably regret not doing so later.

He said, 'I did think of it, and of getting a nurse to witness her signature. But if it were challenged, we'd be on a hiding to nothing because I couldn't honestly say she was of sound mind and knew what she was doing. Would you have got her to sign?'

'I'd have argued it back and forth in my head and then have done as you did.'

He said, 'She kept asking for Giorgio. Fretting. Then she went on about Steve, asking why he hadn't come to fetch her. She said he wants her to go to some hotel or other but she doesn't fancy it because she's no clothes or toiletries with her. She says Steve promised to fetch her her things. She doesn't know about the fire, or even about her father. If she's been told, she hasn't remembered. Alicia was horrified. She went dumb and kept looking at me to tell her mother about the fire, but I didn't. I haven't a clue whether that was the right thing to do or not.'

'You judged her too frail to hear bad news.'

Again he rubbed his eyes. 'She's only, what, thirty-five? I've known her all her life.'

'You think she's not doing as well as she ought?'

'The hospital ought to know what they're doing but yes, I'm worried about her.'

'You've got a headache? A migraine?'

'Headache. Have you any aspirin?'

'Mm. Eat first. You've decided what you're going to do about Alicia?'

'I have an idea.' He picked up Teddy, who had ended up on the central unit. 'Hello, Mr Bear.'

'Mr Bear? Was that your name for your bear when you were little?'

'What was it for you? It is your bear, isn't it?'

'Mm. Teddy. I was told it was "Teddy" when I was given it, and I didn't question it. I was an obedient child.'

He bent over in a gust of laughter. 'You could have fooled me.'

'I was,' she insisted. 'Well, most of the time, anyway. You had a teddy bear, too?'

'Indeed. Not a Steiff. A Merrythought? Have I remembered that correctly?'

'I imagined it might comfort the children to hold it, but it's been picked up and cuddled by all sorts of people today. Even by Steve.'

Bea laid the table, and William stroked the bear. Smiling a little. Back in childhood? She found she was smiling, too. She said, 'In a minute I'm going to dish up and call the others down for food. I don't suppose Steve will wake up. I rather hope he doesn't.'

His mind was on other things.

She said, 'Steve said you were *Lord* Morton. I didn't know. You might have told me.'

He stroked the bear's nose. 'I wasn't sure what your position was. I was told you were Leon's friend.'

Oh. She suspended all movement. Even breathing. Suddenly the situation had changed. He wanted to know . . .? Was he asking her if she were Leon's property? Yes, he was.

Which meant that . . . Her brain zigzagged.

It meant he was interested in her for himself?

Oh. And how did she feel about that? Well, to be honest, she wasn't sure.

He was waiting for a reply. She realized that whatever she said next was going to decide the future for both of them. He was not asking the question lightly. He wanted to know if Leon were serious about her, and if she were serious about Leon. If she said that she was, then he would walk away from her and that would be that. He'd go back to his hotel room tonight. They might meet now and again in the future, or they might not. There'd be no second chances. He wasn't that kind of man.

If she said she was not serious about Leon, he would take it as encouragement to explore their relationship further. It was up to her.

Panic! Permission to panic, Captain Mainwaring!

Do I want to see more of him? Well, yes. Probably.

I like him enormously. I respect him. I think he's rather . . . oh, I'm blushing!

I'm fond of Leon but he can be a pain, and I've never thought of taking him into my bed. No. Well, only occasionally and not with any urgency.

But this man . . . Oh my God! I *am* blushing!

At my age!

I'm lonely, that's all. I've been so lonely since my dear husband died. And yes, sometimes in bed at night . . . Oh, this is ridiculous! I ought to be well past . . . All right, I am interested in taking this further.

My heart is beating so fast that . . .

Calm down, Bea. Let's not rush into anything.

She said, 'Leon? He's a very good friend. We've been through a lot together. We've talked about the future, now and then. Only somehow we've never got round to committing ourselves. We probably never will, now.'

'You were wearing an engagement ring last night.'

'It's the one my dear husband gave me when we married. He died abroad. And yes, I'm sure that says something about my unwillingness to commit to anyone else.'

William smiled. He pressed the bear's stomach, and Teddy obliged with a growl. William liked her answer, and he liked it that the bear still had a growl.

He said, 'I live in a Georgian house just outside Winchester with a married couple to look after me. I busy myself restoring old buildings.'

'You like living in the country?' She wasn't sure she would like it. Not at all.

'I was born and brought up there. Until recently I rented a flat up here in Town, but I found I wasn't getting much use out of it, so when the lease was up, I let it go. Perhaps I'll look around for something else now.'

Now? Did he mean he wanted another flat so that he could see more of her?

If they married and he moved in with her . . .

Marriage? She was thinking he wanted to marry her?

And, did she really want to venture into matrimony again? Er, probably not. At least . . . No, no. This was going too fast. She'd only known him for, what, twenty-four hours? She wanted to say, 'Oh, sir! This is so sudden!'

Be honest with yourself, Bea. You knew you could be serious about this man as soon as you set eyes on him . . . no, in the hall of the burning house last night, when you gave him your phone, knowing that meant you'd be left in the dark, trusting him . . .

She said, speaking in a light tone, 'I'm not ready to retire yet.'

'I've come to that conclusion, too. I need to rethink what I'm going to do next. I have friends who've taken up golf and invite me to join them. Or, I might stand for the council.'

'But you've decided against?'

'Golf is a selfish sport. Politics is a dirty game.'

She drained the vegetables and put them in a serving dish. She wasn't sure where this new relationship was going, but if he was content to take it gently, then she'd go along for the ride. 'I'll call the others down.'

As she reached the stairs, a cluster of rockets went off. Startled, she put her hand to her heart. The authorities frowned on people letting off fireworks in their back gardens, but some householders would always set off a few instead of attending one of the big, organized displays. She hoped the noise wouldn't wake Steve. She hoped it wasn't going to upset the children. She feared they were all in for a broken night.

Thank the Lord for Mel. Which reminded Bea to take a certain precaution. Now, somewhere . . . she went down into the agency . . . yes, Winston was in the stationery cupboard, poor lamb . . . and there was a good thick roll of plastic sheeting which had come wrapped around the new printer and they'd kept because it might come in useful some day. And today was the time to put it to use. Back up the stairs she went.

On her way past the door of the guest room, she peeped inside. Steve was still out for the count. Good. On up the stairs she went to the top floor, walking quietly. The girls were watching television in the sitting room. Mel was setting her night things out in the bedroom with the single bed in it. William had been supposed to occupy it the previous night, but had slept in the chair in Bea's room instead.

Bea entered and shut the door behind her. 'Mel; Bernice said something about Alicia having wet the bed when she was unhappy at school. It might not happen again, but shall we put some plastic under the top sheet of the bed next door, just in case? And I'll show you where the linen is kept?'

Mel straightened her back, hands on her lumbar region. 'But not tell the girls what we've done? Agreed. One of my brothers wet the bed when he was being bullied at school.'

Together they remade the bed.

Bea said, 'I hope we have a quiet night. We could do with it.'

'I doubt it. Is the heating going to be on all night?'

'You mean that if we have to be up in the night, it might be a good idea to have the rooms at a pleasant temperature? I'll see to it. Supper's ready, by the way.'

There was another burst of fireworks as they all trooped downstairs, and it wasn't only the two girls who shuddered. Bea put the radio on in the kitchen to drown out the noises outside, and they ate a little of this and a little of that. Alicia insisted on sitting next to her grandfather, and Bernice gave alternate mouthfuls to Teddy, who was assuming a careworn appearance. Much loving can do that to you.

Bea wondered if it would be a good idea to use a dry cleaner on the bear, and dismissed the idea because it would destroy his scent. For stuffed toys, the scent was all-important to the children who loved them.

When the meal was over, Alicia crept into her grandfather's lap and hid her face against him. 'What was that, chicken?' he said. She repeated her whisper, and he looked up at Bea. 'She wants to know which bed I'm sleeping in tonight.' And to Alicia, 'It's all right, chicken. I'll be just down the road. I can be back here in ten minutes, if you need me.'

She clambered up him to speak into his ear, and he grimaced. 'No, chicken, I can't take you with me. You'll be perfectly all right here, with Mel and Bernice to look after you.'

Bernice tucked Teddy firmly under her arm. 'Lissy wants her grandpa to sleep next door to us. I told her this house is not going to blow up but she's a bit of a 'fraidy cat.' For all her brave words, there was a shadow at the back of Bernice's eyes, too.

'I'm sleeping next door to you,' said Mel, brightly. 'And you can wake me any time you like.'

Bea suspected Mel was going to regret saying that.

William said, 'I can sleep anywhere. On the floor in their room, perhaps?' He looked at Bea for permission.

'Darlings,' said Bea, 'let's take a good look at the problem. We are all of us worn out. We all need a good night's sleep. Steve is in the guest room. William is not going to get a good night's sleep if he has to doss down on the floor somewhere. I agree he should stay within reach and not have to go to a hotel. How about we make him up a bed on the settee down here, and we leave the door open so that he can hear if anyone needs him . . . which I very much hope won't happen. All right?'

She thought of her own beautiful big bed, and of how little space she took up in it, and for at least two seconds entertained the thought of William occupying it with her. And dismissed the idea straight away.

William carried Alicia up to bed. Bernice and Teddy trailed behind him with Mel bringing up the rear. Bea found William a spare duvet and pillows and put them on the settee. She looked at her watch.

William was taking his time, saying goodnight to the children. Did he like to hear them say their prayers? Query: did children automatically say their prayers when they went to bed at night nowadays? Bea did, of course. But other people?

She cleared the table, filled and started the dishwasher. She took Steve's clothes out of the washing machine and put them in the drier. She adjusted the central heating so that it would stay on all night. She turned up the radio to block out the noise of fireworks outside, and fed Winston, who seemed to think the fireworks were getting less noisy . . . and perhaps they were. Just the odd spat and sparkle now and then.

William came down, heavy-eyed. Moving with deliberation. She handed him some aspirins and a glass of water. He nodded, took them, said, 'You should have left me to clear up.'

Humph! As if! Why do men always say that, *after* the work's done?

He refused a hot drink, and plodded off to the sitting room. He took off his shoes. She made sure he knew where the light switches were before she went up the stairs to bed herself.

Steve was still asleep. Hadn't moved, by the look of it.

Time for bed, but she couldn't relax. Told herself it was imperative that she got some sleep. Thought about taking a herbal sedative. Rejected the idea. She was pretty sure they were in for a disturbed night.

She dowsed the lights and stared into the dark. Tried to pray. Couldn't.

Far too anxious.

Lord, have mercy. Lord, have mercy. Lord, have mercy on us.
Shelter us under your wings . . . take care of us this night . . .
all of us under this roof.

Lord, have mercy . . .

She woke with a start and sat upright. The clock said – she squinted at the dial – three fifteen? Had she really slept that long? But . . . what had woken her?

There was a murmur of voices next door, in the guest room. Steve?

She struggled into her dressing gown and investigated. The door to the guest room was open but she could see the bed was unoccupied. So . . .?

Splashing of water. But, *two* voices?

Steve? And . . . Mel? Bea prepared to be scandalized. She pushed open the door to the en suite. Mel looked up. Her hair was loose around her shoulders, and she was wearing a cotton bathrobe over a white cotton nightie. She was bathing Steve's eyes with balls of wet cotton wool. Steve's eyelids were red and swollen.

Mel explained. 'He left his contact lenses in too long. Ought to have taken them out last night but forgot, what with the fire and all. I've done exactly the same myself. It's excruciating. Have you got any Optrex?'

Steve was wearing a vest and boxer shorts and that was all. He looked to be fairly fit. In fact, Bea had heard that 'fit' didn't just mean that you were healthy, but that you were fit for . . . well, anything. Steve looked fit. In both senses.

Bea fetched the eye lotion, and stood by while Mel administered to Steve as if he were a child. Probably, to her, he was just that. After all, he wasn't exactly looking his best, was he?

Mel seemed to feel the need to explain her presence in Steve's room. 'He called out for help. Couldn't see. Couldn't think where he was. I don't think he's disturbed the children.'

Steve was only half awake, even now. Apologizing for his existence. 'Sorry, so sorry. So stupid. I was on my way to the hospital, wasn't I? Daphne's not too good, you know, and I was going to take her . . . Is she all right, do you know? I feel I've failed everyone. It must have been the electrician, don't you think? All my fault. I can't apologize enough for—'

'Shut up,' said Mel. She put her forefinger under his chin and lifted it so that he did shut up. 'You've been having a rough time, what with the fire and your sister, and your dad.'

A hard sob. His throat worked. 'My father . . . I simply can't believe . . .!'

'There, there!' said Mel, putting her arm around his shoulders. 'Have a good cry if it makes you feel better.'

Bea retreated to her bedroom, wondering whether she ought to have interfered. Amused at the thought of how Mel seemed able to act a mother substitute to all and sundry. Pitying Steve, who had lost his father.

Mel must have the sharp hearing of a cat. She'd heard Steve when no one else had.

Lord, have mercy . . . those two looked so innocent . . . I don't think Mel's at risk with Steve . . . What was that about an electrician? I must ask him, in the morning.

She sank back into a half-sleep . . . only to be woken again. A child had wailed? She shot upright and grabbed for her dressing gown, only to realize she was still wearing it.

Out on to the landing. Lights had been left on upstairs, but there was no sign of Mel. The door to Steve's room was ajar, and a light was on within. Perhaps this time Mel had slept through it, or was still comforting Steve?

'What was that? Lissy?' William, bleary-eyed, was struggling up the stairs while trying to pull on his sweater. Thank goodness she'd left the heating on, for the house was reasonably warm.

'I'll go and see.' Up she went. Mel was not in her room.

Alicia was standing beside the bed, hiccupping, distressed. And trying to get her pyjama bottoms off. Oh, dear.

Bea told herself she wasn't too tired to deal with this. Not at all. She said, 'Never mind, poppet. It's quite all right. Let's have you in the shower and get you all nice and clean again.'

Bernice slept, with her head on Teddy.

William was at her heels. 'Tell me what to do.'

Bea led Alicia into the shower, saying to William, 'Mel is looking after Steve. Can you see if she's free to come upstairs now? The children's bed will have to be changed.'

Bea couldn't think what she could dress the child in once she was clean and dry. Perhaps another of her T-shirts? 'Oh, and William! Can you go into my bedroom and fetch me a big T-shirt? Second drawer down, in the chest of drawers by the window.'

Into the shower we go, ta-ra! Scrub-a-dub-dub. Alicia in distress. Gulping sobs.

Mel arrived, also distressed. 'William's just told me. If it isn't one thing, it's another. Shall I take over?'

Bea said, 'Can you dry her while I sort out the bed? William's finding something for her to wear.'

William arrived with a pile of Bea's T-shirts. 'Pink, green or white?'

Bea left them at it and went into the children's room. And was brought up short. For where was Bernice?

ELEVEN

Bernice was not in the bed she'd shared with Alicia. And neither was Teddy.

Before she could stop herself, Bea cried out, 'Bernice! Where are you?'

A scamper of feet. Alicia, wrapped in a towel, huge dark eyes in a paper-white face. 'Berny? Where's Berny?'

Bea snatched at common sense. 'Gone to the loo, I expect.'

William opened doors till he found the loo. 'Not there.'

Bea tried to think. She mustn't upset Alicia any further. 'She's gone downstairs for something, I expect. She's got Teddy with her, so she's perfectly all right.'

She was speaking nonsense, wasn't she? But where else could the child be? She wouldn't have left the house in her pyjamas, would she?

A man lumbered into sight. Leather jacket, bare legs, horn-rimmed glasses. Bea had a moment of dislocation before she recognized Steve. 'What's wrong?'

Alicia ran to the top of the stairs and screamed, 'Berny!'

'Hush, now!' William picked Alicia up, towel and all.

'What's up?' A small figure in pink pyjamas climbed the stairs to join them. She was burdened not only with Teddy and the biscuit tin but also a vibrating smartphone.

Bea said, 'Bernice! Where have you been?'

'I woke up and I was hungry so I thought we could have a midnight feast. I found the biscuit tin and this phone was behind it. I tried to answer it, but the woman on the other end wants to speak to Steve.'

A woman, ringing Steve at this time of night? Equals a nurse. Hospital. Bad news.

Daphne?

Steve wilted.

Mel took Alicia off William, saying in a soft voice, 'Let

me finish rubbing Lissy down. There, there. Everything's all right.' And took her back into the bathroom.

Steve took the phone with a hand that shook. 'Hello . . .?'

William exchanged glances of concern with Bea, and led Bernice off into the sitting room, saying, 'I haven't had a midnight feast for ever. Biscuits are fine, but what do we have to drink?' He closed the door behind them.

Steve sank into a chair, listening. Nodding.

Bea finished stripping the bed, wiped down the plastic sheet, and found clean linen.

'Yes, I understand,' said Steve. 'Yes, of course. No, I don't think I want to see her now. What is the procedure? Yes, my father died last night, too. We can use the same funeral directors, I suppose. I'll try to . . . No, I understand.'

He clicked the phone off, looking shattered. 'A blood clot. I don't even know who her next of kin are. I was going to go into Dad's office tomorrow to see if I could find out. That was my next job, wasn't it? Or one of the urgent things . . . there's so many . . . I need to find out who ought to be responsible for her funeral, but . . . Perhaps Daphne will know? I'll have to ask her. But if there's no next of kin . . . maybe I'm wrong, but I'm not sure . . . then we'll have to be responsible for it.'

He began to shake. He held on to himself, hugging himself. In shock.

Bea's mind did a swoop around and came up with the correct answer. Not Daphne, thank God. Mrs Frost, the housekeeper. Dead. First his father, then the housekeeper.

Steve let his phone slip to the floor.

Mel came back with Alicia, who was now wearing one of Bea's T-shirts and looked as if she were half asleep already.

Mel took one look at Steve and said, 'Bad news?'

He gestured 'no', indicating that he didn't want to talk in front of Alicia.

Mel held the child out for Steve to kiss her goodnight. 'Say goodnight to your uncle.'

Steve mastered his distress sufficiently well to do so and to stroke the child's cheek. 'Sleep tight, Lissy. Nothing to worry your little head about.'

Mel tucked Alicia into bed, dowsed the lights and left the room, leaving the door ajar.

Steve whispered, 'Whatever next?'

Bea also whispered. 'We pray.' She thought he'd probably reject the idea, but he didn't rebuff her, so she went on, keeping her voice low, 'Dear Lord, we seek your help for all of us lost and lonely people. We pray for Mrs Frost, that her passing was swift and easy. We pray for everyone who is grieving. We pray for strength and wisdom to deal with what lies in store.'

Steve nodded. 'That sounds about right. I've never been one for prayer, but perhaps, when everything looks black and there's so much . . . I don't know what to think. Prayer. God. Perhaps He is the answer? It's true we can't rely on anyone else.' He looked, not at Bea, but at Mel.

Mel touched his arm. 'You are not alone. You have your sister and your brother. You have friends.'

He said, 'Daphne. Gideon. They'll have to be told. But not tonight. I've always felt alone. Always. I've learned the hard way not to rely on anyone else.'

Mel gave a narrow look at Bea, who didn't quite know how to react. 'Very well.' Mel urged Steve towards the stairs. 'Let's get you back to bed. You shouldn't be alone tonight.'

Bea wondered if she ought to interfere. She told herself it was no business of hers . . . well, it was under her roof and . . . ought she to offer Mel some birth-control pills? Except, of course, that Bea Abbot, aged sixty something, had no need of such things. Perhaps Mel knew what she was doing? Youngsters nowadays . . .

Steve allowed himself to be shepherded along. 'You'll leave in the morning, Mel. All the girls do. I'm boring, you see. All work and no play.'

'Same here.' They disappeared down the stairs.

Bea retrieved the bundle of dirty linen from the bedroom and chucked it into the kitchen next door. She'd deal with that in the morning. Checking on Alicia, she saw that the child was dozing while sucking her thumb. Tears leaked from the corners of her eyes.

William brought Bernice and Teddy into the room, saying, 'Bedtime, Bernice. Lissy needs you.'

Bernice slid to the ground and sat there. 'I'm not getting into that bed. Stinky-poos.'

'No, it isn't,' said Bea. 'It's lovely and clean now. Come along.' She got into the bed, in the middle, and held out her hand to Bernice to join her.

'No,' said Bernice.

'Yes,' said William. He picked her up and tucked her in beside Bea. 'Now, ladies; just you close your eyes and count to a hundred, and when you wake up the birds will be singing and we'll have bacon for breakfast.'

'Won't,' said Bernice, but her cold feet found Bea's warmth, wriggled a bit, and then were still. She hadn't let go of Teddy, but he wasn't digging in to Bea, so she let him be.

'And I,' William said, with amusement in his voice, 'get to sleep in a decent bed for a change.' He left the room, leaving the door ajar.

William intended to sleep in *her* bed? Bea felt her ribs ache with laughter, but couldn't afford to indulge, lest she disturb the two little waifs beside her.

She lay still, listening to the children breathing softly beside her. She'd never had a girl child. Had sometimes wondered what it would be like. Her only son had been something of a disappointment to her but there . . . you have to make the best of what you're given.

A bird started to sing a carol outside her window. The dawn chorus? Already? She wanted to look at the clock, but couldn't risk moving . . . and anyway, she wasn't sure there was a clock in this room. She'd never slept up here before.

Alicia whimpered in her sleep. Bea kissed the child's forehead, and felt her relax. Poor little mite. Bernice jerked, and Bea kissed her forehead, too. If guardian angels really existed, then there would be three of them in the room. One pink, one peach and one blue. No, that wasn't right. One was blue and green . . . another was pink and . . . peach? But all had some white . . .

Sunday morning

Bea came awake, feeling that something was amiss . . . and smelled bacon. The 'something amiss' was that neither Bernice nor Alicia was in bed with her, but the bacon still smelled delicious.

The two girls came in, one holding Teddy and the other holding a mug of tea with a saucer on top. They were both properly dressed in T-shirts and jeans, their hair was brushed out and braided and, if they looked a little heavy-eyed, they also had some colour in their cheeks.

'Time to get up!'

'Breakfast in ten minutes.'

'He's doing it in relays. We've had ours.'

'He says to ask you if you want one egg or two? He's doing sausages and tomatoes and mushrooms and hash browns as well.'

Bernice said, 'I asked him if he knew how to make hash browns because you have to cook the potatoes first, don't you? And he said you can buy them frozen.'

'He' presumably was William. Bea sipped tea and told herself she'd wake up soon.

Alicia said, 'Mel braided our hair for us. She's wearing glasses today, and so is Uncle Steve. They're having their breakfast now. I asked if they were an item, and she said I had to ask him that, so I did, and he said they were if she thought they were, and I thought they'd go on like that for ever—'

Bernice interrupted, 'And he asked her if he should grow a beard because he hasn't got any shaving things with him.'

'Grandpa has shaved!'

'Yes, but he was up ages ago and has even been out to the shops.'

It was a Sunday but nowadays there were shops open twenty-four hours a day, even on Sundays. Bea wasn't sure this was altogether a good thing, while realizing it could be useful in an emergency.

She tuned out the girls' chatter and forced herself to get out of bed. She noted she was still wearing her dressing gown over her nightie, and caught sight of herself in the mirror . . .

which led to her deciding that there was no way she was going
to expose herself to the sight of any of her guests until she'd
had a shower, washed her hair, and made up her face. Oh, and
dressed in something which didn't remind her of the fire
and its aftermath.

Breakfast in ten minutes? No way. More like half an hour.
She set off down the stairs, closely followed by the girls.

Her own bedroom. How grateful she was to have such a
beautiful room. And, praise be!, it was in perfect order, the
bed made and all sign of an overnight masculine presence
removed. The only remembrance of the recent invasion was
a neat pile of children's clothes in one corner. She showered
and came out to find the two girls sitting on the edge of her
bed, waiting for her.

'We want to watch you put on your makeup,' said Alicia.

'We think you do it rather well. You don't overdo it as
some old people do,' said Bernice.

'Thank you,' said Bea, accepting the compliment in the
spirit in which it was intended. She dressed in her favourite
pale green silk shirt and grey skirt. Grey suede boots. Perhaps
a cashmere sweater over all? Yes. She took her time over her
makeup.

The two girls came to stand one on either side of her,
breathing on her, watching every move.

'Have you tried Botox?' That was Bernice.

Bea said, 'Can't be bothered. If the object is to appeal to
men, then I'll give you a piece of advice. The way to a man's
heart is through his stomach. He can be fooled for a while by
a pretty face but, when his stomach growls, if he's any sense
he heads for the kitchen. And if he hasn't any sense then he's
not worth hanging on to.'

'Marriage is supposed to be for ever.' This from Alicia, who
had seen marriages fail.

'It is supposed to be.' Bea sighed. 'Girls, not everyone keeps
their marriage vows. When you grow up, choose wisely.
Choose someone who wants the same things out of life as you
do.' She picked out some fake pearl earrings to wear until she
remembered Faye and her pearls. She decided to wear her
diamond drops instead. She stood up and inspected her front

and back view in a long mirror. 'Before you leave your bedroom, check yourself out front and back, and then forget what you're wearing.'

Bernice said, 'You were married to the man in the picture downstairs? He looks nice.'

Alicia said, 'Can we be bridesmaids next time?'

'What?!' *Does she mean William – or Leon?* Actually, I don't really fancy either. Not for keeps. 'Sorry. I'm not planning on marrying again.'

William had prepared a highly satisfactory full English breakfast for her, which he decreed she was to eat, not in the kitchen, but in solitary state at the table in the sitting room. Accompanied by the Sunday papers. What luxury!

She hadn't realized how hungry she was, and had completely forgotten what a treat it was to be cooked for. William was more than paying for his overnight stay.

By the time she'd mopped up the last piece of toast, the scent of freshly ground coffee drifted across her nostrils and she almost swooned with pleasure, feeling that she might be able to cope with life again soon.

The only problem was the elephant in the room. The fire.

The children had made themselves a nest on one of the settees while Bea ate. Bernice set to work brushing Teddy's fur with what looked very much like one of Bea's shoe brushes; not one she used for polishing, but the one for buffing up her suede boots. Had the child been into every cupboard in the house? Alicia sat beside her, wearing an expression of wide-eyed innocence, which was possibly misleading . . . and which caused Bea to wonder what the girls had been up to . . . or were planning to do?

Bernice said, 'Can we have the telly on?'

'Must you?' said Bea. Then nodded permission, thinking that at least if they were watching television, they wouldn't be getting up to any mischief. She piled her breakfast things on a tray and took them out to the kitchen, where everyone else had congregated.

William took the tray from her, and piled the dirty dishes into the dishwasher, assisted by Mel. And yes, both Mel and Steve were wearing glasses today. Steve looked older and almost middle-aged in his horn-rims; Mel looked dainty but business-like – an intriguing combination – in her rimless ones.

Steve's eyes still looked slightly swollen. He fingered his phone. 'I rang Gideon and told him about Mrs Frost. He didn't know. He wants to meet at the house soonest. There's so much needs to be done that I . . . I said I'd catch up with my voice-mail, then get back to him. The fire investigator has left an urgent message, wanting to know if we'd hired an electrician to do something in the house recently, which we had. She wants me to ring her back with his number, which I don't have on me. Does she really think the fire was caused by an electrical fault? And if so, are we covered by insurance?'

Bea said, 'Could an electrical fault have caused the lights to fail as well?'

'Lights? I'm missing something.'

William poured coffee for them all. 'Ah, Steve; you left before Act II started. I think we'd better bring one another up to date. Act I was the scene in the dining room, when the curtain caught fire, causing Josh and Daphne to need hospital attention. You think that was an electrical fault? Could be. But the fire investigator talked to us about fireworks. Wanted to know if the children had been playing with them.'

William was looking gaunt today, with two deep lines between his eyes above his nose. He hadn't had a good night's sleep, had he? In spite of being in Bea's bed.

Bea's mind slid away from the thought of William in her bed. She had more than enough on her plate without thinking of . . . well, of that!

Steve looked puzzled. 'Fireworks? There were fireworks outside, but surely the curtain catching fire was due to an electrical fault? As I said, I haven't got the electrician's number on me. I'll have to go back to the house and rummage around in Dad's office to see if I can find it.'

Bea said, 'It's not an electrician you've employed before?'

'The people we usually employed had moved or retired. I think it was Daphne who said someone had recommended these people, and indeed they did a good job in record time – or so we thought.'

'What job?' said Bea.

'Replacing the wiring on the kitchen circuit. One of the lights in the kitchen had been on the blink for a while. The electrician did say the lighting in the rest of the house ought all to be redone because it hasn't been touched for maybe forty years. My father didn't want that because of the upheaval it would cause. Redecoration, and so on. He said just to do the kitchen circuit straight away and he'd think about doing the rest later.'

'You organized it?'

'No, Mrs Frost did.'

'You think the downstairs lighting circuit was dicey, and that some fault in that caused the fire in the dining room? You put out the fire downstairs with the extinguisher, so what caused the fire upstairs?'

'What fire?'

He really didn't know? Oh.

Bea said, 'Steve, things happened after you left. Things you need to know. After you dealt with the fire in the dining room, your priority was to get Daphne and your father to hospital straight away. Panic stations. Quite right, too. The waiting staff also left. Only Faye stayed to search for her broken string of pearls, right?'

'Right. She wanted Gideon to stay behind and help her, but he wanted to go with Dad. He said she could let herself out when she'd finished. I gather she got out all right.'

'Sort of. While you were looking after your father and sister, William and I went upstairs to check on the girls. When we got to the top floor, we found Mrs Frost had broken her leg and was lying on the floor—'

'Poor woman,' said Steve. 'I really have to get on to—'

'Just a minute. A second curtain was on fire on the landing behind her. We got her started on her way down the stairs when the lights went out and the corridor leading to the children's room filled with smoke. We took some towels soaked with water from the bathroom and got to the children's room, which was where the smoke was coming from. We got the girls out, staggered back to the landing and down the stairs, completely missing Mrs Frost, who had collapsed and fallen to one side . . . to find Faye still in the dining room, searching for her pearls by the light of her phone.'

Steve gaped. 'There was another fire on the landing, apart from the one in the dining room? And the children's room was on fire by the time you got there? But . . .'

There was a stir in the doorway and the children came in. 'I'm bored,' said Bernice. 'There's nothing on the telly.' She was tossing Teddy around from one side to the other. Poor Teddy.

'Alicia,' said William, tell your uncle Steve what happened to you and Bernice after you were sent up to your room?'

Alicia went dumb on them, eyes downcast. 'Dunno. Can we go out to play?'

'No,' said Bea and William together.

Bernice shrugged. 'Keep your hair on. Mrs Frost said she'd fetch us a hot drink and a tray to put the fireworks on from downstairs and not to open the box till she'd got back—'

Steve said, 'Of course! I'd forgotten you'd been given—'

'And we didn't,' said Bernice. 'The box exploded and we tried to phone for help but they didn't believe us. Then it all went dark and chokey and we sort of went to sleep until they came and got us out.'

Steve was trying to put it all together. 'The house went dark? The electrics went out when you were upstairs . . . after we'd got Dad and Daphne away? It must have been an electrical fault!'

'Possibly, for the lights,' said Bea. 'Although it's hard to see how one electrical fault in the dining room could set off another at the top of the house, never mind exploding a box of fireworks in the children's room.'

Steve gaped at her. 'You really think the fires were set deliberately?'

The answer was 'yes', but he didn't want to believe it.

Bernice said, 'Can I have some Coca-Cola?'

'May I?' corrected Bea. 'No, I don't have any. You may have milk or orange juice. Choose.'

They chose orange juice. William got a bottle out of the fridge, and poured it into two glasses, one for each child. Giving it to them, he said, 'I have to tell you something sad.

You remember Mrs Frost broke her leg? Well, it didn't mend, but sent a clot up to her heart, and her heart couldn't cope. I'm sorry to say, she didn't make it. I know you liked her, Lissy. Such a shame.'

Bernice shrugged. She had no strong feelings about Mrs Frost, but Alicia's face crumpled in on itself. William scooped her up in his arms and gave her a cuddle. 'There, there. She was good to you, poppet, wasn't she? Now we want to contact her family but don't know where they might live. I wonder if she ever talked to you about them?'

A sniffle. 'Mm. She said her husband was "a scumbag who took off to Spain" and she didn't ever want to see him again. She told me about him after Mummy said we weren't going to live with Alaric any more.'

'I see. That's really helpful. Did Mrs Frost say she got divorced, too?'

'Yes. All she's got left is a son in Dublin. She said he worked in a hospital and I said was he a doctor, but she said No, he was a nurse, which was a bit surprising because I thought only girls could be nurses. But she doesn't like his girlfriend that he lives with because she drinks too much.'

Steve muttered, '"Out of the mouths of babes and sucklings." With that information, we should be able to trace him.'

Bernice stood on tiptoe to whisper that Teddy needed to go to the toilet. Bea nodded and escorted her upstairs . . . and waited outside, thinking the two little mites were having to go through a lot, and Bea wasn't at all sure what could be done about it.

She heard her landline ring and someone answer it. And then she heard William on his phone . . . and Steve on his. They all sounded as if they were at the end of their tether. Ends of their tethers?

Something had to be done. But what? Bea sent up an arrow prayer for help.

When Bernice emerged, looking paler than ever, Bea said, 'Do you know how to get the attention of a room full of people? No? I'll show you, shall I? Take a hold of my skirt so I don't lose you, right?'

The child needed something to hang on to apart from Teddy.

Steve was striding back and forth in the sitting room. 'Yes, but . . . Can't you, just for once . . .?'

William was at the back door, looking down over the garden. 'No, I really think . . .!' with Alicia clinging to his neck.

Mel was on the landline, looking flustered. 'No, but . . . in a minute! I'll call her . . .!'

Bea picked up an empty glass and tapped it with a spoon. Instant silence.

Bea said, 'This is important. Which of you is on the phone to the fire investigator? William? Let me speak to her, please. The rest of you, please put your phones down, turn them off and mute the sound.'

'What!' They all looked stunned.

'Why?' William handed his phone over to Bea and the others slowly obeyed her.

Silence.

Bea spoke into the phone. 'Is that Manisa? Mrs Abbot speaking. I know it's Sunday but can you get over here, soonest? And I mean immediately? Emergency.'

TWELVE

Sunday morning

'Please!' Bea made it an order. 'Whoever rings you, don't answer. Let them leave a message on voicemail and we'll pick it up later. Trust me. I have a very good reason for making this request, which I'll explain when Manisa gets here. In the meantime, let's have some coffee and attempt to relax.'

It was William who made the coffee. Bea reflected that some men had their uses and someone who could make good coffee without a fuss was high up on her approval scale. Imagine Leon being asked to make coffee! Well, no; you wouldn't ask him, would you?

They gathered in the big living room. The girls sat close together on one of the settees, with Teddy on Bernice's lap. Steve sat nearby, fingering his phone, but not venturing to turn it on. Eventually he muttered an excuse, fetched Bea's scratch pad from the kitchen and started making a list of things he had to do. Mel sat near him, not touching but near enough that he could reach out to touch her if he wished to do so.

Bea made small talk with the children. Which Disney film did they like best? What did they want to see first when they went to Disneyland? What food did they like best? Was it McDonald's? Did they like cheese? Could they imagine a world without cheese?

From being two scared little rabbits, they gradually relaxed. Bea suggested they might like to take Teddy into the garden to see if they could find the cat. She said she was worried about him because he hadn't turned up for his breakfast.

Privately, Bea knew he'd taken refuge in the stationery cupboard downstairs for the night and would most likely have been fed by William, who'd been first up that morning . . .

and yes, there was William opening his mouth to tell her that. She silenced him with a frown. It was important to get the girls out of the room before Manisa came, and they couldn't come to harm in the garden, could they?

Mel found the girls their jackets, and they clattered off through French windows at the back of the living room and down the iron staircase into the garden . . . where Winston was probably stalking birds and terrorizing the neighbourhood cats.

William said, 'I'll keep an eye on them,' and stationed himself by the windows.

Steve lifted his phone to make a call, and Bea said, 'Hold on, will you, Steve? I think that's Manisa at the door now.'

It was indeed Manisa, who seemed not best pleased to have been called out. She said, 'You said it was an emergency? Are the children all right? You have some new information for me?'

'They're playing outside. You've met Steve, haven't you? William Morton you know. And this is Mel, who has very kindly agreed to help look after the children. Yes, we have something new for you. The hospital rang early this morning to say that Mrs Frost, the family's housekeeper, has died as a consequence of injuries she received on the night of the fire. You already know that Josh, our host, has died? That makes the case a double manslaughter. Do you have to turn it over to the police now?'

Manisa took a moment to absorb this. Then she nodded and said, 'Oh. I see.' She took a seat. 'Yes, that does put a different complexion on the matter. We automatically send a report to the police when fireworks and children are involved. The police would normally leave the first stages of the investigation to us, but in the case of manslaughter . . . are you sure?'

'Yes. Steve will give you the details in a minute of which hospitals and how they died. I don't think Mrs Frost's death was intended, any more than it was intended that Josh, Steve's father, should have a heart attack. We know that you haven't as yet been able to get up to the top of the house to see where the fire started in the children's room, but we have been able to work out a timeline and would like to share it with you.'

Once again Bea went through the evening's events, this time including the information provided by Steve.

Steve said, 'I admit we panicked, what with my father having a heart attack and Daphne spurting blood everywhere. We took the nearest cars and tore off. Leon had arrived last, so it was easiest to use his car first. Gideon got my father into that and I took Daphne in mine. Alaric followed on behind me with Ninette.'

'And your sister's boyfriend?'

'Giorgio? He arrived at the hospital soon after we did, but didn't stay long. He's allergic to the sight of blood. He says. He'd taken Daphne's car. Probably still got it.' He hit his forehead. 'Another thing I'll have to sort. Alaric and Ninette didn't stay long, either, but you could hardly expect that they would.'

Manisa lifted a finger to attract attention. 'What about your father's car? And I assume your brother Gideon has one, too? Why didn't you use those?'

'Dad's car must still be in the garage. He bought the house partly because it has a double garage at the side. He's very careful – *was* very careful – about his car being garaged all the time. As a matter of fact, he's not used it all that much lately. His eyesight, you know? He ran a tab with a man we know who hires himself out as a chauffeur. As for Gideon, when he arrived with Faye, he didn't want to get boxed into the drive in case he needed to make a swift exit, so he left his car out in the road, some way down. He couldn't find a space nearer. We didn't bother to use his that night. I assume he's moved it by now.'

'Gideon: that's a strange name,' said Manisa.

An attempt at a smile from Steve. 'It's biblical. Some sort of guerrilla fighter. Our mother thought it romantic. He was teased at school, nicknamed "Giddy Gideon", but he's survived. He's a great survivor. He's very charming, you know. Has all the women hanging around him.'

'Which hospital did you go to?'

'Different ones. I knew Charing Cross had a good A & E so I took Daphne there, while Leon took Dad and Gideon to West Middlesex. We only discovered they were in different hospitals when we linked up by phone after we got there. Daphne was hysterical . . . Oh, God! Daphne!' He started to his feet and began to pace. 'She won't have heard about Mrs Frost yet, nor about our father. I keep forgetting! I ought to be at the hospital now, this very minute.'

Bea was soothing. 'Daphne can wait. Let's try to work out what went wrong on Friday night. Leon took Josh and Gideon in his car, and you took Daphne in yours, right?'

With an effort Steve concentrated. 'Yes. When we got to the hospitals, we kept going outside to call one another, find out where everyone was. Leon was great, helped to keep us all calm.'

'How does Leon fit into your family?'

'Well, he's known my father slightly for years, they've sat on the boards of some different companies together, and then his great-niece, Bernice, made friends with Alicia, so they saw more of one another. He certainly came up trumps that night. Daphne kept asking for Dad but of course he couldn't come so we told her he was feeling unwell and would be along later. Then she heard Leon was with Dad and asked if he could come and deal with the doctors for her instead of me. She's my elder sister, you see, and elder sisters don't think much of younger brothers, do they?'

Bea said, 'That's when Leon rang to see if I could go over to look after Daphne, but by that time we'd got the two children on our hands and couldn't help.'

Steve nodded. 'We had no idea about the fire till Uncle Bill called me from our neighbour's house to tell me and to say that the girls were safe.' He passed his hand over his eyes. 'What a shock. I'd forgotten about the girls completely. I rang Gideon and told him what had happened, and then I hared back to the house . . . and found the fire engines there, and Mrs Frost being put into an ambulance. I didn't know which way to turn. Uncle Bill arranged for Mrs Abbot to take the girls in, for which I was very grateful, and then I went back to the hospital to hear the bad news about Dad.'

Manisa said, 'Which hospital did they take Mrs Frost to?'

Steve clapped a hand to his head. 'I do know, don't I? I'm losing my mind! How can I not know? Someone has to contact her family, though I haven't a clue who.' He shot to his feet. 'Look, I really do need to get into Dad's office back at home. You need the name of the electrician and I need Mrs Frost's details. The ground floor's all right and most of the first floor. It's only the top floor we can't get to. There's a builder coming to put a tarpaulin over the roof. I really ought to be there.'

Mel put a hand on his arm. 'Hush, now. Sit down. There's no hurry for poor Mrs Frost, now is there?'

He subsided, reluctantly. 'What a dreadful business this is!'

Manisa collected their attention. 'I have Lord Morton's and Mrs Abbot's statements about getting the girls out. But . . .' Manisa looked at her notes. 'There was someone else left behind, wasn't there? A Faye Starman? She says she stayed behind to look for her pearls and was then assaulted by Mrs Abbot.'

'What nonsense!' said Bea. 'Do you know, she even sent a police officer to see me about it? I saved that brat's life by dragging her out of a burning house, and she wants to sue me for assault and lost wages and the Crown Jewels!'

Manisa half smiled. 'A local policeman, I assume?'

Bea relaxed into a smile, too. 'I suppose she flapped her eyelashes at him, and got him to look into it for her . . . possibly when he got off duty? He was *very* keen that I should pay her off. Perhaps she's promised him a nice tip.'

Manisa almost laughed. 'No win, no fee? He must have been off duty.'

'I take it you haven't yet reported the fire to the police?'

'Not yet. I have to get up to the top of the house to investigate what happened there before I can complete my report.' She turned back to Steve. 'You say the waitresses left at the same time. I'd like to talk to them, too.'

Steve nodded. 'They left when we did. Didn't want to stick around in a house of doom.' He made a gesture of frustration. 'I didn't book them. Daphne did. Or maybe Mrs Frost? When I can get into Dad's office, I'll find out which agency was used and let you know.'

Manisa said, 'Back to the cars. We'll have to check that your father's car is still all right. It should be. The garage wasn't touched by the fire. Lord Morton, what about you? Didn't you have a car there?'

'I'd come up by train. I don't bring a car into London nowadays. Nowhere to park. I arrived by taxi, with a tote bag. I'd been invited to stay overnight. So I didn't have a car with me.'

'And Faye?'

Steve said, 'She arrived with Gideon in his car. I assume she called a taxi when she wanted to go home.'

'And Daphne?'

'She's been living back at home for a while. She let Giorgio use her car. He certainly turned up at the hospital independently, so yes, he must be using her car at the moment.'

Manisa looked over her notes. 'Back to the events of the night. Mrs Abbot and Lord Morton say that the curtain on the top landing was set alight shortly after the one downstairs?'

Bea said, 'The girls had been sent up to bed. About five minutes later, perhaps, the curtain behind me went up in flames. Josh had a heart attack. Daphne became hysterical and cut herself on a broken glass. Leon and Faye attended to her. Steve found a fire extinguisher which he used on the curtain. That was when I heard what I thought was a second explosion inside the house somewhere. Not close. Muffled. Lord Morton heard it, too.'

William abandoned his position by the window to join the circle around Manisa. 'We thought the children might have been frightened by the noise, and went upstairs to see.'

'While we, downstairs,' said Steve, 'had to deal with two medical emergencies. We all left except for Faye, who is Gideon's current girlfriend. She refused to come with us because she'd broken her pearls and wanted to retrieve them.'

Bea said, 'By the time we got to the top of the house, we found Mrs Frost on the floor of the landing, a second burning curtain and smoke rolling down the corridor towards us. As we started Mrs Frost on her way down, all the lights in the house went out. The children say the box of tricks in their bedroom burst into flames without warning, and we assume that's what set furnishings on fire which produced the choking smoke.'

Manisa thought about it. 'If I've understood you correctly, you think timers were used to start three sets of fires?'

Bea nodded. 'And the lights going off.'

Manisa frowned. 'It was a very tight schedule. You are suggesting that they all went off within ten or fifteen minutes of one another?'

'Yes.'

'But you don't think the object was to hospitalize any of the guests, or even to empty the house?'

'The fires setting the curtains alight were not serious arson attacks. Neither was difficult to deal with. Mrs Frost's broken leg was an accident, likewise not intended.'

Manisa narrowed her eyes at them. 'Then you assume that the object of the exercise was . . . what? To frighten the children, who might well have had Mrs Frost still in the room with them, and therefore wouldn't have been seriously harmed?'

'Not exactly, no. On Friday night the children stayed up later than usual. It was way past their usual bedtime when they were sent up to bed. I think that the box of tricks was set to explode at a time when they would normally have been tucked up in bed and asleep. In those circumstances, they'd have died in their beds from the effects of the smoke.'

An indrawn breath from those who hadn't worked it out already. A nod from William.

'A prank that went wrong?' said Manisa, in her gentle, unstressed voice.

'I don't think so. Arson is one thing. A match carelessly dropped. A pile of inflammable material set on fire. The glory of a blazing bonfire. These events are meant to be witnessed by the arsonist, who gets his kick from seeing them happen. A man who uses timers to set fires is something else. He doesn't want to be there when the fire starts. He can be a hundred miles away, or in the next street. He is a deeply disturbed man. I think the object of this exercise was to provide a distraction to the adults by way of not one but two curtains being set on fire and the lights going out, to be followed by the deaths of the two children.'

'Why?' said Manisa.

'Money,' said William. 'They are two valuable little properties.'

'Or,' said Bea, 'they were surplus to requirements in their families.'

Steve said, 'Ouch!'

Manisa looked at each one of them in turn. 'If that is so, which child do you think was the intended victim?'

'Alicia,' said William.

'Alicia,' said Bea.

'Oh my God. My niece?' said Steve.

'Why?' asked Manisa.

'Because,' said Bea, 'Bernice's removal doesn't benefit anyone. Her heirs are in no need of money, and her family – although dysfunctional in some ways – really does care about her.'

'And Alicia?' said Manisa.

'She's a sweet little thing,' said Steve. 'I must confess, I hardly know her. She's away at boarding school most of the time and in the holidays she's stayed with her parents in the country or with friends. Daphne bought a flat in Town when she split with Alaric, but it's not habitable at the moment, so she moved back into the family home with Alicia recently, as a temporary measure. Mrs Frost made over the old nursery for Alicia, and put two beds in there for when she had her friend to stay in the holidays.'

'Nice big rooms?'

He nodded, smiling, remembering. 'Yes, it's pleasant up there; you can look down on the treetops outside. Mrs Frost had her rooms up there, too. Her own bedroom, en suite, and a sitting room. Alicia had the nursery at the end, which was the biggest; the one Gideon and I slept in as kids.'

'She was tucked away from the rest of the family?'

'It's true I didn't see much of her. I'm out early in the morning, don't get back till late. I hardly see Daphne, even. She's out every night. Alicia is so quiet when she's around that I hardly know she's there.'

'You live at home, too?'

'I have my own flat, but when Dad became unwell some time ago, I rented it out. Those heart attacks frightened him and he liked to feel someone was at hand in the night, if . . . so I got in the habit of sleeping in the next room to him and leaving my door open. Sometimes in the night I'd get him a drink and we'd sit and chat for a while. I'm going to miss him something chronic.'

'Daphne didn't share the nursing?'

That amused him. 'No, well, Daphne isn't the sort who . . . I mean, she comes back so late after an evening out and takes a pill, so . . . No, she wouldn't hear him even if . . .'

'What about her new boyfriend?'

A shrug. 'Dad drew the line about his moving in. They plan to move into Daphne's flat together when it's ready.'

'So you hardly knew your niece?'

'I suppose not. Look, Daphne did her best but . . .' A deep breath. 'No, you're right. I've been remiss. The child was no trouble, so I'm sorry to say I didn't concern myself to get to know her.'

William added, 'Daphne was not a good mother. My son was not a good father. When Alaric and Daphne married, he adopted Alicia, and the next thing I knew, they'd sent her off to boarding school. Out of their way. I tried to keep in contact with Alicia but . . . I ought to have tried harder. She didn't thrive at boarding school till Bernice arrived and made friends with her. Since then Alaric and Daphne have separated and both have taken up with new partners. Neither Giorgio nor Ninette are interested in making a home for Alicia. So, yes, I suppose you could say she is surplus to requirements.'

A horrid silence.

Steve gaped. 'Are you accusing Alaric of setting the house on fire to kill Alicia? That's ridiculous! What would he get out of it?'

William was stubborn. 'That old house of Alaric's eats money, and his firm is not doing well in the City. Plus Ninette is an expensive little piece. He took Alicia on to please Daphne, and in marrying her you must remember that he was marrying money, which he needed to maintain his lifestyle. Alaric and Daphne both signed pre-nups, so his ancestral home and estate is not affected by the breakup, but he's lost Daphne's income now, so he must be feeling the pinch.'

'But Alicia's death wouldn't improve Alaric's finances.'

'Yes, it would. Her boarding school fees are horrendous, and the cost of her further education will still have to be paid by him because, by law, he's her father and therefore responsible for her upkeep.'

'Come off it,' said Steve. 'When Daphne divorces Alaric, there'll be a different arrangement and he will cease to be responsible for the child.'

'There you're wrong,' said William. 'An adopted father has, to all intents and purposes, exactly the same responsibilities as a birth parent. He will still be liable. I know, because Josh and I both looked into the matter.'

In the ensuing silence, Manisa coughed. 'Anyone else want Alicia gone? What about Daphne herself?'

That roused Steve. 'No way. Ridiculous! I can't believe that you could even think . . .! I admit she isn't exactly a hands-on smothering mother type, but she does love her daughter in her own way. How can I explain her to you? She lives in the present, doesn't think about tomorrow. She's so pretty, everyone wants to please her; she's always had men clustering around her, and you can understand why. She lights up the room when she arrives.'

William said, 'I don't know how much longer that will last. Too much Botox, too many cosmetic procedures. And, she conveniently forgets if she's promised to take Alicia out and something more interesting turns up.'

Steve was defensive. 'Daphne's very popular. I admit she isn't good with money. Every now and then she comes to me to sort out her finances. It is a bit of a headache, keeping track of what she spends, but she inherited our mother's portfolio of shares so it's just a question of making sure she doesn't do something wildly inappropriate—'

William interrupted, 'Such as buying that studio flat for Giorgio and renting a suite in the south of France for the season so that she could invite all her friends to party with her?'

Steve said, 'She could afford it, so why not? I admit the renovations at the flat in Chelsea are going to cost a bomb and dividends have been dropping, but she wasn't running short of caviar and champagne.'

'Ah, but,' said William, 'could she afford the gigolo *plus* caviar *plus* champagne? I think not. That's why she was on at Sir Leon during dinner to invest in the gigolo.'

Steve said, 'I did warn her that Giorgio might prove an expensive proposition, but she says she has lots of wealthy friends who will be only too pleased to invest in him. I really don't think that would have been a problem in the long run. Dad said that as long as she was happy . . . I doubt if Giorgio would have lasted, but I don't think there's any harm in him. What you see is what you get. And, has he the brains to think up a plot to kill Alicia? No. He's a pretty boy. A toy boy.'

Manisa consulted her notebook. 'What about Gideon?'

Everyone relaxed and smiled except Bea, who frowned. She hadn't taken to that personable young man.

Steve smiled. 'Oh, Gideon! He's all right. Runs the estate agency side of the business. My father thought the world of him, encouraged him to branch out for himself. Gideon has his own flat not far away, and has just got a new car. Girlfriends galore. He hasn't any need to get rid of Alicia. That's ridiculous.'

Manisa looked a question at Bea, who said, 'It's true I don't like him much. I was annoyed that he didn't seem to consider I was worth talking to at dinner. Yes, he's a good-looking lad and knows it. Yes, he was ignoring Alicia and me in order to text his Faye across the table. I admit I thought it impolite. It's a generation thing, I suppose. He has charm and good looks and, to give him credit, he did leap to Josh's side at the first sign that he was in distress.'

'Daddy's favourite,' said Steve, smiling. And if the smile was a trifle rueful, well . . . that was understandable, too, wasn't it?

Bea ran her fingers back through her hair. 'You'll excuse me but I have a feeling, probably unjustified . . . don't you think the girls have been rather quiet lately?'

William shot back to the windows and, November chill or no, threw them wide open. 'Girls?' He disappeared down the outside staircase, closely followed by Mel.

Bea dead-heated to the window with Steve.

Uh oh! What have they got up to? I'm too old to look after such lively children! And Mel has her mind set on other things now.

Bernice was sitting astride the tall boundary wall. Halfway up, Alicia was clinging to the wall, unable either to climb further up, or to let herself down again.

William strode across the flowerbed to lift Alicia off the wall, rather as one detaches a limpet from a rock at the seaside. He ordered, 'Bernice, come off there at once!'

Bernice whined, 'We weren't doing any harm. We saw Winston walk along the wall and drop down into the next garden and we thought it would be fun to see where he went. You needn't have worried about Lissy. She'd have been perfectly all right if you'd let her alone.' She stood up, balancing herself on top of the wall . . . which was enough to give the grown-ups a heart attack.

Mel clapped her hands. 'Bravo! And now you've done showing off, you can climb down and join the party.'

'Poof!' Bernice crossed her arms, teetered, and decided that yes, she might as well descend to earth. She measured the distance to the ground, and hesitated. It was, perhaps, a little further than she'd expected.

Steve held up his arms. 'Jump, and I'll catch you.'

Bernice closed her eyes – they saw her do that quite distinctly – and jumped. Steve caught her, set her on her feet and held on to her till she was steady again.

Mel said, 'Well done, Steve. I'm sorry. My fault. I should never have taken my eyes off them. One of my brothers is just the same. Can't see a wall or a tree without wanting to climb it.'

Bernice picked up Teddy, whom she'd abandoned at the foot of the wall, and led the way back up the stairs, sturdily stomping up them as if she'd never had a moment's failure of nerve. But she did hesitate when she saw Manisa.

'Come along in,' said Manisa, who had also been drawn to the windows to see what was going on. 'There's a couple more questions I'd like to ask you two girls.'

Mel stripped off their jackets and the party resettled them-selves, with the two girls sitting close to one another on one of the settees with Teddy between them, and William hovering behind.

'Now,' said Manisa. 'Just for my own information, did either of you girls ever access any sites selling fireworks on the Internet, either at school or at home?'

'Yes,' said Alicia, in a tiny voice. 'At school. We wanted Grandpa Josh to set some off in his back garden, and we wanted to see what we could get which didn't have bangs. I don't like bangs, and nor does Bernice, much. But he said No, so we didn't do anything more about it.'

'You didn't order any?'

'Of course not. We're not allowed to order anything on the Internet on the school computers.'

Bernice said, 'We didn't need to, anyway. The Head said we were going to go to a big fireworks display, the whole school, on the common land, on the proper date. So we didn't bother.'

'Someone gave you a box of indoor fireworks. Who was it?'

They shook their heads. Bernice said, 'We don't know.'

'We carried them up to our room to open later.' Alicia's eyes welled with tears. 'All my things have gone now. And the presents we'd been given. I had ever such a pretty little watch, and some ballet shoes and a leotard and—'

Steve said, 'We'll replace them. Promise.'

'If I know you two fashionable madams,' said Bea, 'you'll have wanted some of the things in different colours, so next time round you can choose exactly what you want.'

Alicia brightened up at that.

Bernice said, 'I don't need things.' Which was possibly true, except that she definitely needed Teddy at the moment. And then, 'Do you think I could ring Mummy now? If she isn't too busy today and baby bro isn't too spotty, maybe I could go over there and help her look after him?'

Which showed she did need people still, even if she didn't need things.

'Indeed,' said Bea. 'We'll ring her in a minute and see how she's getting on. But don't let's forget your Aunt Sybil will be arriving at Heathrow soon, breathing fire and slaughter and planning to demolish your boarding school. Shall we get a car to go and meet her?'

Reminded of everyday life, Steve looked at his watch. 'Look at the time! I was due at the hospital hours ago to take Daphne her bits and pieces. I took two bags of stuff, which I'd sorted out from home, one for her and one for Uncle Bill. I took them down to the car, which is still parked in the driveway at home. And then what happened?'

He put his hand to his head. 'That's right. I got into the car and put the key in the ignition and nearly passed out, I was so tired. I remember thinking I wasn't safe to drive. I got out my phone and asked for a taxi. I took what I thought was Uncle Bill's bag out of the car to bring here . . . only, it was Daphne's – and they're not really alike, are they? Well, both are black, but . . . I must have left his in my car and it's still there. I'll have to collect it soonest. Daphne will be furious. I must get her stuff to her, and then, if she's well enough, I'll take her down to the spa hotel for a few days, unless . . . I wonder if the boyfriend would take her?'

Mel said, 'Didn't you say you'd asked him to do so, and he'd made some excuse?'

Steve was distracted, fingering his phone. 'Yes, yes. You're right. Daphne first. Then I must speak to the funeral people and start ringing round Dad's old friends and . . . our office manager at work! He mustn't hear it from . . . and Mrs Frost, poor Mrs Frost, I'll have to trace her son, if . . .'

Bea said, 'Steve! Don't turn your phone back on. Everyone, please! Listen to me for a moment.' She turned to Mel. 'I think the children could do with a wash and brush-up after their little adventure in the garden. And perhaps a hot drink and a biscuit?'

'The biscuit tin's empty,' said Bernice. 'And you said I could speak to Mummy.'

'Wait till I can be with you,' said Bea, 'so that we can work out when you can see her.'

'I can ring her myself,' said Bernice. She stalked off to the kitchen, getting out her own phone as she went.

'Wait for me!' cried Alicia, and went off after her.

Mel treated Steve to a look of apology and followed them.

Manisa was smiling, wryly. 'Well, we know who's the dominant partner there.'

'Bernice,' said Bea, with a sigh. 'From a long line of modern buccaneers. She plays chess like a grand master and has only to see a line of figures once to remember it. The blood of the Holland family runs in her veins and my bet is she'll end up as managing director of some multibillion-pound international corporation.'

William laughed. 'So long as she keeps looking after Alicia.'

'Yes,' said Bea. 'That's the point. Are we all agreed that the children are at risk? William? Steve?'

They nodded, if with some reluctance.

Manisa said, 'I'm prepared to consider it as a possible theory, yes.'

Bea said, 'On Friday night a well-prepared attempt was made to kill one or both of them. We don't know who, or even why. But we know that it happened, and that it caused two other deaths and burnt out a family house on the way. I don't think we should assume the killer will stop now. Why should he . . . or, indeed, she? So the question is: what precautions can we take to make sure the girls survive? William, you and Steve were on your phones this morning, answering voice-mail messages, taking new calls. Did anyone at any time suggest separating Alicia from Bernice?'

William said, 'No, but . . .' He looked at Bea. 'I should have told you. Sir Leon rang, wanting to speak to you. He suggests taking you and the children out to Richmond Park for the day. But that's not the sort of thing you meant, was it?'

Bea could imagine how the day would go. Leon would get his chauffeur to drive them there and expect her to look after the children. He would be happy to pay the bill for lunch. He would feel pleased with himself for having arranged the outing. 'Did he say when Sybil is due? Someone must meet her at Heathrow. And, has he sorted out the school situation?'

William shook his head. 'Sorry. There's so much been happening. We haven't had time to stop and think.'

In a few words, Bea put Manisa into the picture about the school, saying, 'I have no right to interfere with the arrangements the families make for the children, but . . .'

Steve produced a wry smile. 'But that's what you're going to do.' He was getting to know her, wasn't he?

Manisa stood up, preparing to go. 'Mrs Abbot has the right idea. I haven't been able to get to the top of the house yet, but I can tell you that, from my examination of the curtain which was set on fire in the dining room, a timer was involved.'

Steve said, 'You mean . . . like a watch?'

'A clock. Yes. Digital. Set to trigger a firework. The mechanism was not particularly sophisticated, but it would be beyond the capacity of those two children.'

'You mean that someone did set out to kill them?'

'That's not proven, yet. Mrs Abbot, Lord Morton; you say the lights went out while you were climbing the stairs to the top floor? I need to take a closer look at the fuse box in the kitchen to see if we can account for that failure, and I need to speak to the electricians recently employed by the family. Until we can get to the top of the house and look at the children's room, I'd prefer not to say any more, but I do agree with Mrs Abbot to a certain extent. Whichever way you look at it, the children have had a rough time. It might be best not to send Alicia back to boarding school for a few days, especially if she has to go without Bernice. And now, I really must go.'

THIRTEEN

Sunday lunchtime

Bea showed Manisa out, saying, 'You'll let us know what you find out? The officer who called on me said he was interested in an alleged assault on Faye, but he was certainly not interested in the fire.'

'I will.' Off went Manisa, looking at her watch. Well, it was a Sunday, wasn't it? Did fire investigators usually have to work on Sundays? Perhaps they did. Which reminded Bea that she usually went to a church service on Sunday mornings . . . well, that would have to go by the wayside today. And – a little shriek as she looked at her watch – it would soon be lunchtime, and what did she have for everyone to eat?

She returned to the living room to find the two men thrusting their chins out at one another. She thought: William will want to keep Alicia safe at all costs, while Steve . . .? Steve doesn't know what to do next. He doesn't want to think Alicia is in danger. And, with so much else on his plate, who can blame him for that?

'Mrs Abbot,' said Steve, 'don't you think we've gone a bit over the top? Electrical accidents happen. There were particularly unfortunate results' – and here he winced – 'but that's all they were. You think Alicia's in danger, but I don't see it. I'm going to take her in to see Daphne, just as soon as I've sorted out one or two—'

William interrupted. 'I'm willing to help you, Steve, if you'll allow me to do so. For a start, I can take Daphne's things in to the hospital for you. If that scumbag of a boyfriend of hers doesn't want to take Daphne down to the hotel, I'll do that for you, too. I'll take Alicia with me. It will make a nice outing for her, and free you up for some of your other tasks.'

'I couldn't let you—'

'Of course you could. Hospital visiting times are flexible at weekends, aren't they?'

Steve sounded relieved. 'I admit it would be a great help. I brought Daphne's bag here by mistake and I see it's in the hall here. I'll give you the details for the hotel and you can liaise with them. Perhaps it would be a good idea for Alicia not to go back to school just yet. If Alaric rings—'

'She won't be here, will she? He can't possibly object if I've taken her to see her mother. As for the rest, I don't like the thought of sending her back to a school which harbours bullies. Perhaps we can find another place for her to go, perhaps with Bernice to look after her.'

Steve could see a light at the end of this particular tunnel, and ran towards it. 'I must say, that sounds sensible. If you really don't mind . . .?'

'Of course I don't mind. When I get back, perhaps you'll let me help you with the phone calls, the funeral arrangements, advising people about Josh. I'm at your disposal, provided I can be sure that Alicia is safe.'

Bea thought that was all well and good, but . . . 'Has anyone checked that the school actually has expelled Bernice? Would they really do that just because someone says her father was a scumbag? Heavens! If they refused to accept anyone whose father has ever had a brush with the law or cheated on their income tax, the schools would be empty overnight. And, by the way, does Alaric even know that we've got Alicia here safe and sound?'

Steve fingered his phone. 'Yes. I told him. He rang me back with a message – which I haven't had time to answer – wanting to know what arrangements we were making to get her back to school. I must ring him, tell him we're not at all sure she ought to . . .' He turned over a page and made another note on his pad.

William would guarantee to keep Alicia safe for today. Steve would identify the electrician. The two men would transfer Daphne to a hotel and get on with the business of Josh's funeral.

Bea struck one fist in the palm of the other hand. She thought the men were dealing with brush fires while a major storm was bearing down upon them, screeching in its thirst for blood. Or whatever. They were not looking at the big picture. Wasn't it even more important to find the man or woman who wanted the children dead? The police would get involved eventually, but how long would it be before they took any action?

In the kitchen, she saw that the dishwasher had finished its routine and was waiting to be emptied. She started to do that, resting her own hand on the top of the machine.

A hand came over her arm and covered hers.

William's hand.

His hand was warm. Large. Capable.

She could withdraw her hand easily enough, or she could turn and link her fingers in his.

With a start she realized she hadn't donned her diamond engagement ring that morning. Had she subconsciously wished to show William that she had decided not to wear it, encouraging him to believe that she was open to receiving his advances?

How old-fashioned.

How strange to feel her pulse quickening. She sought for some mildly amusing remark that she could make, to show him she was neither shaken nor stirred. And came up with 'Lawks!'

Which made her giggle.

He was standing so close to her that she could feel the warmth of his body. She thought he was going to kiss her if she didn't make any move to escape. *Escape?* Was he hunting her down? No, ridiculous.

But, she couldn't make up her mind what to do. Withdraw, or turn towards him . . . in which case, yes, he would kiss her.

She said, her voice uneven, 'I am not in the habit of—'

'I know.'

He *was* going to kiss her. Oh, lawks, indeed! She could do any number of things: bring up her knee, shove him away, scream . . .!

Er, no.

Heavy breathing at hip height.

Oh. The girls, of course. Standing beside them, pink-cheeked and tousle-haired, fascinated to see what the adults were going to do next.

Mel was behind them, laughing, also pink-cheeked and tousle-haired. 'We've played Hide and Seek till we're worn out and in need of sustenance. Can I make them something for lunch before I have to give my old lady hers?'

William stepped away. She rather thought he muttered a bad word as he did so . . . which made her giggle all over again. What? Did Wonderful William actually swear on occasion? How very human.

William said, 'Shall I do cheese on toast all round? Alicia and I are taking her mother down to the hotel where she can be properly looked after and have a good rest. After that, perhaps we can find a place to have a cream tea and . . .' He checked with Bea, 'May I bring Alicia back here tonight?'

'Oh, goody!' Alicia jumped up and down, jack-in-a-box fashion. 'I can sit in the front of the car, can I? Say I can sit in the front.'

'I haven't a car here, remember? So we'll take a cab to the hospital and after that we'll hire a limousine with a chauffeur to take us all down into the country.'

Steve hove into sight, brow furrowed, switching off his phone. 'Uncle Bill, I can't get through to Alaric, but I'm sure it'll be all right for you to take Alicia with you.' Then, catching sight of Mel, he . . . yes, he blushed. 'Oh. Have you been having a good time?'

Mel also blushed. 'Yes, we've had a lovely time.'

Bea thought those two might have slept in the same bed, but they hadn't had sex. There was a delightful innocence hanging around them, which was more than she could say for the two girls, whose heads were turning to each person as they spoke.

Mel released her hair from its ponytail, and shook it back around her face. 'I have to see to an old lady, give her her lunch, but if you like, afterwards . . .? That is, if Mrs Abbot doesn't need me again today? If she does, of course I'll stay. But if Alicia is going out with her grandpa then perhaps I could help you, Steve? Take phone messages for you, drive you around?'

Steve's blush deepened. It really did! 'Oh, I couldn't ask you to do that for me.'

Bea thought, Curses! I really could do with Mel watching out for Bernice. She said, 'Of course we can manage, Bernice. Can't we?'

Bernice nodded, wide-eyed. Probably thinking she could get away with murder if Mel's eye was taken off her. Well, not murder, precisely. But mayhem, definitely. Bea had no illusions about that one.

Steve relaxed. He had a surprisingly charming smile when he wasn't worried half out of his mind. 'That would be wonderful, Mel.'

Young love! Oh well, even if it doesn't last, it will help Steve through a particularly rotten time of his life.

Sunday afternoon

Peace and quiet. After the hustle and bustle of cooking, serving and eating a scratch lunch, everyone departed except for Bernice and Bea. Bea finished emptying the dishwasher and filled it up again. Bernice wandered off with Teddy. When Bea had tidied the kitchen, she found Bernice lying, face down, on the settee in the sitting room, with her head on Teddy. The bear gave Bea a glassy stare, which might or might not indicate that he was fed up with being treated like a pillow.

Bea blew him a kiss and descended to her office. Ah, the wonderful peace of a wet Sunday afternoon. Rain beat on the French windows. Gusts of wind blew across the garden, and the plants bowed and shook before them.

Winston plopped through his cat flap and proceeded to give himself a thorough grooming. He didn't like rain. Bea offered to give him a rub-down with a towel, but he declined, believing he could do the job better himself.

Bea switched on her computer. She was going to look at any work emails that might have come in . . . yes, yes . . . yes. Nothing that couldn't wait. She Googled Josh and his family.

Mm. Yes. Originally builders specializing in property to let at the high end of the market, new prestigious developments, nothing under five million preferred. Film stars, Middle East and Far East buyers, football players . . . tycoons of all descriptions welcome. Also management of properties. Did they locate their main office overseas?

Ah, no. It seemed they had enough of a conscience left to pay tax in the UK.

Josh – picture supplied – son of the founder of the firm, way back . . . more pictures with the great and the good. Wife's death . . . Nothing untoward there.

Two sons. Public school. Son made the sales director . . . aha! Not Steve, but Gideon, looking straight at the camera with what Bea always thought of as 'estate agent sincerity'.

No sign of Steve. How come?

Ah, separate company, of which Steve is managing director. The second company was run from the same headquarters in the City, but was for managing property, leases, repairs, etc. Work which carried no film star kudos. Backstage work, nitty-gritty. Needing meticulous oversight, dealing with difficult clients, builders who didn't do the work properly or . . . yes, Steve would be good at that. And, what was the betting that the Plain Jane company was actually more valuable than the flashy sales front?

Bea leaned back in her chair and thought about that. It seemed to her that Josh had understood his sons' capabilities and given each what they were good at. She also noticed that while Gideon, the lightweight, had been made sales director of his concern, Steve had been made managing director of his. Quite so. Appropriate and very wise.

She put in a request for more information, this time on Facebook. Yes, Gideon was on Facebook, photos of him yachting, golfing, surfing, and squiring a succession of lovelies – though there was no sign of Faye. Steve had said Faye was a recent acquisition, hadn't he?

Nothing for Steve. No, he wouldn't be interested in putting himself on Facebook, would he? It required a certain amount of self-esteem to do that, and Steve was lacking in that direction.

Faye Starman, however, was present in spades. Faye the model. Faye the red carpet starlet (what, really?). Faye the arm-candy for a number of men who looked well heeled and approximately twice her age.

Bea leaned closer to the screen. Was the man in the background of the snap of Faye on a beach somewhere . . . was that, could that be the policeman who had threatened Bea with this and that? Mm. Not proven. Not clear enough an image.

Next up: Alaric. Yes, title. Yes, estate. Nice-looking manor house. Minor racing celebrity. Tuxedos to the fore at various prestigious events. He looked good in black and white. Partner in . . . no, director of . . . various companies. Public Relations? Not clear exactly what he did. Possibly not much? Living on inherited money? Nowadays that might mean living on a dwindling income, hence the marriage to the wealthy Daphne.

His wedding to . . .? Wait a minute. Not Daphne. A fake blonde with fake eyelashes. His first wife? Mm, mm. No photos of him with Daphne. There would have been some, originally, wouldn't there? Taken down recently? Uh-huh.

Nothing of him with Ninette.

Try Ninette. Party organizer. That fits. Weddings, A-list guest lists, stretch limousines, minor film stars, et cetera. Pictures of her, smiling, in the company of important-looking people: the men wore expensive clothes and the women wore not much of anything but had obviously spent money on boobs and Botox. A nice picture of Ninette looking younger and less harassed than she appeared in reality. She was thin enough to model clothes, wasn't she?

There were no photographs of her with Alaric. Why not? Too new a relationship? What was going on there?

Who else?

Giorgio, Daphne's toy boy. A multitude of beefcake stills. Were they still called 'beefcake'? Nice pecs. He stripped well. A face which was handsome without having much in the way of character. The sort of face and body you expected to see on a pin-up calendar or advertising some healthy drink. Or unhealthy junk food.

Heavy breathing at her side.

Bernice, hair in a tangle, trailing Teddy behind her. 'Did you have a look at Uncle Bill's place? I went there with Lissy once. It's big. And noisy, with builders all over the place.'

Bea started. She hadn't thought of looking William up. Or had she? Was that what she'd been working up to all along? Bea Googled him. And yes, up he came. William, Lord Morton. Money made by earlier generations in trade with the Far East. Importer of teas. Later, they'd moved into fine wines. Up came the picture of a sprawling manor house, built in the eighteenth century. The Morton men married heiresses here and there . . . family ennobled in the early twentieth century, services to education. Education!? Ah, founding public libraries, setting up scholarships.

Oh, that sort of charity work; nitty-gritty and out of the public eye.

Like Steve.

William Morton, Harrow and Cambridge. Same as Josh. William went into the family firm . . . took only son into partnership . . . firm sold some years previously.

He'd married, yes, yes. Nice looking. Amateur musician of some fame. She died, et cetera.

Their son – good-looking, weak chin. Took after his mother in looks? Lacking William's strength of character? Son married Daphne, produced one girl child, Alicia. Son divorced. Married again, American girl with a strong chin. Two boys. Now living in Florida.

Bea leaned back in her chair. Bernice leaned against Bea's arm. They contemplated the screen together in silence.

Bernice said, 'There's something about an entail. Lissy doesn't understand it. He did tell her, but she doesn't have a brain for figures. What it means is that William's poor nowadays because he had to pay off his son, who doesn't want to come back here to England to live.'

Ah. To keep landed estates together, the heir would sign an agreement on reaching his majority, which would bind him to hand on the estate to his son or heir. That was it in a nutshell, though Bea believed it could get very complicated, involving trustees and distant relations and . . . well, that wasn't the case here. It sounded as if the son in America had been given money in order to break the entail, which would mean that he had no further right to the estate and William could pass it on to Alicia in due course.

Which was the reason why Alicia was doubly an heiress?

Bea said, 'Does Alicia miss her father?'

A shrug. 'She can't hardly remember him. That's best, really. I can't hardly remember mine. That's best, too. Auntie Sybil says it doesn't matter where you get your loving from, so long as *someone* gives it to you.'

Bea drew the child closer to her. Perhaps she herself was beginning to love Bernice? She'd experienced strong maternal feelings for her own son, but . . . a sigh . . . he'd long since grown up, and she hardly ever saw him and his children, what with this and that and his being so busy.

She'd never thought she'd feel love for a child again. But ups-a-daisy, here it was. The urge to protect. She said, 'Your mother does love you, you know.'

'I know that. And my stepdad is lovely, he really is, but I don't look like them, and I don't think like them. I know it's my fault. I really am a Holland. We don't think like other people. We're different. We don't mean to be, but we're not good with people. Not really. Alicia's different. She needs me.'

'You rang your mother?'

A sharp nod. 'No change there. She says I'm better off here.'

Which was possibly true.

Bernice continued, 'Great-aunt Sybil is lovely but she is awfully old and doesn't want to run around and play games and stuff. I missed out on school when I travelled around with her and it was a bit boring, so really it is best that I go back to boarding school and just see her in the holidays.'

The words, 'And perhaps see you as well?' hung in the air between them. Because the child realized that Bea did understand her, and value her. Bernice wanted another solid presence in her life; someone she could rely on. Someone who understood her. It was a plea from a motherless, father-less child for love. How could Bea refuse?

'Yes,' said Bea, knowing that she might be committing herself to a relationship.

Bernice planted a kiss on Bea's neck and quickly withdrew. She held up Teddy, wrinkling her nose. 'He's got strawberry jam on him, and toast and stuff. He's been a very dirty boy and needs a good spanking.'

Bea switched off her computer. 'How about we try to clean him up with dry shampoo? The only thing is, it might make him smell a bit different for a while.'

Bernice bounced towards the stairs. 'We can always hang him out in the fresh air for a while. When it stops raining.'

The front doorbell rang as Bernice was brushing the last of the dry shampoo out of Teddy's fur.

Bea opened the door to find Alaric and Ninette on the doorstep. He looked as sleepy and disinterested as ever. She looked as if she'd lost weight. Her neck was so long and thin that it made her head with its pile of artificial curls look even larger than usual.

He was smoking another of his cheroots and didn't ask if Bea minded . . . which she did.

Ninette said, 'We've come for the child.' No greetings, no social chitchat. Straight in for the kill.

Bea said, 'Alicia's not here.'

Ninette pushed past Bea into the hall. 'That's what you said this morning. We're not going to be fooled twice.'

Bea shut the front door, and gestured them in. 'See for yourself. You searched the premises before, didn't you? She was not here then, and she is not here now.'

Ninette threw open the door to the sitting room so violently that it banged against the wall. One glance and she dashed past Bea into the kitchen, where Bernice was fluffing up Teddy's ears. 'The wrong girl. Alaric, I bet this one knows where the girl is hiding.'

'My name is Bernice,' said Bernice, being polite. 'Alicia did come here after you left yesterday. But she's not here now.'

Alaric removed the cheroot from his mouth and bent down, nose to nose, grasping one of Bernice's shoulders. He gave her a little shake. 'You are only a little girl, Bernice, and you can't possibly understand what's going on here. I want you to get it into your thick head that Alicia is my daughter, and if I say she goes back to school, then neither you nor this agency madam here can stop me. Understand?'

Agency madam? Bea realized he was trying to insult her. Instead, she was amused. She said, in her creamiest tone, 'I'm sure William told you that the child did eventually turn up here, in a distressed condition. He informed the school and her uncle straight away. I expect you would like to thank us for looking after her.'

'You hid her from us! Admit it!' Ninette almost hissed. As before, she seemed far more angry and upset than he.

Bea was getting bored. 'No, we didn't. And no, she's not here. Now, would you kindly leave, or I shall have to call the police.'

'If we have to wait more than five minutes for you to produce her,' said Ninette, 'then it will be us who call the police.'

Alaric pinched Bernice's ear, bringing tears to her eyes. 'That's enough, Ninette. I believe her when she says Alicia's not here.' He reached out to grasp Bea's arm. And twisted it. 'You! Tell me where she is. Now!'

'Ouch! Do you want me to sue you for assault? Out of my house! Now!'

He smiled, and took his hand away. He put the cheroot to his lips and puffed. 'Please, pretty, please. If you don't tell me, I'll put my cheroot to good use.'

Despite herself, Bea felt fear. There was something coldly repellent about him. She believed him when he said he'd do her an injury. She rubbed her arm. 'If you'd asked me politely in the first place, I would have told you. William has taken Alicia to see her mother in hospital.'

Ninette looked shocked. 'But she's . . .' And stopped herself. Her eyes narrowed. 'Alaric, they're playing games with us. Suppose we take this child instead, just till Alicia is handed over.'

'Nowhere to put her, my dear,' said Alaric. He took the cheroot from his mouth, reached over Bernice's head and pressed the lighted end into Teddy's chest.

Teddy groaned.

Bernice screamed.

Bea dived across the counter. Pulling out a wickedly sharp carving knife, she swished it in the air not at Alaric, but at Ninette's curls. 'Out! Now!'

Ninette screamed and backed away, her mouth awry.

Alaric smiled. 'What a fuss about nothing. Come, Ninette.'

He walked back through the hall, opened the front door wide and went down the steps to the street.

Ninette shuffled sideways till she was out of the range of Bea's knife, and ran after him.

Bea dropped the knife, and took a sobbing Bernice in her arms. 'There, there!'

'He's killed Teddy!'

'No, he hasn't. Look, Teddy's still smiling even though he's been wounded.' She rocked the child to and fro. She was crying herself. 'That wicked man!'

'I hate him!' cried Bernice.

'So do I.' Bea reached for the tissues, and mopped them both up. Slowly they both regained control.

Bea said, 'I've got some red ribbon in my sewing box and some pretty buttons. Suppose we make Teddy a medal to wear over his wound? Then, when we look at him, we'll remember how brave he was.'

'How could they do that to Teddy, who never did them any harm?'

'I can see why William wants to fight them for Alicia. We'll help him in any way we can, right?'

'Tell me what to do. I'm only a child!'

A rather remarkable child. Bea said, 'Bernice, I'm worried. What did Ninette mean by starting to say something about Daphne and not finishing the sentence? And there's another thing. Faye has already tried to sue me for assault, and I did threaten her with a knife. We need some protection here. Do you think you could put on your jacket and take Teddy round the garden a couple of times to get rid of the last of that dry cleaning smell. And then we'll have a nice hot drink and plan what we can do to put those nasty people where they belong.'

FOURTEEN

Sunday afternoon

As soon as Bernice had gone down the steps to the garden, Bea seized her phone and rang the fire investigator.

'Manisa, are you still at the site? Yes? Have you been able to get to the top of the house yet?'

'Soon. Be patient.'

'I'm sorry. Something's happened here which . . . I realize I may be panicking unnecessarily.'

'Tell me.'

'I've had a couple of visitors, Alaric and Ninette. I think you would call them Persons of Interest in the matter of the fire? Certainly they have a motive to . . . No, I have no proof that . . . Start again. They came unannounced, desperate to find Alicia, who has gone with her grandfather to see her mother in hospital. There was no one here but me and Bernice. I asked them to leave, not once but twice. They refused. They threatened to take Bernice until I produced Alicia for them. Alaric twisted my arm. I can still feel it. I was frightened. I am not easily frightened . . .' She tried to laugh. 'I can't believe I did this. I took a knife and threatened them.'

'What!'

'I suspect they will file charges against me. Even though I can claim self-defence, the police might take me down to the station for questioning, and then what would happen to Bernice? She'd be at their mercy. I repeat, I'm all alone in the house, and I'm worried.'

A long pause. Then Manisa said, 'They came looking for Alicia but threatened to take Bernice instead?'

'I didn't cope with the situation very well.'

'You asked them to leave, twice. He laid hands on you first. You're in the clear.'

'Yes, but if he goes to the police and files a complaint, perhaps accuses me of kidnapping . . .'

'You have a rich imagination, Mrs Abbot!'

'You haven't met him. Remember that the child's mother is gravely ill in hospital and he's Alicia's father by adoption. Legally, he has every right to take her away from me, even though her grandfather is strenuously trying to get custody himself.'

'You could file a complaint against him yourself.'

'My witness being a child of ten?'

'If he does take action, you can always refer them to me, but . . . yes. Awkward. Can you not get someone to sit with you?'

'Yes. A good idea. Alaric frightens me. He burned a hole in the teddy bear which the children have been using as a comfort blanket.' Again she tried to laugh. 'Can I get him for assaulting a teddy bear?'

'I'll get back to you as soon as I can.' Manisa disconnected.

Bea tried to get William on the phone. As she did so, she checked that Bernice was all right, down below in the garden. The child was sitting on the bench near the birdbath. She had Teddy on her knee and was talking to him, or maybe just making sure he was all right. Which he was. Of course he was.

An inanimate toy can't communicate, can it?

'William? Thank heaven you picked up. Where are you?'

'In Kew Gardens, feeding the ducks. The river was high so it was too muddy to walk along the towpath. Something's wrong?'

'Yes. No. At least . . . did you see Daphne?'

'Well, no. Not yet. I rang and asked if it was all right to visit and they said to leave it till later this afternoon, as she had some specialist or other there, doing some tests.'

A specialist? More tests? *On a Sunday afternoon?* That sounded serious.

William said, 'Why? Something's happened?'

'I'm not sure. Keep in touch?'

She disconnected and dialled another number. 'Steve? Mrs Abbot here. I know you're busy and I'm probably way out of

line, but have you heard anything from the hospital this afternoon about Daphne? They haven't been trying to get through
to you and failed, have they? Yes, I know you're up to your
eyes, but would you check with them that she's all right?'

Steve was sharp. 'Something's happened?'

'I had Alaric and Ninette here, wanting Alicia, who is out
with her grandfather. Something Ninette said caused me to
wonder if Daphne had taken a turn for the worse. I've contacted
William and he says the hospital put him off as they were
doing more tests on her. I thought that was most unlikely on
a Sunday afternoon, unless . . . You understand?'

'I'll get Mel to check. I've got the information the fire
investigator needs from Dad's desk at home and the address
of Mrs Frost's son, and now I'm back at head office, trying
to deal with, well, everything. I'll ring you back.'

Bea paced up and down. If Alaric came back with a
policeman . . . If what she suspected was true . . . What could
she do to protect herself and the children?

Well, if all else fails, call in the cavalry. She had an old
friend who was a freelance bodyguard. Hari was part Maltese.
He could drift through locked doors like smoke, leaving not
a trace behind. He owed her a favour, so she rang him.

'Mrs Abbot? You don't sound like yourself.'

'That's because I'm not, Hari. At least . . . I am, but . . .
start again. Hari, I'm in trouble. Are you free to look after a
couple of ten-year-old children and their teddy bear for a
couple of days and nights? Oh, sorry; I didn't mean to add
that about the teddy bear, because he's actually mine and not
theirs, although I suppose they'd dispute that. Sorry. Rambling.
Start again. Hari: are you free to do some bodyguarding? I
have two children staying who I believe were the intended
victims of a house fire on Friday night. Various relatives are
buzzing around. Some of them don't seem to have the children's best interests at heart. One has threatened me and . . .
well, I drew a knife on them, which means I may be in trouble
with the police. If you're free, can you get here soonest?'

'Thirty minutes.' He rang off. That was the great thing about
Hari; he knew when to ask questions, and when to act.

Heavy breathing. In the old days, Bernice would have had

her tonsils and adenoids out. Perhaps Bea ought to ask what was being done about that?

Bernice said, 'Teddy's says he's all right now. When Alicia gets back, we'll have a ceremony to present him with his medal.'

Bea nodded. 'My sewing basket's in the cupboard by the fireplace. There should be some red ribbon in there, and a packet of assorted buttons.'

Bernice said, 'My ear feels red where that man twisted it. He does that to Alicia, too.'

'Is that hearsay, Bernice, or have you actually witnessed him doing it? You do know what hearsay is, do you? That's when someone's told you about it, but you haven't seen it for yourself. There's a difference.'

'I've seen it.'

'Have you, now!' Grimly. 'I think you should tell William that.'

'I've been to stay at his place with Lissy twice; no, three times. She'd told me he liked to twist her ear and make her cry, and I said if he did it to me, I'd bite him. I wish I'd been quick enough to bite him today. I liked it when you nearly cut off one of her curls.'

Bea grinned. 'So did I.' She fetched her sewing basket. 'See if you can find some red ribbon and I'll look for a suitable button. I always keep odd buttons. You never know when they'll come in handy.'

Bernice found some bright red ribbon and held it up against Bear's chest. 'Ninette's worse than him, though. She knew Lissy used to wet the bed years ago. She emptied a glass of water into Lissy's bed and made her sleep in it, and she told Alaric that Lissy was still wetting the bed and needed therapy. That's because Ninette doesn't want to be bothered with her.'

'Did you see that happen, too?' asked Bea, picking a gilt button out of her sewing basket. 'Will this do? Order of Bravery for Mr Teddy Bear.'

'I was there,' said Bernice. 'She doesn't think anyone would take any notice of what a little girl says.'

'She's wrong there. I'm listening, and so will Lord Morton.' Bea cut a piece of ribbon off, threaded it through the back of the button, made a loop and sewed it into place over the burn mark on Teddy's chest.

Bernice watched, her expression bleak. 'I was there when Alaric spanked Lissy and said she was a dirty little girl, even though it wasn't her who'd wet the bed.'

Spanking was allowed by law, within reason. But this was abuse, wasn't it?

Bea said, 'We'll see what we can do about that.' She put the teddy bear into Bernice's arms. 'Teddy needs a cuddle.'

Bernice said, 'There, there, Teddy. That didn't hurt a bit, did it?'

Bea's phone rang.

William, sounding distant. 'How did you know, Bea? I'm coming straight back. Fortunately I asked the driver to wait. Thirty minutes? Forty? Depends on traffic. Does Steve know?'

He rang off.

Infuriating man. Did he mean what she thought he meant?

Bernice was close enough to hear every word. 'What is it? Is Lissy all right?'

'Yes, I think so. They're on their way back.' Could Bea ring the hospital and enquire about Daphne in front of the child? But, which hospital?

Her phone rang. A woman. 'Mel here, on Steve's phone. He's lost his voice. When he got through to the hospital, they told him his sister died half an hour ago. He's in shock. Mrs Abbot, may I bring him back to you? I thought of taking him back home with me, but my brothers are home for half-term and the house is bedlam. Steve's a good man . . .' And then, speaking to Steve, 'Yes, you are, Steve. You help everyone else who's in trouble and . . .' And back to Bea. 'I've tried to get hold of his brother, but either I'm not making sense or he doesn't want to listen. Is Lord Morton there? Can you ask him to tell Lissy?'

'He knows, and he'll tell Alicia. Of course you must bring Steve back here. He has found the name and address of the electrician who'd done the wiring?'

'Yes, and we found Mrs Frost's son's address, too. I put in a call to him and he rang back a while ago. He's very shocked. Steve will speak to him again later. That's as far as we've got on that.'

Bea noted the pronoun 'we', and smiled to herself. Steve and Mel were melding into a team, weren't they? She said, 'Thank you, Mel, for everything,' and switched off.

Bernice's eyes were wide with shock. 'Lissy's mother? She's not dead, too, is she?'

Bea nodded. 'I'm afraid so.'

Bernice counted on her fingers. 'One, two, three deaths?'

Bea nodded again.

Bernice climbed on to Bea's lap, with Teddy. She didn't say anything, but clung to Bea as if she were drowning.

Bea held the child, and subdued panic. 'Listen carefully, Bernice. I have a friend coming to look after you and me and Alicia. He's arriving in twenty minutes' time. His name is Hari. You may have met him when you've been hanging around with your uncle Leon, because he's the partner of Anna, who owns and runs the Holland training school for domestic staff. You do remember him? Good. Now, if I'm not able to talk to him, I want you to tell him everything you know. And, I mean, everything! Everything you've seen or heard. You'll be safe with him here. But, if he says "Jump!" you jump. If he says, "Lie on the floor!" you lie on the floor. Understand?'

'He's a sort of bodyguard isn't he? Does he carry a gun concealed, like they do in America?'

'No. But he's a master of judo and all that stuff.'

Bernice sat upright. 'Would he teach me—?'

'Possibly, but you'd have to get permission from your family first. What I think is that he can guard our backs, while we ask questions. We're going to have Steve and Mel and William and Alicia back here soon, and they'll all want supper. So, what shall we cook for them?'

The doorbell rang. It was a little too soon for Hari. Bea looked through the peephole. It was raining – not hard, but with a meaningful persistence.

The man outside was not Steve. Not William. Not Alaric. A stranger in expensive casual wear, with smoothly brushed fair hair and an air of easy confidence; the sort of confidence you get from having wealthy parents and an easy journey through life.

Not a stranger, but someone Bea would very much like to pin to a dissecting board and torture till she obtained the answer to one or two important questions. Of course, torture was out of the question. A pity, really. She had a feeling that this man was Teflon-clad. Whatever he'd done or not done, he'd walk away from the family mess, clad in rectitude and wearing a tin halo.

'Gideon,' she said, letting him in.

He wiped his feet on the doormat – thoughtful of him – and swiped raindrops off his jacket. A diffident smile, full of charm, which he'd probably mastered by the age of two.

'Mrs Abbot, isn't it? I'm so sorry to trouble you, but is Steve here? I rang his phone when I heard the terrible news and got a strange girl who said Steve was coming back here. Is that right?'

'Sort of,' said Bea.

Bernice crept up behind Bea and took hold of her skirt, gazing up at Gideon with a look Bea found hard to interpret. Suspicion? Dislike?

Gideon smiled and bent down to speak to Bernice. 'Ah, Lissy's little friend. Where is she, by the way? I've had the whole boiling lot of them on my back, asking where she is.'

'She's out with her grandfather,' said Bea. 'Will you come in for a minute? We're in the middle of preparing a meal for our guests, aren't we, Bernice?'

'Expected back soon?' Gideon shot his cuff to consult a very expensive, very shiny, very complicated-looking watch.

Bea dodged that one. 'Come into the kitchen. When did you hear the news about Daphne?'

'Alaric rang. He's beside himself, poor chap. Can't think straight. I was out in the sticks – lunch, you know. With Clarissa at her place in the country. Her father has hopes of something in the next Honours List.'

Bea led the way back to the kitchen and the job of peeling potatoes. 'You weren't with Faye?'

'Lord, no. Faye's all right for a spot of this and that. Pretty little thing; but a sleeper, not a keeper, if you know what I mean.'

Bea knew, and thought the worse of him. 'If you didn't

want to get Faye's hopes up, why did you ask her to the family celebration the other night?'

'Clarissa had a prior engagement.' He looked around, assessing what he could see. 'Nice little place, this. Are you thinking of selling . . . perhaps down-sizing when you retire? I can move one of these little doll's houses quickly.'

Bea told herself not to grind her teeth. She took a pot of whipping cream out of the fridge and gave it to Bernice with a bowl and a whisk. 'Empty the cream into the bowl and whisk till the cream is stiff. Then add just four drops of vanilla essence from the rack by the stove, and give it another stir.'

How many potatoes would they need? Better be on the safe side. She counted out eight, nine, ten. 'Tell me, Gideon; did Faye manage to rescue any of her pearls, or is it going to be another insurance job?'

'Who knows? I haven't seen her since the tragedy. What a dreadful thing. I can't get over it.' He didn't look as if he'd suffered much. He talked about it as if he'd mislaid an expensive Parker pen and been forced to use a biro instead. He wasn't going to lose his voice, as Steve had done.

Bea said, 'You took your father into hospital and stayed with him there. He was pretty poorly, wasn't he, but there was hope he'd survive? Until you told him about Daphne and the fire.'

Did a tinge of pink suffuse his cheeks? Possibly. 'Well, yes. I wish I hadn't. He kept on asking where Daphne and Steve were and finally, yes. I was forced, against my better judgement . . . don't you think I haven't wished a hundred times that I'd lied and said everything was all right?'

'Because your news gave him another, and this time fatal, heart attack?'

'I know. I had no idea, none, that . . . but there it is. You do your best and . . . Steve said afterwards . . . but that was nonsense, of course. I couldn't possibly have guessed that Dad would take it so hard. If only Steve had been there . . . but no, he'd gone off with Daphne, our drama queen, always making the most of every cut and bruise. He should have been with me and Dad. That was where he ought to have been.'

Bernice gazed at Gideon, open-mouthed. She seemed to be

familiar with the idea that the guilty often rearranged facts in their minds to prove to themselves that they were whiter than snow, but her wide eyes showed she thought this one took the biscuit!

Bea continued, 'You did the same to Daphne, didn't you? As soon as you were on your own with her. You knew how fragile she was, and you deliberately told her that her father was dead and the family home burned out.'

'Nonsense, my dear. Total, arrant nonsense. I have always acted in the best interests of the family . . .'

In *his* best interests, he meant.

'. . . and no one can say otherwise. Daphne was doing so well, sitting up and worrying about her hair and her makeup. She fretted, worrying why Dad hadn't been to see her, and why Steve had neglected her. He did, you know! He promised to take her a whole list of things. And did he? No, he didn't. It was entirely his fault that she got into such a state and died.'

Bea tried to work out why it might be to Gideon's advantage to have hastened the deaths of his father and sister. Well, Josh had held on to the position of managing director of the estate agency, keeping Gideon as the sales director, whereas he probably thought he ought to be king pin and that it was more than time that his father retired. And Daphne was a drain on the family resources.

Bea didn't think Gideon had planned to cause his father's death, or his sister's. But when the opportunity had arisen he had, to put it bluntly, put the boot in. Steve knew what Gideon had done. He had used the term 'murder'. And he'd known there was nothing anyone could do about it . . . except, perhaps . . .? Well, it depended what sort of wills old Josh and Daphne had left, didn't it?

She put the last peeled potato into the pan of cold water, added a little salt and set it to boil. She found a long narrow dish in the cupboard and two packets of ginger biscuits. Sitting beside Bernice, she said, 'Now we spread a layer of the stiff cream on the plate, quite thickly. And then we put a layer of cream between two biscuits and stand them up on edge in the cream . . . so. Then another two. Add them to the others . . . like a train, one carriage after the other.'

Gideon had his phone out, checking something, frowning. 'Faye, again. Stupid little . . . she must realize I'm far too busy to attend to her now.'

Bea said, 'Did you know the electrician who did the rewiring?'

'Domestic matters . . .' He waved them away. 'I suppose Steve attended to it. It's about his level. Checking on three-pin plugs and all that.'

A tiny voice said, 'Piss artist.'

Bernice?

Bernice.

'What!' Gideon couldn't believe his ears. Bea saw him decide that he must have misheard. Yes. Of course. The child could not possibly have said . . . that!

Bea choked on a laugh, and turned it into a hiccup. Running some water into a glass, she gulped it down.

Gideon beamed a smile at Bernice. 'Alicia's little friend, aren't you? And where has she gone today, eh?' He patted Bernice on the head.

A mistake. Bernice picked up a knife with a blob of cream on it, and waved it towards his sleeve.

'Bernice!' Bea warned her. 'Take care. Gideon, I don't know whether or not you've been properly introduced to Bernice. She's Sir Leon Holland's great-niece and not to be underestimated.'

Gideon withdrew his hand. 'Oh. Well. I don't know where the others have got to. Time marches, et cetera. I'm due at . . .' He shot his cuff to give them another sighting of his expensive watch. 'You know how it is? People to see, places to visit. Moscow one day and Hong Kong the next. I'm rarely in the same city for more than a couple of days at once. This must be the longest I've been back in London for . . . you know? And now there's the funerals . . .' A shake of his head. 'Terrible business. Absolutely terrible. They'll have to find a date when I can make them.'

'Do you know the content of your father's will?'

'What? Do I . . .? Well, naturally. Not in detail, of course, but Dad always used to say we should all update every year, especially me, travelling around, as you know. And insurances, of course. I expect the insurance people will take some chivvying, seeing as the family home is in such a valuable position. Best to sell for redevelopment, block of luxury flats. I can move those, I know just the right developer, must get on to it tomorrow.'

'And the business?' Bea removed the pan of potatoes from the hob, drained off the water, added flour and some powdered mustard, replaced the lid and shook the pan hard.

'Oh. Well. There'll have to be an extraordinary general meeting. Naturally, I will be appointed MD in Dad's place. Better the devil you know, eh?' An empty laugh. 'Poor old Steve will have to arrange everything. Don't envy him. I'll have to give him my dates. Paris next week, then Berlin, and then Hong Kong again. Busy, busy.'

Bea tipped the floured potatoes into a baking tin which was fizzing with melted fat, and shoved it in the oven.

'Smells delicious,' said Gideon. 'Will there be enough for a tiny one?'

He meant himself? 'I don't think so,' said Bea. 'We've got a full house tonight. Now, Bernice, when you've got the biscuits all lined up with a layer of cream between them, you cover the lot with the rest of the cream, leaving not a gap behind. Then we put it in the fridge. The cream softens the ginger biscuits into a cake texture. We sprinkle the top with crystallized ginger just before serving and we cut slices on a slant so we get a sort of roulade of ginger and cream. Oh, and watch out for the cat. He thinks I only get cream out of the fridge for him.'

Gideon's hand hovered over the bowl, and he treated Bernice to a hundred-watt smile. 'You'll let me lick out the bowl?'

'It's not for you. It's for Teddy,' said Bernice, enclosing the bowl with her arm.

'Who's Teddy? Do I know him?'

Sensing confrontation, Bea heard the doorbell with some relief. 'That will either be William with Alicia, or Steve with Mel.'

She opened the door and let William in. He was carrying

a rather damp child, whose eyes were puffy from weeping. His were not much better.

Behind him came Hari, moving like a shadow into the hall.

There was the sound of a slap and Bernice cried out, 'Get off!'

FIFTEEN

Sunday late afternoon

William hadn't heard Bernice's cry. He thrust Alicia into Bea's arms, saying, 'I'm afraid we both got wet. I'm all right but Lissy stepped in a puddle and got soaked.'

Bea cuddled Alicia, who was, indeed, wet and bedraggled. She said, 'There, there. We'll soon have you cleaned up and into fresh things. Hari . . .' She gestured with a sideways movement of her head. 'Kitchen. The other child. She's called Bernice.'

She was about to close the door when Mel and Steve spurted out of a taxi and rushed up the steps to the house. They hadn't an umbrella, either, but they were not as wet as William and Alicia.

Bea said, 'Welcome back, children. Supper's on. Gideon's here, but he's not staying.'

William, relieved of Alicia, gave Steve a hug. 'My dear boy!'

Steve, eyes closed, returned the embrace. The two men patted one another on their backs.

Alicia said, in a tiny voice, 'I did get a bit wet, I'm afraid.'

Mel took one look at Alicia and said, 'Oh, you poor little thing. Come upstairs with me, and we'll get you cleaned up.'

Steve released William. He held out his arms to Alicia and whispered, 'Lissy. So sorry.' He held up his tablet, and mimed writing on it, making everyone smile. Good for Steve! He lifted Alicia from Bea's arms, but it was Mel who kissed the child.

Bea thought, Man, woman, child. There is true love there. How sweet. And with any luck, a happy ending, too. How very fortunate they were that Mel was the girl they'd chosen to help out this weekend.

William shook out his jacket, saying, 'Lissy didn't take it

well. Such a terrible shock, on top of everything else. At least
Daphne's end was peaceful. She'd been upset by a visitor
earlier, hadn't wanted any lunch. She settled down for a nap,
drifted off to sleep and her heart gave out. She's never been
strong, you know. It's a weakness in that family.'

Bea took William's jacket off him and spread it over a
radiator to dry.

'Who was the visitor?'

'Her brother, Gideon.'

'You're squelching, William. Go upstairs, find wherever it
is you've left your clothes, have a shower, rub yourself down
and change into some dry things.'

'I'm all right.'

Men do hate to be told to look after themselves, don't they?
Bea said, 'Move it. Now. Or else you'll be going down with
something and I'll have to nurse you. And I warn you, I'm a
very bad nurse!'

'Not till you tell me—'

'All right. Quick update. Steve went back home, got the
info about the electricians and Mrs Frost's details. Then he
went on to his office with Mel to start telling people about
Josh dying. He lost his voice when he heard the news
about Daphne. Gideon admits that he told his father Daphne
was in hospital and that their house was on fire. He also admits
that he told Daphne that her father had died, and that their
house was in ruins. He rationalizes his actions by saying they
were both fretting for information. How to murder your father
and sister in one easy lesson.'

William gave a long, long sigh. 'I did wonder. Don't tell
Steve.'

'Steve knows. Alaric and Ninette came looking for Alicia
and threatened me when they found she was not here. I asked
them to leave. They wouldn't go, so I pulled a knife on them.
I suspect they'll sue me for assault.'

He blinked. 'Did you really pull a knife on them?'

'Ninette suggested taking Bernice as a hostage for Alicia's
return, and they burned a hole in Teddy . . . which . . .' She
gulped, and snatched at self-control. Just about made it. 'Now,
upstairs and change.'

Surprisingly, he went.

Bea went into the kitchen. There was no sign of Gideon but Bernice was sitting on Hari's knee while they took turns to lick the bowl of cream out. Bernice was looking a bit frayed around the edges. Her eyes were diamond bright and her plaits were unravelling, but she was talking a blue streak . . . 'and then I woke up and it was all dark and Faye was trying to find her pearls by the light of her phone, and we only had Lissy's for a light and my phone was . . .' A shrug. 'I'm not sure. It went. But Uncle William, he's not a real uncle to me but he's a lot better than one of Lissy's. One of hers is a real Wicked Uncle, though the other is all right if a bit soft. Anyway, Uncle William got us new phones, so that's all right.'

Bea put the kettle on. 'So, Bernice; what made you shout out just now?'

Bernice gave her a look of limpid innocence. 'I thought Winston was going to jump on to the table, so I banged the table top and my bang was just near Gideon's hand, and he might have thought I meant it for him.'

'And where is Winston?'

Again that look of innocence. 'He must have slipped out through the cat flap while I wasn't looking.'

Bea tried not to laugh. 'What have you done with our pudding, and where is Gideon?'

'The ginger cake is in the fridge and the Wicked Uncle's gone into the sitting room for "a bit of peace and quiet", he says. If you ask me, he's a waste of space.'

'You called him a "piss artist".'

'Mm,' said Bernice, pleased with herself. 'Is Lissy all right? I saw she was back.'

'She's being cleaned up and changed. She'll be safe with Steve and Mel – and Hari.'

'Mm,' said Bernice, in tones of doubt. 'Now, if Lissy goes one way and I go another, which of us is Hari going to look after?'

'You choose,' said Bea, testing chicken joints which she'd taken out of the freezer, to see if they'd defrosted enough to put in the oven.

Bernice thought about it. Eventually she said, 'I think Hari should go with Lissy, because I can look after myself better than she can.'

'Which is the right answer,' said William, who arrived at that moment, his hair still damp. He was wearing a tracksuit and trainers which made him look larger than ever. And even more formidable. Did he work out at the gym? He didn't look the type, but maybe his looks were misleading.

Bea said, 'William, this is Hari, who is a trained bodyguard and is going to help us keep the children safe. Hari, this is Lord Morton, who is Alicia's grandfather and has her well-being always in mind. William, could you do with a cuppa to warm you up?'

William said, 'I'd kill for one. Shall I make it?' He didn't wait for permission but switched the kettle on. 'Now . . . Hari, is it? How much do you know and how much do you need to know? And your bill comes to me, right?'

Hari said, 'That's for Mrs Abbot to say. I understand there was a fire. Were you there? Tell me about it.'

William told, while making himself the longed-for cuppa.

Bea, listening in case he left anything important out, popped the chicken quarters into the oven with a couple of onions. By the time she'd started on peeling the parsnips, William was on his second cuppa, Hari was frowning in concentration, and Bernice had relaxed, muscle by muscle. Her eyes closed, and opened at half-mast. Closed and . . . fell shut.

Bea said, 'Shall I lay her down on the settee next door for a nap?'

Hari shook his head. 'She feels safe in my arms. Let her be.' He muted his voice to a murmur. 'Mrs Abbot, what do you make of it all?'

Bea also kept her voice down. She finished the parsnips and put them in a pan of cold water, salted them and set them on the hob. 'I'm not sure. There were several people at the dinner party who had reason to wish Alicia harm. First: Ninette and Alaric. Ninette intends to marry Alaric, but I'm told he's not well off and he might be looking for another rich wife to replace the one he's just lost. Also, he'd be better off if he didn't have to pay towards the child's school fees. I'm not sure that that's a strong enough motive for murder.'

Hari thought about it. Shrugged.

Bea continued, 'Second: Giorgio might feel Daphne would have more money to spend on him if Alicia were out of the picture. You could make out a case that any one of them might have paid an electrician to sabotage proceedings . . . but I don't think they did. I don't think anyone at the table had advance warning that all hell was about to be let loose. I didn't notice any tension at the table. Did you, William? Was anyone looking at their watch to check that the fireworks were going to go off as planned?'

William took his time over his second cuppa. 'No,' he said, eventually. 'I didn't notice anything like that. No one was on edge.'

Hari said, 'They could be good actors?'

Both Bea and William shook their heads.

Bea said, 'Alaric looked sleepy. Ninette kept darting looks at Faye, whom she assumed, probably correctly, was the type to make a play for any man under sixty. Faye was texting Gideon, who was amusing himself by texting back. Giorgio only thought of how many calories he was eating. The children had had a lot of expensive presents and were over-excited but beginning to droop with tiredness.'

'Josh,' said William, 'was enjoying being host and grandfather on a family occasion. It wasn't often he could get all his children under his roof. He doted on Alicia, which is why he wanted to celebrate her birthday in style. He ignored Ninette to talk to Alicia.'

'Steve,' said Bea, 'was resigned to going along with the family party. Daphne was a drama queen, showing off her toy boy, shaking her pretty head to settle her hair about her shoulders, admiring the rings on her fingers. Leon was bored, yes. He gets asked to back lame horses all the time, and Daphne was just one more in a long line of people who've tried it on him. He would have seen through Giorgio at a glance. Which left me, also slightly bored but willing to put up with it because it was great to see the children being showered with attention . . . and you, William . . .?'

'Like Leon, I was fighting off Daphne's invitations to take Giorgio to my heart. I can't remember anyone showing signs of tension till the first firework went off.'

Bernice was totally relaxed in Hari's arms. Hari said, 'This is a bright one. Did she see anything?'

'I don't think so,' said Bea. 'We'll ask her when she wakes up.'

William said, 'But if no one at the dinner party organized the fireworks . . .? Bea, you must be mistaken. And, in any case, who else would wish to harm the children? Yes, it looks as if an electrician were involved in some way because of the use of timers . . . but why would an outside workman do such a thing?'

'I don't think it's the sort of simple situation where you have a murderer aiming to kill someone. In fact, the deaths of Josh, Daphne and Mrs Frost were neither planned nor intended. They were accidents along the way. Manslaughter, to be accurate.'

'Agreed.'

'What I think is that several people played a part in creating a situation which was taken advantage of by someone else. For instance, let's take a look at Gideon's part in this affair. He didn't set out to murder his father and his sister, but he fed them information which, for their own good, had been withheld by Steve and William . . . and which killed them. You can argue that Gideon broke the news to them with malice aforethought, but I don't think that's strictly the case. He couldn't *know* for sure that the news would give his father another heart attack, although he must have realized there was a risk of it doing so. He couldn't *know* that his news would distress Daphne enough to kill her, but . . . well, ditto. You could call it manslaughter, I suppose, but no one is ever going to be able to prove it, and he will probably never even be questioned by the police about it.'

'You're right,' said William, sighing. 'For as long as I've known him, Gideon's sailed close to the wind, and got away with it. He must think he's invincible. So you think someone else should bear responsibility for the fire?'

'I'd have to question them all to be sure, but I'm beginning to think the sequence of events was as follows: Josh was informed that the kitchen lights needed rewiring and asked around for the name of an electrician. Quite innocently.

Someone comes up with a name, and again, it could have been a referral without any ulterior motive. The electrician's probably kosher, too. The firm sends someone in to do a survey, he says the whole house really ought to be rewired and reports back to Josh, who doesn't want the upheaval and says the electricians should just do the downstairs circuit. That in itself is quite a big job, which will be done over a number of days and probably involve two men at a time. Mrs Frost arranges for the rewiring to be done.

'Now you know what workmen on a sizeable job are like. They come and go, probably at odd hours because they're fitting it in along with other jobs they're doing. They turn up at the door and are let in, and then they leave and perhaps the next day a different man turns up, or the first one turns up with another man in tow. No one really looks at them, not even Mrs Frost, who probably keeps an eye on their comings and goings, gives them mugs of tea and biscuits, but wouldn't question it if two men turned up one day, and a third the next.

'Meanwhile Josh plans a birthday party for the girls, who pester him for fireworks. He turns them down. Everyone hears that the girls want fireworks. Someone – and it's not necessarily anyone who had dealings with the electricians – buys a box of indoor fireworks for them.'

William said, 'I can confirm that there was no gift tag on the box. The children say they had no idea who had given them the indoor fireworks.'

'Which could mean either that the tag was removed, or that it never had one. The fireworks might have been an innocent gift from someone, which was later tampered with by someone else. Or the villain of the piece might have planted the box of fireworks among the children's presents with the timer already in it. If the latter, then it presupposes that he or she knew the children had been asking for fireworks . . . which means they had the information from a close member of the family. Do you follow my thinking?'

'Someone in the family leaked information to someone employed by the electricians?'

'Or to someone who could pass themselves off as an electrician, infiltrate the household and set up the timers and flares just before the party began. And I mean, that very afternoon. Mrs Frost would have drawn the curtains in the dining room at dusk, which would have been, what, about four o'clock? Not much later. She would have noticed a timer and flare if it had been placed there earlier, wouldn't she?'

Silence while they absorbed this.

William said, 'You're thinking that the firework behind the curtain in the dining room was meant to disrupt, but it wasn't a serious attempt to burn the house down. Likewise, the timer on the landing upstairs. It caused a distraction, but if Mrs Frost hadn't tripped and broken her leg, it probably wouldn't have set the house alight. But the timer in the box of fireworks . . . that's a different matter.'

Bea said, 'Perhaps, perhaps not. The indoor fireworks might not have been taken upstairs by the children that day, but left in the sitting room overnight. It might well have exploded in the sitting room and, if we'd all been in the dining room when it happened, then we might not have known about it until the fire had gained a hold . . . in which case the target could have been any or all of us.'

An indrawn breath. William hadn't thought of that before.

Bea said, 'I think we need to ask the children if anyone suggested they take the box upstairs with them.'

Hari said, 'But why would a strange electrician want to set this up?'

'I think . . .' She hesitated. 'I think it's like King Henry II and Thomas à Becket. Once upon a time the king and Becket had been bosom pals. Then Henry installed Thomas as head of the church. From being a wild youth, up to any lark, Thomas became a devout Christian and withstood all Henry's attempts to control the Church through him. Henry got cross, and burst out with the fatal words, "Who will rid me of this turbulent priest?" Whereupon, four of his knights set out to do just that. Thomas was cut down in front of the altar and Henry got the blame. Was he culpable? Yes. Did he really mean Thomas to be killed? Mm. Yes and no. Was he pleased when it was done? Mm. Yes and no. He spoke in haste and his wishes were fulfilled by others. I think that's what might have happened here.'

'You mean,' said William, 'that Alaric or Ninette, or whoever, learned about the rewiring and suggested to a third party that they'd like us killed, and the third party obliged them by setting the timers? But why would they go to such extremes . . . I'm being stupid. There's some link here, isn't there? Something we don't know about. The fake electrician must have something to gain by acting for . . . whoever. Henry's knights looked for advancement at court. Obviously, you know more history than I do, Bea. Did they get it?'

'I'm not sure, but I do know that Henry had to go to Rome and beg pardon of the Pope on his knees . . . or was it barefoot? Something like that. So we need to look for someone who has a reason to look for advancement by setting the fires.'

William said, 'If we hadn't thought to check on the children—!'

'I know. If we'd been just a few minutes later, they'd have died.'

Footsteps could be heard coming down the stairs. Mel and Steve appeared, Steve carrying Alicia, who'd been washed and dressed in clean clothes, with her long hair tied back in a scrunchie.

'Berny! Berny!' Alicia was full of beans. 'Uncle Steve says I can go to a different school with you if I like.'

Bernice started awake, and looked around, bewildered to find herself sitting on someone's knee. She slid to the floor and pushed her hair back from her face.

Steve held up his hand to get their attention, and whispered, 'Hold on, young 'un. I said "*If* Alaric agrees!"'

'Oh, he will!' Alicia slid out of Steve's arms down to the floor and ran to Bernice. 'He's always saying I should go to a school which doesn't cost so much. Isn't that good?'

Mel clucked over Bernice. 'Come here, lovey, and I'll do your hair for you. You look as if you've been dragged through a hedge backwards!'

Bea registered a pang of guilt. She ought to have seen to Bernice's hair, and hadn't. She really was too old for this mothering lark. She noted that Hari had disappeared. He came and went without so much as disturbing the air around him. He was probably checking out every room in the house to see

if there were any intruders . . . or to see where he might hide
a child who was being sought by the wrong people?

She said, 'Shall we go and sit down next door and see
if we can get the answer to some questions?' It wasn't a
suggestion, but an order.

So they all went next door . . . to find the Wicked Uncle
on Bea's landline phone, lying back in the armchair which
Bea considered 'hers', with his feet up on the coffee table. Bea
was not amused.

Gideon waved to them, took the phone from his ear long
enough to say, 'You don't mind, do you? A client in Hong
Kong.'

Yes, Bea did mind. 'Cut it short, please.'

Steve looked distressed. He opened his mouth to speak.
Everyone turned to him to hear what he had to say, but no
sound came out. He gestured to Gideon to wind his conversation up.

Gideon held up his hand to indicate he wasn't finished yet.

Everyone else found a seat and sat, waiting for Gideon to
finish. Gideon was enquiring about a horse race that he might
fly over to attend. Lots of light laughter and references to
some fillies who were probably not of the four-legged variety.
Finally Steve traced the phone's cable to its power point on
the wall. He looked back at his brother, the message clear.
'I'm pulling the plug on your call.'

Gideon had no option but to put the receiver down after
saying, 'Big Brother's watching me . . .!'

Gideon threw himself back in his chair. 'If you've lost me
a sale . . .!' He smiled brilliantly at the rest of the room. 'You
can see for yourselves that Big Brother has no idea how to
handle clients in the billionaire bracket. All he knows about
is changing fuses and light bulbs in accommodation for
down-and-outs!'

Everyone looked at Steve who threw up his hands as if to
say he wasn't prepared to argue. The opinion of the room
hardened against Gideon.

Bea intervened. 'Thank you, Steve. Gideon, I'll let you
know the cost of that call, shall I, and of any others that you've
made on my phone line without permission?'

It was water off a duck's back. Gideon's attention was focused on Mel, who had seated herself next to Steve on the settee. He said, 'Well, hello-oa, there . . .'

Mel wasn't particularly beautiful; she didn't have a model's figure, and she wasn't dressed to kill. She looked what she was: a nice-looking, intelligent girl with a warm heart. A good, but not a good-time, girl. Not a sleeper, but a keeper.

Mel looked at Gideon and looked through him.

Bea could see that Gideon was intrigued. His track record with women was impressive, and no doubt in the past he'd moved in on any girl Steve fancied. Now he saw fresh meat, sitting rather too close to his despised Big Brother, and he couldn't resist coming on to her . . . which would pay Big Brother back for breaking off his phone call to his prospective client.

He sat upright, and leaned forward. 'Introduce me to this delightful creature.'

Bea recognized the tone of voice and predatory look. Some men needed an elbow in their solar plexus before they would desist. Others could be frozen out. What would Mel do?

Ah, it wasn't only what Mel would do. Steve bristled. He really did. His shoulders seemed to swell and he looked as if he was going to launch himself at Gideon. He had lost weight these last couple of days and now everyone could see his likeness to his father, old Josh. But he didn't lose control. He turned his head, waiting to see if Mel would respond to Gideon's approach . . . or not.

Mel turned away from Gideon to give Steve reassurance. A little shrug said it all. It was clear she'd seen enough of the world to evaluate a would-be Lothario like Gideon.

Hurray!

Mel said, in the polite tone of voice with which one speaks to a casual acquaintance, 'I'm Mel. A friend of Steve's. And you're his younger brother? I suppose you didn't know that Steve lost his voice when he heard about Daphne. I'm afraid he'll have to communicate through me for a while. I'll get him to a doctor in the morning.'

Crash, bang, wallop! Game, set and match!

Bea wanted to cheer.

Steve picked up Mel's hand and put it to his cheek. Mel blushed. Beautifully.

Gideon reddened. He could hardly believe that a girl had turned him down, just like that!

Hari drifted back into the room, gave Bea a thumbs-up and took a seat by the door. He'd searched the house and was giving her the OK?

The phone rang. Gideon reached for it, but Bea was quicker. 'Hello? Leon, where are you?'

'On my way over, in the car. Sybil is arriving at Heathrow in about an hour, add half an hour for retrieving luggage and getting through Customs.'

Bea looked at the clock. It was dark outside, and rain beat on the windows. Not a good night for fireworks, nor for travel. But Leon would be in a big, chauffeur-driven car.

He continued, 'I thought Bernice might like to come. I'll pick her up in ten minutes, perhaps less if the traffic eases up. All right? Do you want to come as well?'

'I can't. I've got guests.' And to Bernice, 'Your great-aunt's arriving at the airport in about an hour and a half. Leon will take you to Heathrow to meet her. Would you like to take Alicia as well? Hari can go with you both, right?'

It was an order, not a suggestion. Both girls nodded.

Bea went back to the phone. 'Alicia will come, too. She'll be company for Bernice while you wait. They'll be ready for you in ten minutes or so. Give me a bell when you arrive and they'll be right with you. And, Leon, I've got Hari here, looking after the girls. You've used him often enough at work and you know how good he is. I'm thinking it would be a good idea for him to come with you. He can look after the girls if there's any delay at the airport. Right?'

She clicked the phone off, and collected everyone's attention. 'Now, we have ten minutes or so before Leon collects the children, so may I suggest we take this opportunity to clear one or two things up. Think back to Friday evening. You were all in the sitting room where the children were opening their presents when Leon and I arrived. Late. I didn't see who was given what. We handed over our own gifts, they were opened and admired, and we went into supper. Agreed?'

Nods all round. Gideon leaned back in his chair, looking bored. His eye was still on Mel, who was conscious of him, but refrained from looking in his direction.

Bea said, 'Children; you had all sorts of lovely presents. Did you make a list of who gave you what?'

Alicia shook her head. 'Mrs Frost was cross about that. When we went upstairs after supper, she asked if we'd written everything down, and we said No, we could remember, and she said we ought to do it straight away or we'd forget. She was strict about writing thank-you notes.'

Bea said, 'So who gave you the box of indoor fireworks?'

Both children shrugged. 'Dunno,' said Bernice.

'Did someone explain what indoor fireworks did? Perhaps they talked about how they had some when they were children?'

'I don't think so. Perhaps it was someone who wasn't there who gave them to us? There was no label.'

William frowned. 'I picked the box up. I knew Josh had vetoed fireworks in the garden. I thought he'd bought it for the children to use instead. There was no label. No wrapping paper. It was just as it had come from the shop or, more probably, been ordered over the Internet.'

No label. No wrapping paper. Bea said to the children, 'Did you carry all your presents upstairs with you after supper, or leave some downstairs?'

The girls looked at one another. 'The croquet set,' said Alicia. 'That was too big and heavy.'

'Some skates,' said Bernice. 'You remember, Lissy? Your granddad gave us both some skates. We left those downstairs as well. Mrs Frost helped us carry everything else upstairs. I don't think we left anything else behind.'

'The box of fireworks was pretty big, wasn't it? Why didn't you leave that downstairs, too?'

'We wanted to set them off straight away, but Granddad said not before supper because it was getting late. He said that when we went upstairs, Mrs Frost would find us a metal tray to put them on and some matches. We didn't have a tray or any matches upstairs.'

'Who carried them upstairs?'

'Mrs Frost helped us, didn't she, Lissy? When your Granddad said we looked as if we were going to fall asleep at the table, he got the waitress to fetch Mrs Frost and she came and got us, and we went into the sitting room and picked up almost everything, and took them upstairs. Mrs Frost helped us. I think she carried the box of fireworks.'

William said, 'I assumed it was a present from someone who knew the children had been disappointed in not being able to set off fireworks outside.'

The phone rang. That would be Leon, announcing his arrival outside.

As Bea picked it up, the front doorbell rang.

What was Leon playing at?

SIXTEEN

Saturday early evening

It was Leon on the phone. 'Are they ready? We're double-parked outside.'

'They're on their way.'

The doorbell rang again. What was going on?

Mel bustled the children into their jackets, while Bea told Leon to let her know when they had successfully retrieved Sybil from the airport. Still on the phone, she followed Hari and Mel as they ushered the children out into the hall.

Hari stopped them there. 'Hold on while I check that your uncle's car is directly outside. It's raining, you see. You don't want to get wet again.' He opened the front door and looked out. Hari didn't trust anyone. Good man!

'About time, too!'

It wasn't Leon at the door.

It was Faye, thrusting past the children as Hari led them out. Faye was dressed in black from head to toe. Her mouth indicated that she was in a shocking temper, but she couldn't frown because of her latest Botox injection.

'Well!' Faye slid out of a fake fur coat and threw it down.

Bea closed the front door on the nasty wet evening. 'To what do I owe the pleasure?'

'Where is he? Where is that scumbag?'

Bea was amused. 'Which scumbag do you mean?'

A glare from eyes almost obscured by false eyelashes. 'Don't act stupid with me. I mean Steve, of course! I know my rights!'

'Steve?' Bea hadn't expected that. 'What did you want him for and how did you know he was here?'

'Giorgio told me, of course! He'll be here in a minute!' She looked into the kitchen, saw no one there, and barged into the sitting room. 'There you are!'

Raised voices. Angry. Bea darted into the kitchen herself,

to check on what was happening in the oven. The parsnips had been par-boiled. She drained them, added them to the baking dish around the meat and potatoes, turned the oven up a fraction, tried to work out if she had enough food if Sybil wanted to join them. Decided she was *not* going to feed Gideon. No way.

Or Giorgio. She had completely forgotten about Daphne's gigolo. How did he fit into the jigsaw puzzle she'd been trying to put together? Or was he an innocent bystander?

Oh. Was that the sound of a slap next door?

She rushed back to the sitting room in time to see William pick up Faye from behind, and dump her, screeching with rage, on to a low chair. She kicked out at him, but he immobilized her by the simple expedient of putting his hands on her shoulders and pressing down.

An overturned chair lay nearby. Steve and Mel were on their feet, Mel holding her hand to her cheek. Faye had slapped Mel? Why?

Gideon was on Bea's landline again. The scumbag.

The front doorbell rang again.

'Enough!' said Bea.

'Lord Morton attacked me!' screeched Faye. Her hair had fallen out of its clasp and was all over her face . . . not to mention her mascara.

Mel took her hand away from her cheek, and hastily put it back again, saying, 'Ouch! No, it's not too bad. I shouldn't have tried to get between them.' She tried to smile.

Steve put his arms around her. Steve was stoking anger but still in control . . . for the time being.

Bea worked it out. 'Faye? You attacked Mel? I suppose she got in the way, trying to tell you that Steve had lost his voice? Is that right, Mel? Yes, I thought so. Shame on you, Faye! First you tried to make out that I'd assaulted you when I dragged you out of a burning building, and now you attack someone who is only trying to help. Save your tears for your lawyer. They won't get you anywhere here!'

Faye sobbed, 'Gideon, tell these horrid people they can't treat me like this!'

Gideon was still on the phone. 'Yes, yes. Well, when I touch down . . .' With a smile. He was not going to hear whatever Faye had to say, was he?

So Bea turned on him. 'Gideon, if that is a private phone call, you'd better ring off before I attack you myself! Oh yes, and please would you move to another chair? That's the one I like to sit in.'

Steve put his arm around Mel and drew her back down to the settee.

William, with care, took his hands off Faye's shoulders. Faye fished a mirror out of her bag, and gave a wail of horror. 'My hair! Look at my hair!' She reached for her handbag to repair the damage. Bea wondered if the girl would go so far as to use heated rollers in front of everyone? No, surely not! But repairing her makeup should keep her quiet for a bit.

Gideon put the down. 'That was someone for you, Mrs Abbot. A cold sales call.'

Did she believe him? No. He'd been making another long-distance call, hadn't he?

The doorbell rang again.

Bea said, 'I suppose I'd better answer that.' She glared at each one in turn. 'Nobody is to say anything or do anything till I get back.'

Who would it be this time? Ah yes. Alaric of the sleepy eyes, not smoking on one of his cheroots for a wonder. And Ninette, who seemed glued to the sleeve of his perfectly tailored Barbour coat. Followed by Daphne's gigolo, Giorgio.

Ninette was looking stressed. So she should.

The gigolo was frowning. He'd have to take care, or he'd get a permanent crease in his forehead.

Bea held the door wide open. 'Alaric, you may come in, because we are about to hold a post mortem on the fire. But please note that I have already informed the authorities of your assault on me earlier today, so you'd better keep your hands to yourself from now on.'

Did he believe her? Maybe.

Giorgio hovered on the doorstep. 'I need to speak to Steve. He is here, isn't he?'

Alaric ignored Bea's words. 'I want my daughter. And I'm not going to be put off any longer. The law is on my side.'

'Steve is here, yes, but he's lost his voice. He's devastated by the loss of his sister, which is more than you seem to be, Alaric. The children have gone to the airport to pick up Bernice's great-aunt. I suggest you come in and take a seat, all three of you, and we'll try to make sense of what's been happening before the fire investigator hands the case over to the police.'

Alaric was not amused. 'Why do you have to bring the police into it?'

Giorgio slipped into the room and looked around for Steve. On discovering him on the settee, he stood over him to say, 'I've come about my car and the flat. Daphne gave them to me, right?'

Steve tried to speak, and failed. Frustration brought colour to his cheeks. He pulled out his tablet and began to write on it. Then he held up his tablet for Mel to read what he'd written.

Mel nodded. 'Giorgio: Steve says this is not the time and place. He'll discuss it with you after Daphne's will is read.'

Giorgio said, 'I can wait.' He drew a chair out from the dining table in the window overlooking the street, and seated himself on it. That way he was still in the room, but keeping at a distance from the others.

Alaric ignored everyone to stand over Mel. 'You're the nanny, aren't you? Where is my daughter?'

Bea intervened. 'Alaric, I told you. Leon's taken the children with him to collect Sybil Holland – that's his elder sister – from the airport. Now, do sit down, please.'

'Why should we?' said Ninette, poised to retreat. 'And what have you been doing to Faye?'

'Lord Morton attacked me!' said Faye, hairspray poised in her hand. Sullen and furious. 'Giddy, tell them!'

Gideon ignored Faye. Since Bea had removed him from 'her' chair, Gideon made as if to sit on the settee beside Mel . . .

. . . or, he would have done, if Steve hadn't given him such a furious look that he decided to sit near the window instead. He, like Giorgio, took one of the chairs by the dining table. He even managed to produce a light laugh. 'Well, here we all are. Alaric, Ninette: welcome to the mad house.'

William looked around. And took the last remaining chair on this side of the dining table. He drew it out into the room, stationed himself behind Faye, and seated himself there.

Bea turned the gas fire out as the room was getting warm with so many people in it. 'Now we are all here, perhaps we can work out exactly what's been going on. Alaric, Ninette – take a seat.'

Alaric said, 'Is this going to take long?' But he took off his coat and settled himself beside Ninette on the settee opposite Bea.

Bea said, 'Before we start, please do remember that Steve's lost his voice. If we need to ask him something then Mel – this is Mel, one of my agency staff – has been helping him and may be able to tell you some of what he's been doing today, or wait for him to write on his tablet.'

'Who cares!' said Faye, and started to toss her hair about her head.

Bea sat down in her favourite chair, from which she could survey the whole room. She said, 'The fire investigator, Manisa, will soon be in a position to make a report to the police, in which she will say that at least one of the fires on Friday night was caused by arson.'

Alaric's eyes narrowed. 'Ah. The children playing tricks, I suppose.'

Giorgio's mouth fell open.

Ninette said, 'What?'

Everyone else nodded.

Bea went on, 'Manisa has already found evidence of one timer, and it is suspected there were at least two more: one on the top landing, and the other in the box of indoor fireworks which exploded in the children's room. It is possible there was also a fourth, in the fuse box which controlled the lights throughout the house. Timers mean arson. Manisa's report will start the police asking questions.'

'Ridiculous!' Ninette exclaimed. 'Isn't it perfectly clear that the children set the fires?'

'You don't seriously think that even if the children had sourced and set at least three timers, they'd have been so foolish as to put one in their own box of fireworks?'

'Anyone can see that they were totally out of hand, egging one another on. Alicia wets the bed. Alicia is a very disturbed child and needs to see a psychiatrist. And as for Bernice! Well! What can you expect of a criminal's child?'

William and Steve stirred, but Bea held up her hand. 'Ninette, just because you don't fancy looking after a ten-year-old girl, it doesn't mean that she set out to murder you. Perhaps you haven't realized it, but if that box of tricks had been left in the sitting room on Friday evening, then it would have exploded while we were all at dinner and caused a fire which might have threatened all our lives . . . you included.'

Ninette went a greenish-white.

Alaric paused in the act of lighting another of his cheroots.

Faye's mouth fell open, as did Giorgio's.

Ninette squeaked, 'Who would want to kill me?'

Bea said to Alaric, 'Please, no smoking. Did anyone apart from William comment on the box of fireworks before it was taken upstairs?'

Giorgio lifted his hand, not very far. 'Daphne did. She said it was nice of someone to have given it to the children. She thought I'd got it for them, but it never occurred to me.'

No. He probably hadn't bothered to get the children a present of any kind.

Ninette said, 'Didn't the kids ask if they could have the fireworks before supper and Josh said "no"?'

Alaric nodded. 'He did.' He still held the cheroot between his fingers, turning it round with strong fingers. But he didn't light it.

'When the children left the dinner table,' said Bea, 'did anyone hear Mrs Frost arguing with the children about taking their presents upstairs?'

'Well, yes,' said Ninette. 'I suppose I did. I was seated nearest to the door to the hall. The door was open because the waitresses were coming in and out. I heard Mrs Frost telling the children to leave some of the big presents downstairs till the following day. She helped them carry the rest upstairs.'

Bea sighed. It seemed they were no further in finding out who'd supplied the indoor fireworks. 'Let's move on to something else the fire investigator wants to know. Who chose the electrician to do the rewiring? It is quite possible they had nothing whatever to do with the fire.'

'You mean that you "need the name to eliminate them from your enquiries"?' Alaric put his cheroot to his mouth, felt Bea's eye on him, and took it away again. 'Don't look at me; I wasn't asked.'

Steve snapped his fingers, and nodded.

Mel said, 'We found the name in Josh's papers. A firm called BEC Electrics, based in Chiswick.'

Ninette stared. 'Oh, them. They have an office downstairs in our building. They're good. I recommend them to people all the time.'

'Did you recommend them to Josh?'

'No. Why would I?'

Giorgio said, 'I think I saw a van with those initials painted on its side a couple of times. It was parked in front of the garage and I had to ask them to move, so I could get Daphne's – I mean my – car out. She gave it to me. Honest!'

No one believed him.

Bea said, 'You spoke to the electricians, Giorgio? What did they look like?'

A shrug. 'Like any other workmen. Overalls. One was shorter. One was taller. Neither of them worked out, I can tell you that.'

'Polish, Albanian, what?'

'Er.' Trying to think. 'British. Ordinary. South London accent. Bobble caps. Tattoos? Yes, one of them had tattoos on both his arms. I don't hold with them myself.'

'You saw the same two men on several occasions?'

Deep thought. Painful. 'Dunno. Daphne said she never knew who she was going to meet when she walked into the house, but that was Daphne. She might not have meant it.'

Alaric threw up his eyes. 'Come off it. Daphne would have noticed any man who entered her orbit.'

Bea tried once more to extract information from Giorgio. 'So, one tall man, one shorter and fatter? Bobble caps, overalls.' She thought about that. So where did the fake policeman come in? Suppose . . .? She ventured a guess. 'Was the third man the same, or different?'

Deep thought. The lad really was trying hard. 'Different. Irish? Black hair. Blue overalls, not grey. He worked out. Good biceps. Strong neck. You know? But . . . tattoos?' He shook his head. 'No, I don't think so.'

'You've done so well,' said Bea. And indeed he had.

Black hair. No, it couldn't be . . . could it? The query 'off-duty' policeman who'd called on her and . . . what was his name? Thurrock? Manisa hadn't officially informed the police about his visit to Bea yet, so they'd assumed he'd been doing Faye a favour. But . . . where did he fit in?

What had a plain-clothes policeman to do with an electrical firm? No, it couldn't possibly be the same man. Could it? A man with black hair who worked out. There must be quite a few of those around.

Of course, if he hadn't been a policeman at all, but someone impersonating one . . . No, that was ridiculous! Everyone knew the penalties for impersonating a policeman were horrendous.

True black hair wasn't that common in a man with Caucasian looks. Irish, yes. Indian, yes. Pakistani, yes. West Indian, Somalian, Afghan? Yes, all of those. But Caucasian, no.

She said, 'Excuse me a moment . . . the supper . . . be back in a sec.' She had to think. She went out to the kitchen and checked that everything was boiling or roasting or . . . whatever.

She turned the oven down. It was possible she might have to ditch the lot. Her brain had gone into overdrive. It lurched from 'possible' to 'impossible' and back again.

Someone was calling her name. 'Bea!' Sharply.

She started.

William. 'Wakey, wakey. What's got into you? We were making some progress, I thought, and then you storm out, leaving us . . .'

She tuned him out. *Possible, if . . . But then, who was Henry II?*

He snapped his fingers under her nose.

She blinked. 'Don't do that!'

He was not amused. Probably not used to women telling him off. 'Look here, Bea . . .!'

She said, 'Which of them is Henry II?'

'What! Look, Bea, I don't know where you think you're going with this but I've been having second thoughts about allowing Alicia to go off with—'

'Sorry, William. A bit distracted. I want you to watch them when—'

'Watch who? I don't understand what—'

'Alaric and Ninette. I want to know if either of them—'

A shout of alarm. A crash.

Bea said, 'What's going on?'

'Gideon making a nuisance of himself, I suppose.'

It sounded like a minor riot. Voices raised, the sound of a blow?

Bea rushed back in to see an overturned chair and upraised arms. She raged at them. 'I turn my back for five minutes!'

Gideon was on his feet, nose to nose with his brother. Mel was half on and half off the settee.

Gideon's cheek was red this time.

'Oh, for heaven's sake!' said Bea. 'Children! Sit down and behave!'

Gideon shouted, 'He hit me!'

'Yeah, yeah,' said Bea. 'And what did you do to deserve it! Make a pass at his girl? Sit! All of you!' She waited till they'd shamefacedly groped back into their seats.

Bea swung round on Faye, who had ignored the fracas and was now working on her lips. 'Faye, you know this man Giorgio's been talking about. The third electrician?'

'Mm?' The perfect brow wrinkled.

But somewhere in the room a breath of unease stirred the air. Bea wasn't sure where it had originated. She couldn't watch everyone all the time. William had followed her in, but he probably hadn't grasped the importance of what she'd asked him to do.

'Concentrate, Faye. Tall man. Black hair. Works out.'

Faye said, 'Huh?'

'Narrow eyes,' said Bea, crossing fingers and toes that she'd got it right.

Faye's expression went from blank to recognition. 'You mean Neil?'

Someone had made a sharp movement. Who?

'Neil.' Bea repeated the name, checking everyone's faces for a reaction. 'You sent him to me, pretending to be a policeman, trying to screw money out of me to cover your losses on Friday night.'

Faye nodded, pleased. 'It was a good idea, wasn't it? We thought you'd pay up straight away' – a cloud crossing her brow – 'but you didn't.'

'Is he really a policeman?'

'No, silly! Of course not. He's a chauffeur. Has his own limo. Top of the range.'

'What's Neil's surname?'

'Thorough. No, that's not quite right. It's what I call him.' Giggle. Faye tried to engage her brain. The slightest of frowns depressed her perfect eyebrows. She turned to Gideon. 'Tell her. You use him all the time.'

Steve frowned. He'd known the name. He reached for his tablet.

Gideon flushed. 'You mean Neil Thurrock?' Uneasy. Why?

Faye widened her eyes. 'Thurrock. That's it. I told him he should try modelling, but I think maybe he's too old now?' She made it a question.

Bea said, 'How did you meet him?'

'I see him at home, everywhere. Often at Giddy's evenings. Lots of bubbly, and on to a nightclub. I go along to make sure the clients have a good time.' She pouted. 'You needn't all look at me like that. Giddy used Neil and his limo all the time. Or he used to. Something happened, didn't it, Giddy? I asked Neil but he wouldn't say.'

Gideon was terse. 'I don't use him any longer.'

Steve held his tablet up for Mel to read. She took it from him, frowning. Then looked up. 'Is this true, Gideon? Steve says you sacked Neil's father after thirty years with the firm?'

Gideon's colour deepened. 'I did, and yes, he took it badly, threatened to sue . . .!' He was incredulous. 'How dare he! I caught him red-handed with his hand in the till, and he had the nerve to say I'd framed him for the job. Dad always made excuses for him, but he was nothing but a dead weight in the firm, obstructing my ideas, working against me, whispering to people behind my back. I should have got rid of him ages ago. He lost me my biggest sale to date, didn't he? I can't tell you the relief it was to see the last of his sour face.'

Steve shook his head from side to side, fingers flying on his tablet.

William had been hovering in the doorway, but now he came right into the room, picked up the fallen chair, righted it, and sat down. 'Relax, Steve. Let me tell them how it was.'

SEVENTEEN

Sunday evening

William said, 'No, Steve, let me speak. It's about time we put the record straight. Your father and I have been friends since before you were born, and we've shared all our triumphs and disappointments. Our children have intermarried; our businesses have had their ups and downs.'

Gideon raised his eyes to the ceiling. 'Here it comes: tell me the old, old story of how you two dinosaurs refuse to step into the modern world—'

Steve made a sudden, violent movement. Mel calmed him with a hand on his arm and a smile.

William said, 'It's all right, lad. I know exactly what's been going on. Gideon: you will agree that you and Steve are as different as chalk from cheese. Your father knew that, and tried to help you both to develop according to your characters. Steve took over the Maintenance Division, while you, Gideon, were handed the Sales branch.'

Gideon huffed, 'Steve would have been less than useless in Sales, whereas I . . . you only have to look at the turnover to see what can be done by someone with a flair for it.'

'Turnover is one thing,' said William. 'Profit is another. Your idea was to spend lavishly to attract the wealthiest of buyers with holidays, trips on chartered yachts, suites at the Dorchester, provision of girls, entry to the most exclusive of nightclubs and tickets to sold-out concerts.'

Gideon chuckled. 'I know how to do it in style, don't I?'

'It's one way of doing it, certainly, though not your father's way. Nor mine. However, you miscalculated—'

'Nonsense!'

'The wealthy don't object to being wooed, but are usually canny with their money. If what is on offer amuses them, they take the bait, but don't necessarily follow through with a purchase. For the last two years you have made a thumping loss, and for the five years before that you only made the slenderest of profits. Your father carried your losses but knew he couldn't do so for ever. He foresaw that if you continued to spend money without making the sales, you would bring the company down. He did try to talk to you about it, didn't he?'

Gideon puffed out his cheeks. 'Poor old Dad. Still living in the past. He couldn't understand that nowadays you have to invest in order to prosper.'

William sighed. 'He knew he'd always been weak where you were concerned. He wanted to save you from yourself, so he asked Steve to let the Maintenance Department's own office manager, Cecil Thurrock, move to Sales. He hoped Cecil would be able to act as a brake on your spending. Cecil had been due to retire and was reluctant to go . . . wasn't he, Steve?'

Steve nodded violently.

William sighed. 'Gideon, if only you'd listened to Cecil, who—'

'Listen to that marionette, who only danced to my father's tune? He hadn't a clue about how to run a Sales Department. He came to work in a suit, for heaven's sake, complaining about the hotel bills, or the limousine or . . . anything and everything. He'd say, "Mr Gideon, you can't do this," and "Your father wouldn't like you to do that!" I tell you, when I saw his yellow face come round the door, it used to give me heartburn!'

'Perhaps it was a mistake to ask him to work for you—'

'He obstructed me in every way!'

William shook his head. 'He could read the writing on the wall quicker than most. He told your father how much you proposed to spend on a weekend on a yacht with girls in tow in order to persuade a client to buy a penthouse suite in Knightsbridge—'

'It would have been money well spent if my father hadn't nixed the deal. I could have strangled the little—'

'But you did, didn't you? Well, not physically strangled. You trumped up some excuse to give him the sack—'

'He walked off with my iPad—'

'Which found its way somehow into his briefcase while he was out for lunch—'

'He meant to take it home with him, to extract information which he could sell to our competitors—'

'That's nonsense,' said William, 'and you know it.'

Gideon reddened. 'How dare you call me a liar!'

'Cecil would never, ever, have stolen from you. You arranged the theft to give you an excuse to sack him. When he got back from lunch you told him to clear his desk and leave, or you'd report him to the police. You said he could kiss goodbye to his company pension. He was shattered. He couldn't believe what had happened. He went home and died that night.'

Gideon moved uneasily in his chair. 'More fool him. I suppose my father and Steve would have come up with something to ease his way into retirement—'

'The shame of it! That good old man, who'd worked for the firm for so many years, accused of a crime which he hadn't committed. And when his son Neil confronted you about it—'

'When he forced his way into my office and threatened me—'

'You told him you wouldn't be using him any more and he should vacate his flat and the one his father rented from the business . . . which meant that, as he was a freelance, his future looked bleak, too.'

Steve blundered over to the window. He put his hands on the glass and leaned against the pane, his head bowed.

Everyone turned to look at him. Mel said, 'Steve, what is it?'

He swung his head from side to side.

Mel went to him. 'Steve? Tell me.'

He mouthed something.

She said, 'You're guilty? What do you mean, guilty?'

He grasped her wrist, trying to speak. Mel did her best to follow what he was trying to tell her. 'You went to see Cecil that night, after he got the sack? Right? Well, that's good, isn't it?'

Steve was shaking his head violently. She handed him his tablet and he bent over it, fingers flying.

Mel read it out. 'He wanted job back. Dad told me to say "No". Time he retired.'

Steve nodded, hard, and continued to type.

Mel read out. 'I was supposed to say pension OK. Cecil too tired to talk. Told me to go. I didn't tell him. He died that night. Guilty.'

William said, 'You did your best, boy. You couldn't have known Cecil would have a stroke before you had a chance to put things right. His death affected Josh, too. All those years he'd spent making excuses for Gideon, always hoping that next time the boy would come up trumps. Poor old Josh. No wonder he decided to take precautions to safeguard the future of the business.'

Those words sank like lead into silence.

'You mean . . .? What do you mean?' Gideon lost all his colour. 'My father would never have done anything to hurt me.'

Bea guessed, 'Josh changed his will? Someone said something about Josh remaking his will every so often, and getting Daphne to do so as well. Is that true?'

Giorgio, who'd been sitting there with his mouth open, trying to follow the conversation, now stirred in his seat. 'Daphne gave me the car. She did. It was a gift. And my flat.' His voice trailed away because no one was taking any interest in what he said.

Faye's mouth was also open. 'You mean, he cut Giddy off without a penny?'

'He can't have done!' Gideon passed his tongue over his lips. 'He can't, anyway. I'm the sales director. I occupy the ground and first floors at our head office. I employ twenty or so members of staff. Do you know how much per square foot that's worth in today's money?'

William said, 'Josh transferred the freehold of the building to a limited company. Steve has forty-five per cent of the shares, I have a few, and the rest are held in trust for Alicia. The Maintenance Department has always paid its way, but you haven't. Your father's idea was that if you reorganized your business and started to pay a market rent, then you could stay. But if not, you would have to leave. Even if Steve were agreeable to your staying rent-free, he couldn't do so, because the rest of us can outvote him. Your father ought to have told you what he intended to do, but he put it off. He was always hoping you'd see sense.'

'What!' Gideon shot out of his seat. 'He can't have done that! Anyway, Steve, you wouldn't turn me out! I couldn't survive!'

Steve lifted his hands in the air. In defeat.

Gideon turned on William. 'Who are Alicia's trustees? They'll see me right.'

William managed a small, tired smile. 'A firm of solicitors who can neither be bribed or bought. They will look after her interests and take their cut. They are currently assessing how much the property should be let for in the event that you fail to pay your share of the rent. It may be that Steve himself will be advised to find new premises which are somewhat cheaper, but we all know he'll manage to pay his way.'

Gideon gaped. 'But I need offices in the right part of town! How can I attract customers if I'm working out of a hole in the wall?'

Yes, exactly.

Alaric clicked a gold lighter. On. Off. Face wooden.

Ninette however, couldn't sit still. 'But if Gideon goes out of business, what about me? My party business depends on a whole raft of clients, of course it does. I'm doing very well, of course I am, but without the work he puts my way . . .'

Party organizer. Limousines. Neil Thurrock. Faye.

Connection?

Bea held up her hand. 'Just a thought. Parking has become an increasingly difficult matter in London. Many people are leaving their cars at home and using a cab if they go out for the evening. How many of you regularly used Neil Thurrock as chauffeur?'

William said, 'Josh has been driving himself less and less recently. He didn't want to use a black cab. He told me he's been using a local man with a car. Was that Neil Thurrock, Cecil's son? Keeping it in the family, so to speak?'

Steve nodded. Mouthed, 'Yes.'

Bea said, 'I wonder . . .? Does anyone have a picture of him?'

Faye said, 'He's on Facebook.'

Steve scrabbled on his tablet, relaxed into a smile and held a picture up.

Mel peered over Steve's shoulder to say, 'Neil Thurrock's on Facebook advertising himself and his limo. There's pictures of him on a motorbike, too. I wouldn't know him from Adam, but . . . shall I pass this around?'

Bea almost snatched the tablet from Mel. Yes, this was the man who'd visited her, posing as a policeman. She said, 'This is the man who visited me, pretending to be from the police, trying to make me pay for Faye's pearls. Giorgio?' She handed the picture over to him. 'Giorgio, did the third electrician working at Josh's house look like this man?'

A blank look. 'Dunno. Might have. I didn't notice, did I?'

Gideon took the tablet off Giorgio. 'Yes, that's him. I used him all the time for entertainment, tax deductible of course. As a chauffeur. Not socially, of course.'

Bea homed in on Faye, who was concentrating on teasing out her hair. 'You knew him very well, Faye, or you wouldn't have sent him to me to ask for money. How intimate were you?'

'Hunh? Oh, not *that* way. Well, only occasionally. I had to be careful because we both knew Giddy wouldn't like it if he was spending time with me. Yeah, we saw one another all the time, living in the same building, and him being handy with a screwdriver if the electrics went wrong or anything.' She looked around. 'What are you all looking at me like that for?'

'You live in the same building?' Bea was incredulous. Hadn't the girl any idea at all about, well . . . anything?

'Sure. Why not? Giddy arranged for me to rent a studio flat for free, in one of the company's properties. Old Man Thurrock had the ground-floor flat, and Neil had the basement, where he kept the limo and his motorbike and all. He was mad about that car. He was at it, polishing, cleaning, every day. Giddy's old man had pretty well given up driving, so Neil usually took him to and from work. Me, too.'

She looked around blankly. 'But you knew I work part-time for Giddy? When he needs extra, and when his receptionist is off in the evenings, that sort of thing. I don't touch his computer, because she, his receptionist, proper old dragon, said she'd cut me off with a squeak if I did. So I don't. Except for Facebook, of course.'

William was open-mouthed. 'You work for Gideon? And so does Neil? Gideon, is that true?'

'Why not?' Gideon was abrupt.

Faye nodded. 'Almost nine months, now.' She concentrated on painting colour on to her eyelids.

Bea handed the tablet to Ninette. 'You employed him in your party business. How well did you know him?'

Ninette was caught up in a censorship battle, not knowing what to admit or deny. She shot a glance at Alaric, who looked boot-faced as usual. No help there. 'Well, yes, I knew him. On a strictly employer and employee basis. He was a competent chauffeur and kept his limo spotless. He was always on time. What's not to like?'

Faye put the boot in. 'But you sampled what else he had to offer, didn't you? You think I didn't know what it meant when you made him go back for you after he'd taken me and the clients back home?'

Alaric clicked his lighter on again, and lit his cheroot. He'd heard. Had he understood what Faye meant? Yes, of course he had.

Bea said, 'Alaric, I have already asked you not to smoke here. If you don't put your cheroot out, I shall have a short-sighted moment, assume you're on fire and dowse you with a jug of water.'

Alaric ground out his cheroot and got to his feet. 'Well, I'd best be going then. Ninette, I'll speak to you later.' He turned away from Ninette. He was shedding Ninette because she'd granted favours to Neil? Did he no longer consider that Ninette was a suitable partner?

Ninette jumped up and pawed at Alaric's arm. 'Don't go yet. Not without Alicia. And . . . well, with Neil . . . that wasn't anything, you know. Faye is making far too much of it. She's jealous, I suppose.'

That stung Faye into action. 'Of you? That's rich! Neil told me every time he had it off with you in the back of his car. We used to laugh about it. I mean, you really are a bit old for him!'

Ninette went a sickly pale. And yes, they could all see for the first time that she was mutton dressed as lamb. Late thirties or even early forties, trying to look twenty-five?

Bea's eyes were on Alaric, who was so very, very hard to read. She said, 'Alaric, I really don't understand why you want to hang on to Alicia. She was costing you a lot in school fees and you can't pretend you feel for her as a father should. Why not let her go?'

Ninette lost it completely. 'Can't you see why? Oh, in the old days he wanted to be rid of her because he had to pay her school fees, or as much of them as Daphne couldn't manage, and she threw money around like water, so he often did have to come up with the readies when she discovered a hole in her finances which, let me tell you, was far oftener than he expected when he married her, but now is different. He's Alicia's next of kin now. Can't you see that – with Josh and Daphne dead – Alicia inherits the lot, which means that Alaric will be able to use her money to keep himself going!'

Alaric back-handed her. 'Shut it! Slut!'

Ninette fell back into her chair. Spurting tears of humiliation and rage, she screamed, 'I'm not a slut! And if they can't work it out, I can! If the girl dies, you inherit the lot!'

Bea was appalled. She'd suspected . . . no, she'd half thought and dismissed the idea. She looked around to see what reaction the others had had.

William's eyes narrowed. He'd worked it out, too.

Heavy breathing and rounded eyes from everyone else.

Except Steve, who clambered to his feet, took aim . . . and knocked Alaric into the fireplace! Where he lay, too shocked to move.

Someone cheered. Bea thought it might have been herself.

A sense of satisfaction spread through the room.

Steve nursed a bruised fist. Mel put her arms around him and drew him back to the settee. Kissing him, wherever she could reach. 'Oh, Steve! You are wonderful!'

Ninette gave a little hiccup. 'Oh!' Was she smiling? Yes, she was. She wasn't displeased to see Alaric take some punishment.

William stepped over to the fireplace, reached down and jerked Alaric to his feet. William was breathing hard. He was going to hit Alaric, too?

'No, William!' Bea caught his arm. She could feel him stiffen under her hand, but then, slowly, he relaxed his hold on Alaric.

Alaric slumped to the floor with one hand to his jaw. His hair had been ruffled, and so had his dignity. 'I'll sue the lot of you!' He spoke indistinctly. Perhaps Steve had loosened a tooth or two?

'No, you won't, Alaric,' said Bea, 'because this stops right here. Sit down, everyone who's standing. William, sit! Alaric, back in your chair! Ninette, shut it!'

Heavy breathing. Slowly, they resumed their seats. Even Alaric.

Bea fixed them with a beady eye. 'Now that we've uncovered some of the poison that's been circulating, we can work out precisely what each of you did to bring about the tragedy on Friday night. And then perhaps we can think up a solution to the case which may avoid criminal proceedings. Yes, Alaric, I said "criminal proceedings". So shut up and listen.'

Alaric mumbled something, hand clasped to jaw.

Bea cut him off with a gesture. 'Let's see if I've got it right. Some time ago Josh became disillusioned with Gideon's business practices. Josh had always taken his eldest son Steve for granted, but had come to appreciate him more when Steve moved back home to look after his father. Josh was anxious for the future of his granddaughter and worried about his daughter Daphne, who spent money like water, and who was about to link up with a young man who didn't give a toss about Alicia . . . No, Giorgio: you can't make us believe you loved the child. You were far too young to take her on.'

Giorgio shrugged, then nodded agreement. 'Yeah, maybe. Though I'd have tried, you know.'

Perhaps he would.

Bea continued, 'Meanwhile Alaric – who had formally adopted Alicia when married to Daphne – was feeling the pinch financially as she wasn't the cash cow he'd thought she'd be, plus he would have to go on contributing to Alicia's school fees, even after the divorce went through. Also, he'd collected Ninette who didn't fancy taking on a stepdaughter. So far so good? Yes, everyone?'

Everyone nodded, some with reluctance.

Bea said, 'Acting with the best of intentions, Josh asked Steve to let his office manager, Cecil Thurrock, transfer to Gideon's department. Cecil did so, and confirmed Josh's worse fears. Gideon sacked Cecil on a trumped-up charge. Josh failed to confront Gideon, and Steve failed to reassure Cecil that he'd still get his pension. Cecil died, and his son Neil – who was already working for most of the personnel concerned – confronted Gideon, who sacked him as well and told him to vacate his flat.

'Now we have to think how Neil would take this. I imagine that he seethed with rage. How dare they treat him and his father like that! He wanted to hurt the family as he had been hurt. He wanted revenge and he was well placed for that, wasn't he? He knew all the family secrets from his father, who'd worked for Josh for thirty years. He knew Faye because they lived in the same building and because she worked for Gideon. He knew Ninette because she employed him in her capacity as party organizer for Gideon. He listened to the family's phone calls and conversations while he was driving them around. He listened to the tittle-tattle which Ninette and Faye fed him. He knew who was doing what, when, why and to whom. He was an angry time bomb, primed with background information, waiting for someone to light the fuse.'

She swung round on Alaric. 'You supplied the match, didn't you? You knew Ninette was on good terms with Neil. You heard from Ninette how badly Neil had been treated, and how angry he was. And one day, struggling with a mountain of bills, you said, "Who will rid me of this turbulent priest?" Or, in other words, "How wonderful it would be if Alicia were to meet with an accident, and then I wouldn't have to find the money for her school fees!"'

Alaric laughed in her face. 'Prove it!' And then said, 'Ouch!' and put his hand back to his jaw.

Bea said, 'Ninette?'

Ninette shrugged. 'I suppose. Yes, something like that.'

'And you told Neil, half in jest.'

Another shrug from Ninette. 'I might have. I thought he'd be interested. He was always interested in bits of gossip about my clients. I told him in confidence, of course.'

'Ninette, you told him with malice aforethought because you knew Neil was furiously angry with the family already and you didn't want to have to look after a ten-year-old child. Alaric lit the match, and you applied it to the fuse.'

'Nonsense.' With a flounce. But then she chewed her lip.

Bea said, 'All right. Let's move on. How did Neil hear about the problem at Josh's house with the electrics?'

Ninette said, hesitantly, 'Oh, that? Josh asked Neil if he knew of anyone. Neil asked me if he should volunteer to look at the problem because he's good with his hands, but he wasn't qualified to tackle such a big job. I gave him the address of the electrical firm we'd used in my office building. And he told Josh.'

'Josh contacted the firm you recommended, and gave them the work. Finally, Neil heard about the party Josh was arranging for his granddaughter and her little friend from – well, it could have been from Josh, or Faye, or Ninette.'

Faye spoke up. 'We were all invited. We all knew. We all heard the fuss the kids were making about fireworks, and I suppose I did tell Neil, just casually, not thinking . . . And Neil asked me if I needed him that night, and I said "No", because Giddy was taking me . . . only when my pearls got broken, Giddy abandoned me! He left me there, in the dark!' She produced a realistic sob.

'So there it was,' said Bea. 'Not just one but every member of the family and their past and present girlfriends were all going to be there that night. What a stroke of luck! Neil found out which days the official electricians were working at the house, and which they weren't. He went in to suss the place out. Working so much for Josh, Mrs Frost would have let him in, and not thought anything of it. If challenged, he could say

he'd been sent to pick up a coat which Josh had forgotten . . .
but I doubt if he were ever challenged. He was seen by Giorgio
and probably also by Daphne, but it never occurred to either
of them that he wasn't kosher. Faye says he was clever with
electrics. He bought and sabotaged a box of indoor fireworks,
which he was pretty sure the children would want to set off
that night. On the afternoon of the party, he entered the house
for one last time, to add the box of fireworks to the children's
presents, and to set the timers in the kitchen, in the dining
room and on the top landing. Then he walked out and went
about his business. He was not going to be anywhere near
when the fires started. And what was more, *no one at the table
knew that anything was going to happen, and behaved innocently when it did!*'

'That's right,' said Faye, and shuddered. 'I was shattered,
wasn't I! I told him, I . . . What are you all looking at me like
that for?'

'You told him . . . what?' said Bea. 'And, when? Ah, I've
got it. You called all sorts of people asking for a lift home
after the fire. Was Neil one of those you called?'

'What if it was? He knew I was out at a party, but he's
chauffeured Giddy around long enough to know that I can be
ready for bed long before him, and he rang me – or I rang
him, I can't remember – to ask if he were free and he came
and fetched me and took me home, and why shouldn't he?'

'When he'd been the one to cause the fire in the first
place!'

'No, no,' said Faye, biting her lip and squinting. Trying
to think straight. 'I'm sure he wouldn't have. Though of
course he was very cross with Giddy and Steve and, well,
all of the family. But he wouldn't . . . no, really, that's going
too far.'

'Don't you see?' said Bea. 'He didn't care if the children
took the fireworks up to their room or not. His aim was to
hurt as many people as possible. If he got Alicia, then Josh
would lose his beloved grandchild, as Neil had lost his father.
If the fireworks went off in the drawing room while we were
at dinner, then fire would engulf the ground floor and, Faye,
we would all be in danger . . . you included!'

Faye flushed. 'I don't believe it. He wouldn't have done that to me.'

'And you told him all about the fire in the dining room and how Daphne and Josh had been taken off to hospital, but that the children had been rescued. You told him that that horrid Mrs Abbot had forced you to abandon your search for the pearls and how you wished someone would take the woman down a peg. He realized that his revenge on the family was incomplete. That's why he came to see me the next day, to try a little gentle blackmail and to find out what had happened to the survivors from the fire. Which he did, more or less. And so, he lived to plot another day.'

Faye's face crumpled in a bout of childish tears. Bea handed her the box of tissues.

Alaric was concentrating on building his own defence. 'It's clear the man was holding a grudge against Gideon. You can't blame any of this on me. I knew nothing. And I am appalled, yes, appalled, that you should think I would begrudge paying my daughter's school fees.'

Ninette tossed her head. 'I don't mind telling the police what you said, more than once, calling the child retarded, and wondering why you'd ever been so stupid as to adopt her.'

Alaric rounded on Ninette. 'You didn't want her around. Admit it! You were always whining, saying she was in the way, wanting me to get rid of her—'

Ninette shouted, 'You should have let her grandfather take her! Then none of this would have happened.'

'Well, I would have, eventually, if he'd agreed to refund the cost of her school fees. She'd cost me a small fortune in the years Daphne and I were together. Daphne shopped in Paris and left me to pick up the tab for the child's expenses. But he,' glaring at William, 'was too mean to cough up.'

'What was that?' said Bea.

William reddened. 'I . . . yes, he did make some stupid suggestion . . . but I turned him down. He said he'd not fight for custody if I paid him back all the money he'd expended on Alicia to date. It would have been like buying the child. Naturally, I refused.'

'It was a fair offer,' said Alaric. 'You could have asked Josh to help you out. He was as crazy about the child as you were.'

'I did discuss it with him, yes. But we decided we shouldn't play. Ethically, it was all wrong. Also, Josh was strapped for cash like me. His business was running at a loss and Daphne's extravagance had caught him on the hop.'

Bea said, 'Alaric, why don't you cut your losses now, and let William have custody of a child you don't care about?'

He grinned, relishing the ace in his hand. 'This threat to her has made me realize how much she means to me. I am her father. I don't mind paying her school fees.'

His unctuous tone set Bea's teeth on edge. She said, 'That's very noble of you, since she's going to be a very wealthy little girl, and I suppose you are already working out how to persuade her trustees to let you control her income. However, if I tell her trustees and the police what Ninette recollects of your attitude to the child, they will certainly be looking very hard at your motives for getting rid of her.'

A shrug. 'They wouldn't believe Ninette, anyway. A party girl, for hire!'

Ninette grinned. 'Try me! You ditch me, and my memory will become a hundred per cent certain that you put Neil up to murdering the girl.'

'Alternatively,' said Bea, in her creamiest of tones, 'you agree to let William have custody of his granddaughter, without trying to recover past fees. Come; that's a decent offer. Off with the old. Face the future without ties.'

'That's blackmail,' Alaric said, dabbing at his chin. 'I don't give in to blackmail.' There was a trickle of blood at the corner of his mouth, hooray.

'It's an arrangement to suit all parties,' said Bea. 'We tell the fire investigator everything we've learned about Neil. Neil will be arrested but put forward a good defence. He hasn't killed anybody, except by accident. The deaths of Josh, Daphne and Mrs Frost can all be put down to man- or woman-slaughter. Does everyone agree that that will be justice?'

'I don't,' said Alaric, dabbing at his mouth.

'Everyone else does,' said William.

And that was when Bea realized what she'd done. She shot to her feet. 'Leon's own chauffeur is on holiday. Who . . . he wouldn't be using Neil, would he? Because, if so . . . Alicia is in the car with him at this moment!'

Alaric fell back in his chair, laughing. 'I don't believe it! Missus Know-all has put them all in danger!'

EIGHTEEN

William caught Bea's arm. 'You can't have sent Alicia off in a car with Neil as chauffeur!'

'Calm down,' said Bea, trying not to panic. 'It might not be him driving them. Leon might be using any old car firm.'

Steve was at his tablet again. Mel read out, 'Josh recommended Neil to everyone.'

William said, 'You've got to stop them!'

'How? If I ring Leon, what will he do? Order his chauffeur to let them out on the side of the motorway? Suppose it's not Neil? And if it were Neil, well, he might obey . . . if he's no further plans to destroy Alicia. But suppose he does still want to get back at the family . . . would he obey?'

William put his hand to his head. 'But if it is Neil! Do you think he still wishes her harm, after everything that's happened? Surely not.'

Bea said, 'It might not be him who—'

Faye was amused. 'I suppose he could poison them, with bottles of soft drinks left in the back for them to take, or biscuits that he's doctored?'

William made a dismissive gesture. He didn't want to hear that.

Faye continued, 'He wouldn't crash the car, would he? Out of spite? Hoping to kill his passengers and leave himself unscathed? No, no. He might be injured himself if he tried that.'

Everyone was on their feet except for Alaric, who continued to lie back in his chair, grinning.

To do her credit, Ninette was as worried as everyone else. She said, 'Would Neil care about getting hurt himself? I don't think he would, he's so bitter against the family. He might fake an accident, and set the car on fire?'

William strode up and down. 'He could have booby-trapped

the car already. He could set off a fire, and walk away on some pretext, getting petrol, perhaps, or buying sweets for the children—'

Bea said, 'He wouldn't risk his own life, would he?'

'No, surely not.' William couldn't accept that idea.

'Yes,' said Ninette, frowning. 'I don't want to think so, but yes . . . I really think he might.'

Faye's eyes were huge. She was high on excitement. 'You don't understand him, any of you! He's been so hurt!'

William pounded one fist against the other. 'Let's get the police to stop the car!'

'I suppose so,' said Gideon, showing anxiety for his niece for the first time. 'This has gone beyond a joke.'

Steve nodded, eyes wild. His arm went round Mel, and hers around him.

Bea said, 'Let's not jump to conclusions. It might not be Neil driving. Let's first of all find out if he really is the chauffeur.' She got out her phone, and hesitated. 'If it is Neil driving, we don't want to alert him to the fact that we've worked it out that he caused the fires. If he thinks the police are after him, he might panic. He might even crash the car, not caring what happens to him.'

Tears stood out on Faye's eyelashes. 'Neil's not a bad man. He isn't!' She wrung her hands, prettily.

William ordered Bea, 'Ring Leon. Tell him to stop the car!'

Bea tried to think. 'Leon knows nothing of the background to this case. He would need endless explanations, which would alert Neil to what we've worked out, and precipitate the very act of revenge that we're trying to prevent. I have a better idea. Hari's in the car with them, and he's quick on the uptake. I'll try him first. But, let me think! I must phrase my questions in such a way that Hari replies without alarming Neil.'

William got out his own phone. 'I don't care what you say. I'm ringing the police.'

'Don't! At least, not until we know if it's Neil in the car or not. It might be a plump, fifty-year-old baldie who isn't a threat to anyone. Let me speak to Hari first.'

She dialled Hari. 'Hari, this is Bea! Trouble! I'm going to ask you some questions to which you should answer yes or no, while pretending to discuss what we're having for supper. Say hello to the children and Leon for me, will you? And smile.'

She heard Hari say, 'Hi, kids! Bea's on the phone. Wants to know if you'll be back in time for supper or not.' Murmurs in the background. Bea heard Leon say, 'Tell her we're stuck in traffic and the children are watching a video.'

'I heard that,' said Bea. 'Tell me, Hari: are you sitting in front with the chauffeur, and do you like salad with your meal?'

'Yes, I love salad. Why would you need to ask?'

'Is your chauffeur called Neil, black hair, looks fit, narrow eyes? Do you like cucumber with your salad?'

'Yes, of course I like cucumber.'

So Neil was the chauffeur.

Bea signalled to William, mouthing, 'Yes!' She returned to her phone. 'Is it an open car, no division between the front seats and the passengers? Tomatoes as well?'

'Yes, I'm heavily into tomatoes. Bernice, do you like tomatoes? . . . She says she likes tomatoes, but Alicia . . . she's pretty well worn out, poor kid.'

Bea was alarmed. 'Did Neil give her anything to eat or drink?'

'No, nothing like that. She's just worn out . . . aren't you, poppet?'

'He can hear everything you say?'

'Yes, and onions, too.'

'Is everyone wearing seat belts? In case of a car crash. What about peppers in the salad?'

'No, peppers are an acquired taste.'

So they weren't wearing seat belts. They ought to be. In those big limos, they'd be thrown around like dried peas in a tin if the car crashed.

'Listen carefully. We think Neil was responsible for setting the fires at the house. He holds a grudge against the family because they sacked him and his father. Are you near the airport yet?'

'Oh, it's quite a drag. Traffic, you know. Leon, are we going to be late, do you think?' A muttered conversation. 'Leon thinks it will be a close-run thing. His sister's plane is on time, but then there's Customs and luggage clearance, so we might make it yet.'

'Is there central locking in the car?'

'Yes, we're all looking forward to our supper. We'll be on our way back as soon as we've collected Sybil.'

'Could Neil get out of the car and lock it so that you couldn't leave?'

'Mm. Probably. But I hope we won't be that late.'

'I'll speak to Leon on the other line in a moment. The best scenario is that when Neil drops you at the airport, you collect Sybil and get another car to bring you back. Should I keep some hot food on the go for you?'

'Hot food sounds even better than salads. I'll give you a bell when we're on our way back. The traffic is heavy . . .' There was a muttered conversation which Bea couldn't hear properly. Then Hari was back. 'The chauffeur says he knows a short cut. Leon thinks it a good idea. Back roads. You know?'

'Red alert, Hari. If he dumps the car with you all in it and it goes up in flames—'

'Gotcha. I'll keep you updated. We're turning off the motorway now. *Ciao.*'

William was practically dancing with agony. Bea held up her hand and then put her finger to her lips, holding her other hand over the mouthpiece of her phone.

Gideon and the rest were all agog. Ninette whispered, 'Hari's not broken the connection? He's still on the phone?'

Bea nodded, putting her finger to her mouth to signal that they keep quiet.

William mimed going out to the kitchen, and disappeared. To ring the police?

Bea beckoned to Mel. Murmured, 'Get the licence number of Neil's car from his pictures on Facebook. Give it to William.'

'What?' said Gideon who, as usual, was slow to catch on.

Steve worked on his tablet. Faye was interested enough to get up and look over their shoulders. Ninette snapped her fingers. 'I ought to know it . . .'

Steve held up his tablet, shaking his head. Mel said, 'You can't see it properly.'

Faye reached for the tablet. 'I think it's . . .' She typed. Frowned at the number, handed the tablet to Ninette . . . who also frowned, changed one digit and nodded.

Mel took the tablet off to the kitchen with Steve following. They would ring the police . . . who might or might not be in time to intercept Neil before he did . . . whatever . . . and it was always possible that he had no plans to hurt anyone any more. In which case everyone was going to look extremely foolish.

Bea told herself to relax. And failed.

She prayed. *Lord, have mercy; Lord have mercy . . . look after the children . . . look after Leon, who is completely unaware of what's happening . . . I can't think how to alert him without advising Neil that we're on to him. Think, Bea! Pray!*

She could hear the murmur of voices inside the limousine. Bernice asking permission to change the DVD on the television set in the car?

The thrum of the powerful car, a smooth ride, going through the countryside taking back lanes to the airport.

Back lanes meant little traffic. The police would have difficulty finding them if they took back lanes.

Bea held the phone to her ear, while continuing to cover the mouthpiece with her hand. If Neil heard noises from her end, he'd understand that his cover was blown and he might act . . . how would he act? What was he planning? Was his suggestion to turn off the motorway meant to get them to the airport more speedily, or was it to take them away from other traffic so that he could finish off his passengers without having any witnesses. He was good with timers and rockets, he could set the car on fire and jump out, leave everyone to burn.

Neil wouldn't have agreed to chauffeur the girls today if he hadn't planned something for them. Or would he? Perhaps he felt he had done enough to avenge his father and the rotten way Gideon had treated him? Perhaps.

Don't take chances with their lives, Bea.

Think, Bea! Think!

Pray, Bea! Pray.

Driven to action, Gideon and the girls had followed Steve

and William out to the kitchen to ring the police. Alaric remained. Watching her. Cat and mouse.

But, who was the mouse? Alaric or Bea?

And what did the cat have to gain by sticking around? Ah, if Alicia died in the car, then Alaric, as her father, would inherit a nice little fortune. He was going to hang around till he discovered what the future would hold for him . . . penury or a prince's ransom.

In the kitchen they were keeping their voices down. Good.

In the car, Leon was telling Bernice how to change the DVD, although it seemed likely to Bea that the child would know how to do it herself. Alicia seemed to be . . . snoring? Lightly. Had she been doped? What had she eaten or drunk lately? Had Neil left some crisps or lemonade in the car, which he'd adulterated with poison? Ought the child to be on her way to hospital instead of to the airport?

No, Neil's weapon of choice was not poison, but fire, so she was probably just worn out. Hopefully.

Oh, dear Lord! Please look after her . . .

Hari was humming a tune. Bea couldn't place it.

Mel came out of the kitchen, eyes wide, trying to ask a question?

Bea showed the girl that she'd covered the mouthpiece of the phone. 'What is it?' keeping her own voice low, just in case.

Mel murmured the words. 'The police think we're hoaxing them. Won't take William seriously. I've turned off the oven. Everything's cooked. We can heat it up later.'

Bea nodded. Held out her phone to Mel. 'Can you hold my phone, covering the mouthpiece, while I ring Leon on the landline? Hari's humming a tune. I can't recognize it. It may be important.'

Mel took over Bea's phone.

Bea rang Leon's mobile from the landline. 'Leon, my dear; Hari tells me you're running late. Are you planning to bring Sybil back here with you? In which case we can all have supper together. What do you think?'

'Good idea. I'll put it to her when we meet up.' He was relaxed.

Bea could hear the thrum of the car, on a steady forty miles per hour?

What was Neil planning? Or perhaps they'd got it all wrong and he wasn't planning anything?

Bea said, 'What about your chauffeur. Do you usually feed him after a long session? Would he like to join us, perhaps, when you get back?'

Leon wasn't a snob, exactly, but she didn't think he would normally invite his chauffeur to share a dish with him. She was snatching at straws. If Leon passed on the suggestion and Neil accepted it, then he might not carry through whatever plan he had in mind for the car. He might decide to postpone whatever he'd planned for Alicia so that he could pot more than one bird at a time.

Leon laughed, a little surprised, a little annoyed. 'I think he'd rather get off home at the end of a long day. Good of you to ask.' She could hear him mentally chalking one up against her for the suggestion. *Not* what Sir Leon Holland expected of his friends.

Mel was making gestures to Bea, who said, 'See you later, then!' and cut off the call to Leon.

Mel whispered, 'Hari's singing, "Short of petrol" to the tune of "Baa Baa Black Sheep"!'

The two women stared at one another. Bea whispered, 'Neil's planning to stop in a back lane somewhere . . .? He'll leave the car to get a can of petrol from the boot . . .?'

Mel whispered, too, 'Locking them in?'

Bea wanted to scream, but refrained – with an effort. 'And then the car bursts into flames?'

Mel nodded. Big eyes.

Bea made up her mind. 'Hari's there. He knows what to do. I'll try to warn Leon, though I realize he might not listen.' She pressed the number for Leon again. 'Leon, a problem. Don't panic. Follow Hari's lead. Your chauffeur today is the man who set the fires the other night. He's holding a grudge against Josh and his entire family – including Alicia.'

'What!' He was amused, rather than worried.

She'd *known* he'd be slow on the uptake! 'I'm serious, Leon. He doesn't care who he hurts. You, or Alicia or himself!'

'Ridiculous! Honestly, Bea! What will you think of next!'
And he cut the connection.

Bea stared at Mel, and Mel stared back. Eyes wide, breathing
rapid.

What next?

Pray!

Bea reached forward and took her mobile from Mel. Hari
was the last resort. 'Hari, I tried to warn Leon. He won't listen
and the police think we're mad.'

'Roger. We're going through some pretty back lanes. Not
another car in sight.'

'Perfect for an ambush, you'd say?'

'Do you want me to take action?'

Hari was perfectly capable of disabling Neil, but in the
process the car might run out of control and crash, injuring
the passengers. If only Leon had listened to Bea . . . if only the
passengers had all been belted up . . . but they weren't. So,
no. They couldn't take that route.

Bea said, 'Last resort. Get ready to grab the girls and
abandon ship. I'm going to speak to Neil direct, tell him we
know what he's done and suggest he surrenders. It's a long
shot but it might work. Would you hold this phone up so that
he can hear me?'

On the phone Bea heard Hari say, 'Mrs Abbot wants to
speak to you, Neil.'

Which gave away that Hari knew who Neil was and what
he'd done.

The pace of the car didn't slow.

'Yes, Mrs Abbot?' Neil's voice. The voice of the pseudo-
policeman who'd visited her the previous day. The voice of a
man who'd killed by misadventure.

'Neil, we've worked out that it was you who set the fires
on Friday evening, and why. You haven't murdered anyone.
We understand your reasons for what you did.'

Silence, except for the smooth purr of the car.

Bea said, 'You are carrying a precious load in the back of
your car, Neil, none of whom have ever done you any harm.
I don't think you really bear them any malice, do you?'

Again, silence.

'Hari is a trained martial arts instructor. He is in the car with you, sitting beside you, to act as bodyguard to your passengers. Slow down and let your passengers out. After all, you can't be charged with anything but arson at the moment. Not murder. And I believe Steve would spring to employing legal representation for you. He's distressed that your father died before he could reassure him that his work pension was safe.'

Again, nothing. Except . . . did the car's pace begin to slow?

She said, 'You are short of petrol, Hari says. I suppose you have a spare can in the boot?'

Yes, the car was definitely slowing down. The engine sound was changing.

Bea said, 'When the car stops, tell Sir Leon that you have a mechanical problem with the car and let everyone get out to stretch their legs. Sir Leon can phone for another car to take them to the airport. Then you can go to the police and tell them what you've done, without getting any blood on your hands.'

She heard the car slow to a stop.

Neil spoke, 'Sir Leon, we seem to have a technical fault. Would you and the children like to get out to stretch your legs while I see what can be done about it?'

Leon's voice, grumbling. 'We're going to be late picking up my sister.'

Bernice: 'Wake up, sleepyhead. Bring Teddy, he'll like a spot of fresh air.'

A whine from Alicia. 'Must I?'

Doors opening. Doors shutting.

Hari, 'OK, Mrs A. Safely out, all of us.'

Bea said, 'Hari, get them away from the car, now!'

She heard Leon say, 'What? What the—!'

A child shrieked.

The phone crackled.

Whoooomph!

Another shriek, faintly. 'Mummy, Mummy!'

Bea held on to the phone so tightly that her fingers hurt. 'Hari . . .?'

Lord, have mercy. Lord, have mercy!

Heavy breathing. Children, crying.

Hari, calm as always. 'Sorry, I dropped the phone when I grabbed the children. They're all right. A bit muddy. I threw them into the ditch. And the bear is losing an ear. Leon's OK, torn his coat. He landed in the hedge.'

'Neil?'

'He's had it. He detonated charges under his seat and in the back. He's still in the car, burning. I'll switch off now and phone the fire brigade.'

NINETEEN

Sunday evening

Giorgio left, saying he was glad the kids were all right. He probably meant it.

Alaric left, looking grim. Ninette followed him down the street, crying his name. He didn't look round.

Gideon asked Mel if he could give her a lift home. She said 'No, thank you. I'm here to look after the children. And when I'm no longer needed, I'm taking Steve home to introduce him to my family.'

Nice one, Mel!

Gideon went off by himself, not looking at all happy.

Hari arranged for a car to take himself and the children back to Bea's while Leon stayed to do his 'Captain of Industry' act with the police and fire brigade. 'No, I have no idea why my chauffeur should want to blow himself up . . .'

Leon phoned his sister to tell her what had happened, advising her to make her own way home.

Alicia was enveloped by loving arms when she arrived back at Bea's house. Her grandfather and uncle made much of her.

Mel tried to give equal attention to Bernice, but it was clear that Alicia had won her heart.

Bernice was mute. Her eyes looked black against the white of her face. She was still clutching a rather dirty and even ragged Teddy. She rebuffed all Mel's attempts to cuddle her. Mel bore both children off for a bath and to deal with their various scratches and bruises. Being thrown into a ditch hadn't done them much good though, to be fair, Bernice had fallen on Teddy, who had come off even worse than her.

Bea rang Manisa and told her what had happened, concluding, 'They are all going to heap the blame on Neil, who is conveniently dead. Greed and self-delusion are not crimes in the eyes of the law, and I don't think you can prove that any of the others was at fault.'

Manisa said, 'It's protocol to pass a report on to the police in any fire which involves children, and that I will have to do. I shall report that Neil had as good as confessed to setting the fires and that, when the truth came out, he committed suicide. I shall recommend that that verdict is accepted, and in all likelihood the file will be closed. Arson, manslaughter, and suicide.'

'Thank you. Yes, I suppose that is the best we can hope for. You have been most understanding.'

'I recommend you get some therapy for the children; I'll leave you to enjoy the remainder of the day of rest.'

Mel and Steve decided to take the children and some reheated portions of food up to the flat at the top of the house. Alicia refused to walk, and made her grandpa carry her up the stairs. Alicia was relishing physical contact with everyone. Alicia was probably going to come out of this all right, perhaps even a little spoiled.

Bernice? She wouldn't be so lucky. Bea watched the child plod up the stairs carrying the cream-and-ginger-biscuit cake she'd made earlier and trailing Teddy behind her. Would she turn back and ask for a kiss? No way.

Bea decided she wouldn't enquire whether Steve intended to share the single bed on the top floor with Mel that night, or whether she would descend to join him in the spare room on the first floor.

Leon rang a second time, to say he'd been released by the police and was on his way back into London in another chauffeur-driven car. He had convinced himself that it was only his quick thinking that led him to rescue the children from a fiery tomb. But he'd collected a couple of nasty bruises from landing up in the hedge and torn his expensive new cashmere coat, so he was glad enough to go straight to his own home, especially as his sister Sybil was expected there at any minute.

William came down from seeing Alicia cleaned up, working himself into a paddy. 'Alaric is just as guilty as Neil, but he's going to get away with it, mark my words.'

'No, he's not,' said Bea. 'We've all heard Alaric promise to let you have custody of the child. Alaric won't have to pay Alicia's school fees any longer, but he's still in deep doo-doos as far as the upkeep of the estate goes. And I doubt if Ninette is going to be much of a comfort to him in future.'

'I suppose, but the cold-blooded way he would have sold the child to me . . . and Ninette's worse! Fancy saying that my granddaughter wets the bed!'

'I'm sure she'll grow out of it now she's got herself a new family.' Bea thought Ninette would probably come out of it all right, too, even if she lost Alaric, because she would still have her party-organizer business.

'Gideon says he's sure Steve will see sense in the morning, and that there was no way his brother would make him bankrupt. Hah! Well, he's going to have to look round for different premises to rent. I foresee he'll be out of business within the year.'

Bea wondered would it have served any purpose to have Gideon arrested for his duplicity in dealing with the Thurrocks, or for giving the bad news to his father and sister? But what could be proved? Nothing.

Bea prayed, *What should I do, Lord?* And seemed to hear, *Leave it to me.*

Bea wondered if Faye might indeed be able to hang on to Gideon. Perhaps she might, and perhaps not. Either way, Bea thought Faye was a survivor and would recoup the value of her lost pearls one way or another.

Mel and Steve? There was hope for the future there.

'Food?' said William.

'Of course. Masses.' Bea wasn't hungry, but made herself eat.

William had two helpings, which made inroads into the remaining food pile. As the ginger-and-cream cake had disappeared upstairs, they had ice cream for afters.

William sat back as Bea cleared the table. He sighed, replete, and eyed her sideways. 'I suppose you'll want me to toddle off to my hotel now?'

'I'm aching for an early night. You've been just great. We'd never have managed without you.' Which was partially true, and what he needed to hear. What she needed was time to recuperate. And no more complications in her life.

She let him out into the night, and set her back against the door as a firework party started up not far away.

'I'm off fireworks for good,' she said. She turned out the lights, made sure the alarm was set, and plodded up to her room. She had a shower and was just about to crawl into bed when a small, barefoot child appeared in her doorway.

Bernice said, 'Alicia's asleep, and so are Mel and Steve. Teddy can't sleep. His ear hurts.'

The child was white-faced, but tearless.

Bea held back a sigh, told Bernice to pop herself into the big bed and went to fetch her sewing basket. She mended Bear's ear, watched by Bernice.

Bea said, 'Poor Teddy's been through the wars. Can you sew, Bernice? He's so accident prone, he's going to need running repairs.'

'He's not mine. He's yours. He's only on loan to me.'

Bea thought about that. She could give Teddy to Bernice, but would it be right for such an ancient bear to be taken off to boarding school? She said, 'He belongs to you now, but perhaps he is a bit old for school. We could find him a comfortable place to sleep here, and you could visit him in the holidays. Perhaps he can go with us to the shops to choose a younger bear who can go back to school with you, but won't need so much looking after. What do you think?'

A shrug. 'Maybe.'

Bea finished the repair job, and tried to brush some of the mud off the bear. She said, 'Shall we give him another dry-cleaning session tomorrow?'

Bernice didn't reply. She took the bear into her arms, and held him tightly. She closed her eyes. After a while she began to shake.

Delayed shock.

Bea took the child in her arms. A thin arm went round Bea's neck and clung to her with surprising strength. Bea prayed and sang a lullaby, over and over. They shook and shivered together, till eventually Bernice relaxed her hold on Bea and fell asleep.

Bea gave thanks, thanks and yet more thanks. The outcome of the day's events might have been horribly different. And so . . . she gave thanks.

Five days later

Sybil Holland descended upon London like a tornado, whirling people around in her wake. She sorted out the school – Bea wished she'd been a fly on the wall for that! She visited Bernice's mother and stepfather, told Leon to get off his backside and start working on a golf handicap, and arrived at Bea's house as the agency was closing for the day.

Forewarned, Bea opened the door as Sybil alighted from a stretch limo, bony legs wayward under the weight of mink hat and coat, cashmere pashmina, and a scintillation of diamond rings.

Sybil shook herself out, informed the chauffeur that she didn't know how long she'd be, but she expected him to be on call nearby as she was not in the habit of being kept waiting, and demanded he give her his arm to help her up the steps to the front door. Her words were severe but her tone was soft, for her chauffeur for that visit was Hari.

Sybil had bright orange hair this week, with purple eye shadow, false eyelashes and scarlet lipstick and nail varnish. She was dressed to impress in a scarlet two-piece, but Bea noticed that – now Sybil had reached her late eighties – she'd abandoned her high heels for more sensible shoes.

Though, as Bea reflected, there wasn't much else that was sensible about the habits of a cigarette-smoking harridan who could have bought the Tower of London over twice or thrice, with change left for Buckingham Palace.

But oh . . . how grotesquely thin Sybil had become!

Bea's heart beat faster. Sybil was ill? Bea liked and admired Leon's much older sister.

'My young brother Leon,' said Sybil, 'hasn't the sense he was born with. But you'll have worked that out long ago.' She processed into the sitting room on knees that tottered and arranged herself on the settee. 'Hand me an ashtray, will you? I know you don't smoke but you can't expect me to give up the habits of a lifetime. Open a window, if you must . . . but not too far. I feel the cold, here in London. Can't wait to get back to California.'

Bea opened the window a crack and provided the ashtray, without comment.

Yes, Sybil had aged considerably since her last trip to the UK. No application of powder and paint, no amount of Botox could conceal that the hand of death was hovering about her.

Sybil lit a cigarette, and coughed. Lung cancer? 'Leon has suggested giving you some tomfoolery jewellery as a thank-you for saving his and Bernice's life. I have observed you only ever wear two items at a time, usually your pearls and your engagement ring. I have therefore told him to buy you a mews cottage. There is a mews at the end of this street, is there not? It will have a garage for your car, to keep it off the street and safe from vandals. The upstairs rooms you can let out, or use as an extra office, as you see fit.'

Bea's jaw dropped. This was a magnificent gift. Those mews cottages went for princely sums, and a garage in Kensington was beyond price.

'No need to thank me,' said Sybil, grinning. 'It's not me that'll foot the bill. I'm giving you something else. A gift you won't thank me for. One that you'll be cursing me for, endlessly, over the next eight years.'

The hairs prickled down the back of Bea's neck. 'You're giving me Bernice.'

The woman flicked ash on to the carpet. 'You'll say you are too old. And you are. You'll say you're too busy. Which you are. I have discovered the child has never been christened. That omission is to be rectified and you will stand as her godmother.'

Bea took a deep breath, but Sybil forestalled her.

'There are no alternatives, and you know it. Bernice's mother has no sense. Her stepfather is a good man, but out of his depth when it comes to handling large sums of money. The boy child they've produced together is a chip off the old block . . . hers, not his. I've looked into his eyes and I foresee that he'll grow up to be of middling intelligence; a worthy sort, a probation officer, or policeman. Something of that sort. He'll love his parents, and they'll love him. A total love-fest. And Bernice will always be on the outside, looking in.'

Bea winced. What Sybil said was true.

The harridan lit one cigarette from the other, and tossed the spent stub in the direction of the ashtray. She missed.

Bea picked up the stub and put it in the ashtray so that it wouldn't start a fire on the rug.

Sybil admired the multiplicity of rings on her right hand. 'Leon is awkward around children. He'll never marry, never have children of his own. His last chance was when he met you, but he muffed it. You took a good look at him, and knew exactly who was going to have to play Daddy to his Mummy if you married him. So you didn't. And now he's realized he's past it. He's thinking of buying a yacht. A life without involvement. No responsibilities.'

Bea nodded. That was true, too.

Sybil tapped ash on to the rug. 'Bernice knows I'm dying. I see it in her eyes. And I see her fear. It wrings my heart.'

Bea nodded again.

'The child has chosen you. She said to me that you would look after her. Love her. She doesn't need much looking after physically. She'll make her own way in the world. She'll get scholarships, go up to university early. She'll find her way into the business world on her own merits. But she needs someone to return to . . .'

'Like a boomerang?' Bea's tone was dry.

Sybil cackled. Then coughed.

Bea stood. 'I'll get you some water.'

Sybil spurned the offer. 'Water is for tadpoles. I haven't much time. I get tired, you know.'

Bea sighed. There was no point avoiding the issue. 'Are you ready to go?'

'Some days, yes. Others, no. I'm not afraid, much. One has doubts, occasionally. Bound to. On the whole, no. I'm tired. I've had enough. But I have to see the girl settled. What Leon does with his money is his affair, but I've set up a trust fund for the girl which should see her through. You and my solicitor are to be her trustees. You'll let her have the flat at the top of your house. Somewhere she can call her own. Her room at Leon's is pretty enough, but it's not a home. You will pray for her and scold her. You'll tell her her skirts are too short, and that she has to be in by ten or whatever time you decide. You'll worry about her and listen to her when she wants to talk, and you'll remind her of her manners and teach her to cook and how to look after her clothes. If she makes mistakes, you'll be there to scream at her, and forgive her, and help her to put them right. Understood?'

Bea sighed. 'You've got a nerve.'

'Mm. Haven't I just? I'm not offering you a fortune for looking after her. An income of sorts in case you eventually decide to retire. Running this house must cost a penny or two. Bernice will have an allowance, of course, but it won't be lavish. She has to learn the value of money.'

'Yes, but—'

'You're not interested in money, are you? Or a title? Otherwise you'd have taken Leon, or that other dog that's been sniffing around your skirts.'

Bea tried to be amused. 'William is not—'

'Yes, he is. But you won't take him either because he's not up to your weight. If you marry again you'll want it to be a partnership of equals.'

Ouch. Sybil had put her finger on the problem with William. Bea had admired him tremendously when he'd rescued the children from the fire, but since then she'd come to understand that he wasn't that clever with people. He'd fumbled his attempts to get custody of Alicia, hadn't he?

She said, 'Looking after Bernice means I won't ever have the energy to think of marrying again.'

'Well, Bernice might find you someone, when she's ready to move on to the next stage of her life.'

Sybil stubbed out her cigarette, actually making it into the ashtray, and struggled to her feet, hauling a bejewelled cell phone out of her Mulberry handbag. 'Now where's that driver of yours? I'm due for lunch at Fortnum's and then a nap. The beds at Leon's are too soft for me, but I'll not be using them for long. Don't look like that. I mean, I'm on my way back to the US of A this weekend. I'll have Bernice with me for the Christmas holidays if I last that long. If not, she'll be coming to you, with or without Alicia. Understood?'

'Yes,' said Bea, with a thrill of horror. What on earth was she agreeing to? She must be mad.

Sybil grinned. 'I envy you. She'll keep you young. Tell her I love her every now and again, will you?'

[END]